SIXTY DAYS OF VIRGIL

ORION GRACE

Sixty Days of Virgil

Copyright © 2025 by Orion Grace
All rights reserved.

No part of this book may be reproduced, stored in a retrieval system, or transmitted in any form or by any means—electronic, mechanical, photocopying, recording, or otherwise—without the prior written permission of the author, except in the case of brief quotations used in reviews, articles, or scholarly works.
This is a work of fiction. Names, characters, places, and incidents are either the product of the author's imagination or used fictitiously. Any resemblance to actual persons, living or dead, events, or locales is entirely coincidental.

First edition

Published in the United Kingdom by Orion Grace
www.oriongracebooks.com
ISBN: 9798289818614

Cover art and design by Damonza.com

CONTENT WARNINGS

This novel contains references to childhood trauma, emotional child abuse, physical child abuse, infanticide, and sexual child abuse. These elements are discussed or alluded to through character backstories but are not graphically depicted.

The narrative does include scenes or descriptions involving: psychological manipulation, psychosis and mental illness, murder and graphic violence, suicide, sexual assault and genital injury, animal death (cat), references to human leather, blood, drugging and sedation, psychological torment, and gun violence.

Reader discretion is advised.

1

VIRGIL FRANCOPAN

Virgil heard it in their wary footsteps and the unnatural silence: dread clung to the correctional officers like a second skin.

"Stand back," shouted Johnson. Virgil called him 'Lord Farquaad' for his resemblance to the Shrek character, though not to his face. He liked his morning porridge snot-free.

He rose to his feet and stood in front of the raised concrete slab they called a bed.

"Stand *back*," Johnson repeated.

Virgil looked up at the camera, a little black, shiny eye in the corner of the cell, and without breaking eye contact, he moved back the remaining three inches between his slippers and the concrete slab.

The solid steel door opened in a metallic shriek and revealed six correctional officers standing in a line, each dressed in protective bulletproof vests, wearing riot helmets complete with impact-resistant visors, and carrying black tactical nightsticks.

Virgil stood in his orange jumpsuit, bare hands limp on

the side of his body, and watched Johnson unlock the door of traditional prison bars, the last barrier separating the officers from him. A six-officer unlock did nothing but stroke his ego.

"Strip," Johnson ordered.

Virgil straightened his back, raised his head slightly, looked down on Johnson, and did nothing.

"Strip. Naked." Johnson's voice quavered, and the urgency with which he lifted his nightstick, ready for a pre-emptive strike, was enough to satisfy Virgil.

He undressed, then he turned around before the order came. He knew the dance. He bent over, spread his buttocks, and allowed them to have a good look.

"Squat and cough."

He obeyed, and when they were satisfied he wasn't hiding any contraband, they proceeded to inspect his mouth and ears. They gave him a fresh jumpsuit, and a second officer came forward holding leg irons. With Johnson holding his nightstick in a striking position, the other officer bent down and attached the restraints around Virgil's ankles. He recovered his position behind Johnson, and a third officer stepped out of line holding wrist irons.

Virgil stuck his arms out in front of him.

"Stand back!" shouted both Johnson and the officer behind him, lifting their nightsticks above their heads in unison. The other four officers were so cramped in the doorway they couldn't see Virgil's hands, let alone raise their weapon for any practical purpose.

Virgil lifted his hands in the 'I'm unarmed' position. His lips curved into a weak grin. "I was just making it easier for him to cuff me."

"Only move when you're told," Johnson said, lowering his stick a fraction.

"Jeez, Johnson, you're not so nervous when you slip my ice-cold mash through the hatch, sprinkled with love whispers. Wonderful what a solid steel door, or absence thereof, will do, isn't it?"

They restrained his wrists and led him upstairs to the building's entrance hall. There they made him sit in a wheelchair and further restrained him so he couldn't move his arms or legs. They rolled him into the prison yard and onto a prison van's ramp. It was still dark outside, but a blueish-orange glimmer of light rose on the horizon. One black car waited in front of the van, another behind it.

"Where are we going today?" Virgil asked.

No reply came.

"Ah, a surprise then. My favourite."

They secured his wheelchair, and the correctional officers occupied six of the old brown leather seats around him. Virgil picked up on when they stopped at a traffic light, went round a roundabout, merged onto a motorway. Nobody talked, not even the usual chatter between officers, or the derogatory comments they liked to throw at Virgil. Maybe they were reluctant to fog up their impact-resistant visors.

Fifteen minutes into the journey, the van made a couple of right turns and pulled to the side of a small city road, judging by the van's speed. The officers' behaviour told Virgil this was unexpected. They were careful not to say anything, or to look at each other with puzzled expressions, but all of them, at different moments, glanced at the tiny reinforced window leading to the driver's cabin, the only link to the outside world. All of them, except one. A man with a short, neatly trimmed beard, instead glanced behind his neighbour's backrest.

Two doors slammed, distant voices filled the air, but no sign of alarm. Besides the officers' subtle hints of perplexity, the van reaching its journey so soon after leaving made no sense. Virgil didn't need a medical treatment, and he had no scheduled court appearance, which were the only two reasons he would need to be moved out of the prison for such a short journey. The only purpose for this trip was a transfer to another correctional facility, and prisons with the right level of security for Virgil Francopan were few and far between. This could not be a scheduled stop.

Shoes walked over gravel behind Virgil and made their way to the car. Faint voices rose, then one loud unintelligible shout, and silence.

The officers tensed, gripped their nightsticks, and watched the van's door intently. Johnson's knuckles were white around his nightstick's handle. The bearded officer's right hand held the stick, but his left hand hung by his left hip. Metallic clunks rang out on the other side as someone engaged the mechanism to open the doors, and as the van's double doors flung open, Virgil watched everything unfold as if in slow motion.

The people on the outside started shooting inside. The bearded officer grabbed a gun strapped behind the backrest and shot his colleagues. Because they had only nightsticks for weapons against guns, they couldn't put up much of a fight, especially because it took them a moment to understand the bearded officer – one of them – was attacking them too.

Johnson fell into Virgil's lap, but instead of kicking him off – or, more accurately, wriggling under his restraints to make him fall to the floor – Virgil studied him. He'd been shot in the arm, but it wasn't a bullet, and no blood gushed out of a visible wound. Instead, a game dart stuck out of his deltoid muscle, with a small chamber holding a liquid and tail fins at the back.

The man still breathed. And when Virgil moved his head to try and catch a glimpse of Johnson's face, he was staring back at him. His eyes were wide open, and they moved. Virgil could imagine only too well what foul language the little man was using in his head. Or perhaps he was scared to death, it was hard to tell.

Some officers crawled under and over the seats, trying to lift themselves up, but they were too weak. Within thirty seconds they dropped to the floor, hardly any better than corpses.

Despite the peculiar carnage, not a single drop of blood had been spilled. They must have been injected with large doses of some neuromuscular blocker, most likely succinylcholine. It worked by interrupting the transmission of nerve impulses to muscles, resulting in paralysis of the muscles, but it did not affect consciousness, cognitive function, or pain sensation. The advantage of succinylcholine, as opposed to other neuromuscular blocking agents, was its very rapid onset. Virgil had used it himself in the past. Extensively.

The bearded officer dropped the dart gun, rolled Johnson to the side, and undid the wheelchair's straps restraining Virgil's limbs. He nudged him out of the van, and as Virgil jumped out of the back, he noticed a pen clipped onto one of his liberators' shirt pocket. He faked landing at the wrong angle and stumbled into the man, nearly knocking him down.

"Do we need to shoot you too?" the third man said, tall and lanky, pointing the dart gun at Virgil.

He recognised the two men as the van's drivers.

"It depends," Virgil said, lifting himself back up. His lips stretched into a thin grin. His head was inclined slightly downwards so that his gaze was that of a parent calmly chastising a child. "You may have to, if you expect me to follow quietly."

"Mate," said the man Virgil had nearly knocked down, "what are you doing? You're being freed."

"Freed?" Virgil's grin grew larger. "Am I really? Wonderful. Can I just walk off, then?"

All three men looked at each other.

"Oh," Virgil went on, "and will you remove these leg and wrist irons too, while you're at it?" He nodded at the silence. "Didn't think so. I am so free that I must remain in your custody. Where are we going? Am I walking to a fate worse than solitary confinement?"

The bearded officer pointed the dart gun at Virgil.

Virgil raised a pen. An ordinary blue capped biro, but the way he held it, they had travelled back in time and he was unveiling the atomic bomb. "If you do not answer my questions, I will drive this pen into my carotid artery and expire." His movement may be limited by the leg and wrist irons, but that he could still do.

Hands balled into fists, jaws clenched, and Virgil had them where he wanted.

"You've been told to bring me alive, haven't you?"

"We need to go," the bearded officer said. "The drug will wear out soon and they'll be on us."

"I'll be quick," Virgil assured him. "Who is–"

"He wouldn't dare kill himself now that he's so much closer to freedom," said the lanky driver.

"Do you not know my history?" Virgil said. "My previous correctional facilities have gone to great lengths to prevent me from harming myself. Trust me, I am itching to use this." He stared longingly at the pen. "I've not been so close in many, many a year."

Virgil could taste freedom, the sweet acridity of petrol

and burnt tyres in the air; not the type of smells you commonly encountered in a solitary confinement cell. No, he had no intention of using the pen other than to write.

A phone rang. The officers' eyes shot down, Virgil's lit up.

"Turn the speaker on," Virgil said. "Don't mention I'm listening."

They paused, and the ringtone went on. Virgil pressed the tip of the biro to his neck, marking the centre of his carotid artery with a tiny blue spot.

The lanky driver slid a finger across the phone's screen and put the call on speaker.

"We've got him," the voice at the other end said, and paused, expecting a reply, but the driver merely stared at Virgil.

"Jones, did you hear me?" the voice went on. "Bardeaux, we're driving away with him. What's your update?"

"Bardeaux?" Virgil raised his eyebrows.

"Who's this?"

"As in, Rocky Bardeaux?" Virgil went on, staring at the lanky driver. "Now, that's interesting."

The caller hung up, and the lanky driver put the phone away.

"We really need to go now," said the bearded officer. "They're starting to move over there, in the car."

"Where are we going?" Virgil said.

"To an apartment."

"By myself?"

"With Bardeaux. And...others."

Virgil flicked the pen at the lanky man, and extended his cuffed hands out. "Show the way."

2

ROCKY BARDEAUX

(two and a half days earlier)

He would not go so far as to say it would be a nice and peaceful place without that blasted phone, but it would be nice enough.

Sure, the light was left on all the time. Every second of every day. Tube lights hanging over him like a dooming blanket of white poison, forever altering his quality of sleep. And all in all, total solitary was more of a slow constant peeling of the skin, stripping of the flesh, like the nerve-wracking sound of water dripping from a leaky tap while he's trying to sleep. *Drip, drip, drip*, the minutes, hours, days, weeks, months, years constantly dripping away with no end or relief in sight.

But when that Klein scumbag went off and called that fucking phone next to his cell and let it ring for fifteen minutes at a time, all night long, preventing him from falling asleep... Now that was what created repeat offenders in prison. The fellow prisoner Rocky killed all those years ago had nothing on Klein. Nothing. Given half a chance, Rocky would sort him out. Every time that tinny, excruciating, brain-drilling ringtone went off, he imagined a different way to pay him back. And to his detriment, his creativity in that respect knew no bound.

Well...in truth, no one compared to the sexually depraved degenerate Rocky had killed, but sleep deprivation altered brain function, and on those painfully hazy mornings, he considered Klein just as much of a scumbag.

Solitary confinement may be bearable if he could spend decent nights, if he could face the day after a full rest. With Klein snatching his nights away, worse than a newborn baby, he wondered how he hadn't yet gone clinically insane. He wasn't far off now.

When morning came, Klein knew better than to come to the cell's hatch himself to hand Rocky his mail, but he had no doubt his grubby fingers had already run all over the letters, looking for contraband or merely to satisfy his curiosity.

Only two letters today. He opened the one he looked forward to reading the most; from his sister, his only family member who still bothered to keep in touch. People may not expect this of him, but he lived for the news she delivered monthly. Not that he was much of a family man – in Rocky's world, nobody could be such a thing, not an upstanding one anyway – but it enabled him to leave the confines of his cell for a brief moment, to immerse himself in someone else's life, and imagine it being his own. A rare gulp of fresh air.

His sister wrote about the new car she and her boyfriend had just purchased – new to them, but secondhand and already full of problems. She caught her daughter, Rocky's niece, with a bag of weed, and that broke Rocky's heart. So young, fourteen, and already following in the family's footsteps. Was there no end to the generational downward spiral?

His nephew, Stevie, had just won his first football tournament, and he'd scored the winning goal in the final. Rocky could only imagine how much that meant to little Stevie; he'd questioned his worth as a footballer in the last few months. How Rocky wished he could have been there, cheering him on, congratulating him at the end, taking hundreds of photos, buying him an ice cream as a treat. He would do everything in his power, however little he had, to keep Stevie away from trouble; at only ten, there was still time to set him on a different path, on the right path. Rocky's sister was trying, and her latest boyfriend was a good man. If only she could hold on to him long enough. It may be too late for his niece, but Stevie could still have a bright future.

His sister wrote that she'd enclosed a photo of Stevie and his football team posing with their medals, so he jumped to the end, but saw nothing. He double checked inside the envelope...nothing.

"Oy," he shouted through his door's food tray hatch. "There's meant to be a picture with this letter, where is it?"

"All your mail is with you," a male voice replied.

"Officer Klein kept my fucking picture, didn't he, where is it?"

"He did no such thing," the officer said, but Rocky could detect a grin in his voice.

"Scumbags," he muttered as he stepped away from the hatch.

He'd wanted to see Stevie so bad, to see the joy on his face, how he fitted in with the rest of his team. Were the other boys holding his shoulder, leaning towards him, showing their affection and respect for his part in the final? The winning goal! Was he in the centre of the team, or on the outside? How did he style his hair these days? Had he visibly grown since the last photo?

"Scumbags," he muttered again to himself, grabbing the second letter.

It was from Lynda. He groaned. Who the fuck wrote Lynda with a Y, anyway? This nymphomaniac, apparently. She'd been writing to him for weeks, months, had it been years? It was hard to get a sense of time in this cell. Some woman with a fetish for dangerous prisoners, describing all the things she'd do to him if she could. At first Rocky had replied, intrigued by the interest in him. Now he no longer bothered – but he didn't tell her to stop, either. He'd learned not to be picky when it came to entertainment, because boredom was always worse.

She often sent photographs of herself in suggestive positions and outlandish outfits, including this time. Klein hadn't taken those away, of course he hadn't. Rocky would trade all the photos she'd ever sent, and a week's worth of dinners, just for the one photo of Stevie and his football team.

The photos were distraction enough, but they didn't do much for him. If there was a prospect of ever seeing her in person, he might find this relationship, or interaction, more interesting, but he knew that was impossible. He could only be allowed in the same room as someone else if they were related or already knew him before his incarceration.

Today's letter started like all the other ones, with Lynda describing where she was when she suddenly got the urge to see him. She went into detail about what she was wearing, how she imagined he would remove each item of clothing, each strap. She wasn't a born writer, so it made for fairly boring reading. But midway through the second page, the narration changed. Rocky had to read twice, and a third time, a fourth, and a fifth time for good measure.

One sentence read: *I would let you suck on my toe, the pinky, it turns me on real good and it'll make me open up like a flower for you.* And the very next sentence, without so much as a paragraph break: *On the thirtieth of June, at one in the morning, you will complain of intense stomach pains.*

Certain he wasn't imagining it, Rocky kept on reading: *Bite your cheek or tongue so you spit out blood. The correctional officers will have no choice but to escort you out to give you medical attention. Once in a secure hospital, they will keep you until morning, which is when we will intervene. We are acting in your best interest. You will be in prison and possibly in solitary for the rest of your life, with no chance of parole. With nothing to lose, you might as well trust us. If you detect any sign that the staff have read this part of the letter and are watching you, ignore this plan.*

After this, it was back to the bad sex talk. A lot of things now made sense, but at the same time...had Lynda been a long-thought out plot from the beginning? All for these few sentences? Rocky saw no other explanation, and he was dumbfounded. He almost felt violated, in a way.

One in the morning on the thirtieth of June was in two days and fifteen hours. He had plenty of time to think on it, but it turned out to be a long, long wait. Because...

It was a no-brainer.

3

ANNA KIMPER

You cannot understand the meaning of remoteness and being in the middle of nowhere until you've been on a boat in the middle of the Atlantic Ocean.

The sea is still, a gentle swell hinting at the life bursting below the surface. Petrel and shearwater birds are perched on the yacht's mast, grateful for the only place on which to rest for hundreds – thousands? – of miles around. It's a chilling thought, to know that there is no land, nothing but water, for an area several times the size of Great Britain around us.

It brings mixed feelings. Safety, definitely, from the law, from any kind of human-made danger. But isolated, secluded, totally on our own, and hours and hours from any kind of help. Even with Lawrence's helicopter. Danger, so much danger.

And then there's the radio, connecting us to the mainland, to the civilised world out there, reminding us of our mission and that something historical is taking place. Because, yes, our operation is the only thing anyone can talk about online and on the radio. Now that it's real, that it's finally happening, I live with the constant dread of being found out, of hearing the distant rumbling of a plane engine, or a boat. What if a cargo ship happens to cross our path? Or a fishing boat. They'd find a luxury yacht this far out into the Atlantic mightily suspicious, wouldn't they? I keep reminding myself that the ocean is a big, big place, so the chances of this happening are infinitely slim, especially because we are steering clear of the shipping lanes. But it's not impossible.

Of the consortium, only Lawrence, Stephen, and I are present today, and I wish it were only Lawrence and I. Stephen makes me uncomfortable. We can hear the staff below us. Is a captain, an engineer, a chef, a nurse, and four deckhands enough for a big yacht this far out at sea? I have to trust Lawrence on this, and I try not to dwell on it too much.

The news agencies have latched onto the prison breakouts ever since they started yesterday. At first, only in the UK, with most foreign news broadcasts mentioning it in passing. But ever since yesterday, when the US supermax prison was broken into, the entire world has become frantic. It's like until America is involved, nobody really cares, or it's not quite real. I suppose Lawrence was right, after all, to insist on getting American prisoners too.

Stephen arrived about an hour ago; it's his first time on the boat. Lawrence showed him the surveillance room, with all the screens, and started showing him how it works, because he'll have to do a few shifts over the course of the experiment. But the lesson didn't last long; Stephen's a large, unfit man, and beyond his physical restrictions, it seems using his brain drains him too.

I can't stand him; can't stand the sight of him, his stench, his nasal voice, his frequent coughs and his continuously sweaty forehead. But he's the consortium's largest investor, and God knows this whole thing is money-hungry. His aide, or servant, or whatever he calls him, made sure he has a selection of snacks and a cold drink, a portable fan set at the right angle, and his phone connected to our satellite internet connection.

The radio is going on about the Van Helmont twins' breakout from ADX Naples, the American maximum security penitentiary which was believed to be unbreakable. The breakout that 'rocked the world.' I wish we would turn the radio off for a bit, just for a break, but Lawrence wants to hoard every bit of information he can.

"So, Lawrence," Stephen says after draining his sweating glass of peach juice, "I've been waiting for this moment for a long time. Tell me how you managed it."

Lawrence briefly glances at the large man before looking at the radio in a way which makes me think he's faking interest in what is being said. I recognise disdain in his expression, and I realise this must mean I've gotten to a stage where I know Lawrence quite well. I suppose it's normal when you spend most of the past two years in each other's presence. I've grown fond of him, in the same way I might've grown fond of my grandfather, if I'd had one. His unshakable calm helps still my nerves, a much welcome benefit in our situation. Before he even opens his mouth, the way he holds his head high, keeps a straight back, and the serene but confident look in his eyes command respect. He may be the least wealthy member of the consortium, but his looks say the opposite. I couldn't think of a better person to lead the experiment.

"What do you mean?" His voice is neutral, flat.

Stephen gives a garbled chuckle. "This." He points to the

radio. "What the entire world is talking about. How are you getting all these dangerous criminals out of the most protected prisons?"

Lawrence tut-tuts. "I can't reveal the details, you know this. It would be careless of me, and against our interest."

A short pause as Stephen takes this in. I can't imagine he hears 'no' often. He looks at me, and I immediately scratch at my long-sleeved glove. Convenient that I actually have an itch.

"You mean my help doesn't entitle me to knowing the inner workings? Or at least some details?"

"A simple security procedure, it would go against protocol." Lawrence lays his hands flat on his lap. "Even Anna here doesn't know everything, and she's joined me in organising this almost from the very beginning."

I'm still moving my glove around, trying to get to the source of the itch, and it's starting to piss me off. I needn't have avoided Stephen's gaze, though, because he doesn't even look my way. As if me not knowing everything is entirely normal.

An uncomfortable silence settles. A sea breeze picks up, weaves around the mast, the table, and our drinks. The sun deck is peaceful, but now that we can no longer hear the staff below, the absence of noise becomes oppressive. I'm grateful when Lawrence breaks the silence at last.

"But I can give you a good idea of how we did it – or rather, how we are doing it."

He takes the leaf of mint out of his glass of Pimm's, sucks it dry, places it delicately on the table, and takes a sip.

"Imagine you're a prison guard," he resumes, "or a prison van driver, hardly the most exciting of jobs, and not incredibly well paid. You risk your life every day being around dangerous criminals, sometimes lunatics, some of whom have already murdered colleagues of yours while on duty, and you're offered one million pounds to make a silly mistake you can easily blame on absent-mindedness, or the argument you just had with your wife, or sleep deprivation due to your newborn baby. Something like leaving the van unlocked and unattended for a minute while you go to the toilet. Or falling asleep while guarding an inmate's door in hospital. You might get fired when they find out your mistake led to an escape spree, and no one will hire you for a similar role ever again, but there won't be any criminal charges pressed against you. Do you give two fucks?"

This last word doesn't feel right coming out of Lawrence's mouth, but then it adds some spice to his story, especially paired with his imperceptible grin. I can't get rid of the itch so I remove the glove, slowly, careful not to irritate the skin. As the sleeve uncovers my bare forearm, I tilt my body so that Stephen can't see it. He's too engrossed by Lawrence's speech anyway. I shake the glove out, but nothing falls out.

"You don't need to work another day in your life," Lawrence goes on. "In a standard savings account nowadays, you'll get thirty thousand pounds a year in interest. That's the same or more than you received working a full time, miserable job. To echo our Italian friends, it's an offer most can't refuse."

Aha, there it is. Just a fold of skin at the wrong angle. My skin is looking redder than it should be, maybe the lack of shade on this sun deck isn't good for me; I hurry to slip my arm back inside the glove.

Stephen gives Lawrence the same kind of grin I imagine he has when he watches one of his sick videos. I've heard things, and I do not doubt their truth one second. "That is all I needed to know," he says.

The jingle announcing a breaking news announcement comes on the radio.

"And of course," Lawrence says, leaning forwards, "when a member of our consortium owns the company which operates a prison where one of our prisoners is held in solitary confinement, it makes it even easier."

He turns the volume up as BBC Radio 5 Live announce the breakout of inmates Teddy Brandt and Quentin McQueen from HMP Wandsworth.

"McQueen?" I check, frowning.

"McQueen," Lawrence says calmly. "Why not? Better than missing one."

"So is that it?" I ask.

"That's it," he confirms, giving me a restrained smile. "We have everyone."

4

Official trailer of the streaming of the UPC, as seen on social media platforms

Numbers in black and white count down, the image flickering like in old film productions. When it reaches zero, close up of a man wearing a black leather mask. He is plunged in darkness, standing on what looks like an abandoned theatre stage. The mask's most distinctive feature is its long, curved beak, like a crow's. Metal strips frame eye openings covered with clear crystal. The man wears a long hood and robe, gloves, and boots, all made of black leather. He is wearing a plague doctor's outfit, but instead of holding a wooden staff in his hand, he holds a gavel.

"Welcome, to the rise against inhumanity," *rises a voice from behind the mask. A modified, deep voice.* "You can call me the plague barrister. I have extensive experience in the legal establishment, and I have seen firsthand how ineffective our system is. It is high time we reform our penitentiary systems in the United Kingdom and the United States, and we model them on Scandinavian countries. As you may have noticed, all of the prisoners whom have been liberated were held in solitary confinement, some for many years. Serving time should not include cutting off family ties, livelihood, inhumane treatment, attacking mental health, and ultimately destroying a person.

"I believe in humans, regardless of who they are, and what they have done. I believe that in the right environment, circumstances, and if they are treated with respect and dignity, they can better themselves and not reoffend. In my vision of a perfect world, instead of a mandatory military service for all young persons, I would install mandatory weekly mental health therapy sessions for at least one year. But that's a debate for another day.

"Today, we have gathered some of the world's most dangerous criminals in one place, and I will show you they are not the monsters you think they are. If you treat a man like a feral dog, he will become a feral dog. So we will treat him like a brother, and see what happens next.

"Our seven prisoners will be locked in a secret location for sixty days. Cameras have been placed inside, and a continuous live stream of the lounge will be shown on our website. Every day, we will publish a video of the day's highlights, using the cameras placed in all rooms. The prisoners will have to work as a team. If at Day 60 all of them are alive, and they haven't caused severe injuries to their teammates, we will release them all in an unknown location, thereby gifting them freedom. We will also provide them with a new identity, short-term financial assistance, and funding for a new career path, or help further a previous career or profession, in order to help rehabilitate them, ensuring they stay away from prisons and trouble.

"If, however, a death occurs as a result of malicious intent, a ranking system will take over. Everybody will start with sixty points, and points will be deducted for every act of violence, physical or psychological. These will be deducted retroactively, too. If a prisoner assaults another, for instance, before a death has occurred, they will not have points deducted. But in the event a death subsequently takes place, the offending prisoner will have points deducted for their past action. We will take notes.

"The prisoner with the highest score on Day 60 will be freed, but will not receive any further help from us, and a week later, we will inform the authorities where they have been released. The prisoner with the second highest score will be freed, but three days later, we will contact the authorities. The rest of the prisoners will be returned to the authorities of his or her country. Any prisoner who reaches a score of twenty or below will receive an undesirable execution. We have a psychiatrist on our team who will determine that offender's worst nightmare, or greatest fear, and use it to devise a suitable execution.

"Now for a brief introduction of our participants."

The feed switches to a live broadcast of the apartment, where the seven prisoners are sat on the sofa, armchairs, or standing in the living room. They all wear the same indigo jumpsuit.

"Teddy Brandt, also known as the Tattooed Beast, and considered Britain's most violent prisoner. He was first incarcerated at twenty years old for armed robbery, was released a few times but never lasted long on the outside. He has been in prison for ten straight years.

"Glenys Murphy, our only female participant. Coming to us from America, you may know her from headlines as the Manhunter. She is one of America's most prolific serial killers.

"Quentin McQueen, from Berkshire, your everyday man who descended into hell following his wife's suicide.

"The Van Helmont twins, Jan and Edmond, from America, one known as the Vampire of Delray Beach, the other dubbed as the Firestorm Slayer.

"Rocky Bardeaux, the world's longest-serving prisoner held in solitary confinement while serving an active sentence, this year marking his thirtieth anniversary. Held in HMP Wakefield, England, before his liberation.

"And finally, Virgil Francopan, recognised widely as the world's most dangerous prisoner, and our second and last serial killer. A psychiatrist, he notoriously killed more people inside prison than outside – that we know of. Including a correctional officer, a nurse, and fellow inmates.

"Participants, society gave up on you. The prison system in both Britain and the United States is determined to hold your head under water by placing you in solitary confinement. I believe you are better than that, that you can be rehabilitated. Please prove the world I am right, and the system wrong.

"To help make your stay enjoyable, we will provide you with good food, unlimited films, offline video games, books, music, and calls with family and friends.

The feed switches back to the plague barrister.

"We want to emphasise our gratitude to the invaluable assistance we have received from the Anonymous hacktivist collective and movement, and consider them a trusted partner of our consortium.

"Let the Ultimate Psycho Championships begin."

5

ANONYMOUS UPC RANKINGS

Day 1 of the Ultimate Psycho Championships (UPC)

Rocky Bardeaux

"Let the Ultimate Psycho Championships begin."

They all stared at each other. At first, in silence. Then, Teddy Brandt gave a bark of laughter, and everyone started speaking at once. Everyone, except Rocky.

He couldn't quite believe what they'd been thrown into, and he wasn't sure what to feel about it. He'd been eager to seize any opportunity to get the hell out of that solitary cell, and after hearing what that man-bird had to say, like everybody else, he allowed himself to dream of a new life in the wild. It may not be as good as being legally released – he wouldn't be able to hang out with his sister and niece and nephew, though he might find a way to watch one of little Stevie's football games – but it was a sight better than being locked up until his last breath, which was his fate before a couple of days ago. Yet he didn't feel hopeful, or elated like that fool Teddy. He just didn't believe they would make it to sixty days without a tragedy, or that the man-bird would live up to his word if they did.

And the other part which didn't sit well with him, was the cameras. It was a terrible feeling, to be continuously monitored, every second of every day. He would know. But here, thousands of people would see him, maybe more. Normal people, not just prison staff. His family, the families of his victims, all the people he knew. Like a zoo featuring the scum of humanity, and he was powerless to stop it. He hoped his sister would keep the children away.

He looked around at this cast of lunatics, his people really, all wearing matching jumpsuits, a drawing of the plague doctor's mask sewn onto their left breast, silver on purple. Teddy was the one who stood out the most, naturally, with his face tattoos. Rocky knew of him, he'd seen a picture in the papers before, but seeing him in person was another experience altogether. He felt like if he were caught staring, Teddy's hollow eyes would latch onto him and devour him.

A jagged, thorny crown with sharp edges had been inked across his forehead, above blackout eyes. The black shading around his eyes made them appear hollow, and unnerving. Gave them an inhuman nature. No wonder his media nickname was the Tattooed Beast. A string of barbed wire wrapped around his neck and led up to his jaw. A mean-looking snake coiled up from the back of his neck, its maw open with fangs ready to crunch near his left temple.

Rocky quickly looked away when Teddy turned his head in his direction.

He couldn't bring himself to see this situation as a good thing. How could anyone expect him to work with and trust them, the least trustworthy people in the world? He knew the Brits by name, the Americans he'd never heard of, and Francopan…they'd been held in solitary in the same wing in Wakefield for a couple of years, before they moved Francopan away. They could only communicate by shouting to each other, the voices carried by the ventilation system's metal pipes, but they'd managed to alleviate their solitude somewhat. Francopan was a talker, and when he'd started prodding too hard, Rocky had retracted into his shell, so by the time Francopan had moved away, their interactions had turned cold.

Teddy twisted on the sofa and pointed to the back of his bald head, where a set of bars with broken chains were etched into his skin. "Looks like I predicted this, doesn't it?" He cackled. "Where d'you reckon they'll release us? Somewhere in the Philippines I say." He lifted his feet onto the coffee table and leaned back on the sofa with his hands laced behind his head. "Set me up with a nice little bed-and-breakfast on a secluded beach, with a pretty Filipino bird by my side, and I'll be happy for the rest of my days."

"Releasing you won't do you any good, will it?" Glenys said. "You'll be the most recognisable man in the world, once your picture gets out."

"Not in the Philippines I won't be, especially if I have my bird do the shopping for me. I won't need to leave the house."

Glenys shrugged. "All we have to do is not kill anyone. Seems easy enough. Unless any of you piss me off, I have no patience for assholes." She gave everyone a stern glance.

"Try anything dirty, and it might be the last thing you do. You've been warned. Especially you, pretty boy McQueen, I don't care if you're a pretty boy or not, I got zero tolerance."

Quentin shook his head. "You have nothing to worry about."

Rocky couldn't help but agree with Quentin's reputation; in fact, he was more striking in real life. Classic salt-and-pepper hair, large and vivid hazelnut eyes, lines around his eyes and mouth which could easily give in to laughter. He had an air of George Clooney about him, albeit a less smiley version. It marked him as an outcast in most prisons, let alone this masquerade – and let alone sat next to Teddy on the sofa.

"I don't think I can wait around for sixty days to see if that masked dude thinks I'm a good enough boy to let me go," said Edmond, "not without trying to get out of here first." He got up from the armchair and started inspecting the walls from up close.

"Hey, careful," Glenys said, "we're being watched, remember?"

Edmond shrugged. "By the time someone gets here, we could be far away."

"You don't know," said his twin, Jan. "They could be next door."

"What d'you think these cushions are for?" Edmond asked, trying to poke a hole in one of the wall-mounted mats. "Brings back bad memories. Do they think we'll try to smash our heads in? Hate to break it to them, but there's a very good-looking coffee table here waiting to crack some skulls."

"Noise cancellation," Francopan said. "We could be screaming our lungs out for days on end, nobody would hear us, with the amount of cushioning they fitted. I suspect it means without this, we could be heard by people our masters do not want to alert. So there must be inhabited flats around us, though I would assume not directly above or below us, or to the sides."

"Anyone know where we are?" Quentin asked. He was sat next to Teddy on the sofa, but leaned away from him, as if he didn't want anything to do with him. "Were we all drugged? I woke up here, no idea how I got here." Everybody shrugged. "Nobody knows how long it took to get here," he went on, "or even if we had to fly to get here?" No reply. "So we could be in Uzbekistan, for all we know."

"Or in the Philippines," Teddy said, and cackled.

It was a scary prospect, to have no idea where they were. Rocky had been placed in a campervan immediately after the breakout from the 'secure' hospital, then had been injected with something and had woken up in a single bed in this apartment, alone in his own room.

"Why are you grinning like a fool?" Glenys asked, raising an eyebrow at Francopan.

He lifted his hands in the air, smiling like a child. "I'm just taking this in. All of it. I am a sucker for human nature, understanding a person's inner workings, why they do what they do, how someone became who they are. So I am thrilled to be stuck in here with you, all of you, possibly the most interesting people in the world. I mean, I've always been curious about you two," he pointed at the Van Helmonts. "As twins, even though only fraternal ones, your genetics are very close together, and for both of you to become such dangerous criminals, and to have such rare mental health conditions..."

Rocky tensed, but the Van Helmonts seemed indifferent, almost bored.

Francopan brought his hands together out of excitement. Rocky always wondered if he was homosexual, but he never made up his mind. In fact, thinking about it, he'd never gotten any kind of sexual vibe from him. "And you're both here," Francopan went on, "I can't wait to talk to you in private."

"Ain't gonna happen," Edmond said.

"What do you mean?"

"I'm not talking to you in private." Edmond moved to a different panel along the wall, studying the seams from up close. "I heard what the masked dude said, I'm not letting you psychoanalyse me or whatever it is you want to do."

Francopan smiled, as if he found it funny.

"Can you believe it, though?" Teddy said, now sitting up to lean on his knees. "We've been given a second chance. It's so bloody unexpected. I mean, yesterday, at this time, I was in my cell, dreaming about my parole hearing five years from now. And we all know what they were going to say anyway."

"Yes," Francopan said, "they were not going to let you out, you can be sure of that. When was the last time you assaulted an officer? Last year?"

Teddy made a face, then muttered: "A few months ago. But hang on." He stood up and pointed a finger at Francopan. Standing next to Glenys, who was of average height, it made his own short stature stand out. He was built like a bull; wide neck, strong shoulders, thick arms, narrow waist, but his head only reached Glenys' nose. "You make it sound like I'm this mad fucker, but I never killed. Not once. Any of you can say the same?"

Nobody met his smug gaze, save for Quentin. He stared at him long and hard, and didn't waver until Francopan spoke.

"But you committed rape, didn't you?" Francopan fixed

him with his eyes in this way he had, which drilled through you and grounded you. "Some here rate plain old murders lower on the scale of despicable crimes."

"Ha, you're one to talk, eh?" Teddy said. "I wonder how the others rate *your* crimes, Virgil. Say what you will, I've never taken a life, and I'm proud of that."

"I don't know what you lot are getting excited about," Rocky said, sensing it could go downhill easily. "The only exciting part is potentially getting out, as a free man. Nothing exciting about our time here, or being thrown in here."

"The food, mate," Teddy said. "The films, the music, the proper beds with a fluffy duvet, an actual bathroom with a lockable door, the freedom to live in a flat, not in a small box with a concrete slab for a bed, or shitting in front of your cellmate. Bloody hell, I'm well chuffed!"

"You realise we won't get through sixty days of this new prison without killing each other, don't you?" Rocky said. "The world's most dangerous people trapped together for two months. It won't end well. No wonder they're making it into a show."

"Not the most dangerous people," Glenys said, lifting a finger, "just the most dangerous prisoners. The most dangerous people are those who don't get caught, and who are still plying their trade out there."

"And those who hide in plain sight and rule the world," Francopan added. "Those who are untouchable by the law, and those who have others do their dirty deeds."

"Eh, I don't know," said Teddy. "You're a pretty dangerous bastard yourself, aren't you? I'd rather be stuck in a room with a *dangerous* billionaire than you."

"Oh, you're hurting my feelings," Francopan said. "I have

no intention of harming any of you here. Freedom is too valuable to waste it."

"What's with everyone pissing their pants in front of this guy?" Edmond said, glancing at Francopan. "I don't get a good vibe from him, sure, but what's so special about him?"

"Well," Teddy said, "if you don't know anything about him, it's best you stay that way. But here's a little story that should explain what kind of man he is. He once killed a man while restrained with belts, a full-on restraining suit, lying on a bed with a strap holding his head tight against the mattress. Couldn't move anything other than his toes." He tapped the side of his head with his finger. "All by manipulating the mind. He made the nurse kill himself, using only the gift of the gab."

Rocky had heard of that, though he'd never known if it had just been a rumour, the kind of thing which the media loved, and made inmates run wild. A heavy silence settled in the room. The lack of natural light created a sense of claustrophobia as it was, but in that moment it took things one notch higher. No doors, no windows, no way out of a space filled with madmen and a dark wizard with words. No flight possible in a fight-or-flight situation made for seven sacks of knots ready to snap at any moment.

Jan spoke at last and broke the spell: "That true?"

The Van Helmont twin had shoulder-length greasy hair, his body thin as a picket fence, but though he was known in the media as the Vampire, he wasn't quite as pale as his brother. Edmond looked like he could benefit from a few days in the sun, as well as several burgers shoved down his throat. If they hadn't been known as twins, no one could have guessed they were related. Jan was brown-haired, Edmond blond. Jan was the tallest here, Edmond was taller than Teddy – that wasn't hard – but only an inch taller than Glenys.

Francopan's extended pause only contributed to the general sense of unease. Then he pointed to his mouth. "You see this?" At first, Rocky wasn't sure what he meant. Then he saw it, though it was faint: a dark, reddish mark at the corner of his lips, on both sides. "That's from being gagged for weeks while in confinement, to stop me from speaking to correctional officers. They had to feed me soup through a syringe they slipped in between the gagging ball and my teeth. But," he lifted his hands, as if to show he was unarmed, "lady and gentlemen, I am not here to harm you, and I have no grudge against any of you. I want this promised freedom more than anything, and I have no doubt that the consortium, or the public, are convinced this will fail because of me, or in part because of me, but I will prove them wrong. Believe me, I have my reasons for wanting to get out of here alive. For the next sixty days, I am your friend. You are my friends. We are a team, and we will make it through, with God as my witness."

He marked a pause, glanced at the ceiling, then wrinkled his nose and grinned at the inmates. "No, I'm not a religious man, so I retract that. It just sounded good in the moment. But I mean the rest."

Rocky did not believe a single word which came out of Francopan's mouth, and he never would. Only a fool could take him seriously, not after knowing all the things he'd done.

"So, Rocky," Glenys said, not at all subtle. "I've actually heard of you before. That fella's eyeball. Did you really eat it?"

Rocky walked to the dining area and circled the long dining table. He wasn't sure yet where the lounge's cameras were, but he hoped it put him out of their sight. "No," he said simply. He knew full well how far a story could explode out of proportion; the rumours which had been born of his murder of a convicted paedophile in a prison cell had been exaggerated, so he could easily imagine the same had been done with Francopan. But he had no game in keeping these rumours alive, in fooling everyone there into thinking he was this monster. As opposed to Francopan.

"So how d'you explain a plastic fork sticking out of his eyeball, and a chunk missing?" asked Glenys.

Rocky shrugged. "I was in a frenzy, not totally myself. I just lashed out with whatever I could get my hands on, and that's where the fork ended. And things tend to go missing when you stab frantically."

Glenys chuckled. "Don't we know that."

"Right," said Teddy, getting up from the sofa. "Time to explore this kitchenette of ours."

He made his way to the corner of the dining area where the consortium had placed a small fridge and screwed a couple of shelves to the wall. Wooden – maybe bamboo? – plates and bowls, and bamboo cutlery lay on one shelf. A kettle and two loaves of pre-sliced packaged bread, along with a bunch of bananas.

"Oh yeah," Teddy said, opening the fridge door. "Butter, cream cheese, chutney, marmalade, ketchup, milk. What more do you want?" He proceeded to open the bag of bread and spread some butter on a slice. "Oh my word, this butter." He closed his eyes. "All light and whipped and fluffy. Mates, you'll want a piece of this."

Rocky turned away. He made for the bookshelves by the telly, but before he reached it, a noise came from behind the lounge's wall. Then the plague barrister's voice entered the flat again.

"Participants, you will now receive the one item you each requested for yourselves. We trust you not to try anything silly."

A hatch door low in the wall, about a foot high, opened, and through the gap came a male hand pushing a colourful piece of cloth inside the flat. Rocky picked it up and unfolded it.

"What is this?" he said, grimacing.

"My bandana!" Teddy shrieked.

He hurried to wrap it around his bald tattooed head, and ran around the flat looking for a reflective surface.

"What's the story behind that?" Glenys asked, amused.

"I've had this since I was thirteen," came Teddy's voice from the bathroom. "Used to wear it with my mates on the streets of Stevenage. Red and black, they were our colours." He came back into the lounge, still tying the knot behind his head. "Kind of washed out now, but man oh man, I didn't think they'd manage to find it. Brings back loads of memories, that does."

The hatch opened again, this time it spat out a watch. An old-fashioned Casio digital watch. Quentin picked it up and wrapped it around his wrist. When he looked up, he found all six pairs of eyes staring at him.

"To keep time," he said, shrugging. "I've not been able to do that in solitary. Drove me mad."

Glenys raised an eyebrow. "Is that yours from before you were put behind bars?"

"No. I just asked for a watch. Any watch. With date and time."

The hatch opened again, and a beige blanket came out, with tassels all along the edges.

"That'll be mine," said Edmond. "Reminds me of home,

and I tend to get cold." He breathed it in. "Still smells of my dog."

The hatch operator didn't bother to close it again, and pushed some dark leather gloves forward.

"Wonderful," said Virgil. He put the gloves on, and they fitted to a tee. "Finest leather you'll find around. And the smell...hmmm. A beauty."

"Are you a keen driver, or motorcyclist?" Glenys asked, eying him sideways.

"No, I just enjoy gloves and leather. A thing of mine."

Right, Rocky thought. He exchanged a look with Teddy, who seemed to be the only other person here to know enough about Francopan to understand what he meant. He preferred not to draw anyone's attention to it, and was grateful Teddy kept his mouth shut.

Next came a potted plant, small enough to fit through the hatch.

"Ah, come to mama," said Glenys. "This, gentlemen," she added, holding the pot in front of her, "is a snake plant. It purifies the air, and is fine with low light. Which here might still be an issue, since there is no natural light at all, but we'll see. I'll take good care of it. And you can thank me later, when it helps purify this male-infested oxygen." She swatted at the air with a grimace.

A pair of socks materialised inside the hatch, and Rocky felt himself go red. They were a light brown, and trimmed with white and dark brown fluff. A squirrel's head had been knitted into the bottom of the socks, where the toes went, mouth half open, as if about to nibble on other people's toes.

"Now that," said Glenys, who was still there with her plant, "that is good. That is hilarious. Jan and Rocky are the only ones left, so whose is it?"

Rocky chose to put them out of their misery quickly. He grabbed the socks and shoved them in his jumpsuit's pocket. "You can't get funny socks in solitary, can you?" he said. "It's the ultimate sign that I'm out."

"Mate, I love them," Teddy said, catching his breath from laughing. "I just hope we won't get any nuts, or they might go missing." More laughing.

"Also," Rocky added, "I didn't really think about it. Just said the first thing which came to mind. I didn't think they were serious, that they were actually going to go through with it and give you what you asked for. I knew they wouldn't allow a Swiss knife, or anything else actually useful, and my mind couldn't get past socks. If I'd known I could ask for a plant, I probably would've gone for that. That was actually a good idea."

Glenys shrugged. "I have my moments."

Rocky was relieved when the hatch opened again and the attention was diverted away from him. A rolled up poster came out, and Jan snatched it up and went back to his chair around the dining table.

"Mate," Teddy said, "what is it? A Playboy poster?"

Jan ignored him. He kept the cardboard tube pressed against his chest, crossed his arms in front of it, and stared ahead with a blank look on his face.

"Come on man," Glenys said, "you know what we all got."

"It's only fair," added Francopan.

Edmond stepped in front of his brother and faced the rest of them. "Leave him alone. He's entitled to some privacy, if he wants it."

"Any privacy he has will quickly dissipate," Quentin said, still sat on the sofa. "We're constantly monitored, remember? And by thousands of people. Bye bye privacy."

Jan audibly sighed, but Edmond didn't let down: "He can choose how and when–"

Teddy quickly moved past Rocky, snuck between the dining table and the wall, and coming behind Jan, he snatched the poster from under his arms.

Jan just sat on his chair, peering at Teddy like an injured dog. At Rocky's surprise, Francopan was quicker than Edmond and he darted off and caught the poster as Teddy was about to unravel it. In a few rapid and precise moves, he forced the poster out of Teddy's hands and held it out of his reach.

"That is not how we will handle things in here," Francopan said. "As much as I want to see what this is, your method is the perfect way for us to fail. Do this on day 41 when we're all on edge and have cabin fever, and you will get killed. We will respect each other's wishes, even if we're displeased. Do you understand?"

Teddy grumbled and snatched his arm out of Francopan's grip.

"Theodore Brandt, *do you understand*?"

"Who the fuck do you think you are, mate?" Teddy got up in Francopan's face, even though he only reached his chin. "No one is above anyone else in here, why d'you think you can make the rules?"

Francopan calmly handed the poster back to Jan, then suddenly, quick as a praying mantis striking a cricket, he grabbed Teddy's wide and strong neck with both hands, and held tight. The sinews in his hands stuck out like a web, and his fingers turned white from the pressure. Teddy's facial expression, from one second to the next, changed from tense and angry to drowsy. His eyes started going, and Francopan released his grip. It all happened in the space of two or three seconds. He then stepped behind Teddy and held him up with contrasting care. Teddy's eyes became alert again and he jumped out of Francopan's embrace.

"Get off me, you mad fuck. What the hell was that?"

"Not to worry," Francopan said, calm as a leaf. "I only stimulated your vagal nerve to force a vasovagal syncope. A sudden drop in your heart rate and blood pressure. Harmless, as long as I don't do it for too long. You must understand that we need some order in here, or we will never make it. And unfortunately, violence is your only language."

Teddy massaged his neck.

Francopan defending someone else didn't suit him, or inspire trust, but Rocky could not help but be grateful he had acted the way he had. Francopan did sort of look like a praying mantis; a wiry body, a long neck, a small, flat head. And Rocky imagined Francopan to be the type to eat his mates and skip the part with sex.

Everyone forgot about the poster for a while, until Jan hung it in his room. Rocky snuck in while Jan was in the bathroom. It took him a moment to understand what he was looking at, but eventually he recognised it.

It was a map of the human anatomy.

6

ANNA KIMPER

I'm glad to find Lawrence by himself on the sun deck, and no sign of Porker Stephen. The weather has been brilliant lately, and we're lucky because I don't want to imagine what it'll be like on this yacht in the middle of the Atlantic if it gets stormy.

Lawrence is lying on a chaise longue with a glass of Pimm's by his side, his usual. Eyes closed behind his sunglasses, but airpods in his ears so I know he's listening to the radio, or the audio feed from the UPC unit. I sit on the chaise longue next to his, and he slowly opens his eyes.

"I got off a video call with the university, for their fundraising event–"

"What are you donating?" he asks.

"A tennis lesson, one hour."

"That will be popular, I'm sure."

"But I talked with the staff for a while about our experiment, and the public reaction is quite a lot bigger than I imagined it would be. I didn't bring it up, they did, and it seems people are panicking about all these dangerous freaks being released into society."

"Yes, that's consistent with what I've heard on the radio," Lawrence says. "Good, that's what we wanted."

"The public outcry is so strong the government will make it a priority to get to the bottom of this," I say. "They're being humiliated; they were meant to keep us safe from these prisoners, and they've failed miserably, and now they're endangering everyone. They will stop at nothing, if only to save face. They will want to make an example of us."

"I expect nothing less from them. And in our preparations, we always planned for them to go full-on." He lifts his sunglasses to have a better look at me. "Are you getting nervous, Anna?"

"No." I look down at my elbow-high glove, and fiddle with the leather patches' seams. "Well, maybe a bit, I suppose. We've prodded a dangerous beast, a beast with more means than us."

"I'm not so sure about that. We've got a lot of means – less than a government if taken in general, certainly, especially the British and the American governments put together – but their budget for this specific case is likely comparable to the budget we've had. And we've got cyber experts no government has, in addition to using politics to our advantage. Don't fret, we'll be fine."

His confidence, his unwavering serenity goes a long way in calming my nerves, it always does. He is human, so he must be nervous too; a situation with such high stakes, there is no other way. But he is masterful at hiding it.

I just can't help but think of my son, Ollie, and how this could all catch up to him. I've done my best to keep him out of it, but I simply couldn't. I had to talk about all this to someone, and he's…he's my best friend, really. There is no one else I could share this with. Talking to Lawrence and the rest of the consortium provides some relief, but it's not the same. I'm not intimate with them as I am with Ollie. Would he be liable in any way, if I were to be found out, just because he knew all about it and chose to say nothing? And beyond that, having his mother locked up, all the stigma that would come with it, because let's not pretend the media wouldn't have a whale of a time with this information. I suppose he'd drop out of uni, and then what?

I go back to the video call I just had, to think of something else. "A government spokesman said they're analysing our website, the stream, every detail of the trailer's footage we put out. They've put teams of computer experts on the case, cyber people, they're linking with Interpol and US agencies. I imagine you know what they're saying in America, I've made a point of not looking at any American news site."

"Yes, but I sense it might be better if I didn't tell you anything about it." He gives me a slight, teasing smile. "Everything is going to plan so far. They're reacting the way I thought they would. No reason to worry just yet. What is more worrying, as far as I'm concerned, is that our participants do not kill each other in the first week of the experiment. That would be a great shame. I'm not accustomed to failure."

The tell-tale signs of Stephen approaching make my heart beat faster. His aide telling him to watch out for a half-concealed step, the heavy breathing and grunting as he climbs up the stairs, and the loud exclamation as he reaches the top.

"My PA has just gotten back to me with very interesting information," he says, grabbing one of the patio chairs and turning it around to join Lawrence and myself. "It seems I am the person with the most cash sitting in bank accounts in the world. Hard cash." He chuckles to himself, and is totally oblivious to Lawrence's and my blatant lack of reaction.

How silly of me to think his *very interesting information* had anything to do with our experiment.

"You'll wonder how I can possibly know this. Well, the people who are wealthier than me on the list of the world's richest all have their wealth in assets, you know, property, companies, it's all tied up, so they can't actually see or use it. All highly illiquid. That sums up Alexey perfectly, all in his new company, nothing left to pay the bills." He chuckles again.

I much prefer Alexey, mainly because he's declined to ever come to the yacht or meet us in person.

"Everyone below me on the list has a lower worth than what I've got in the banks," Stephen resumes. "I've just sold a company and a string of properties, and I'm holding on on investing the cash for the time being, so right now, I'm the world's most liquid individual. I had one of my assistants research those I wasn't sure about, so we're positive."

"You had your assistant look this up?" I ask. "How long did it take?"

He waved my question away. "A few days, a week at most."

"So for a few days, maybe a week, you paid someone's salary, a good one too I imagine, to look up whether you were the world's most liquid person?"

Stephen glares at me, then after a pause: "Do you have something you'd like to say, Mrs Kimper?"

I meet his stare but say nothing.

"Have you heard what the media is saying about our experiment?" Lawrence asks, and Stephen looks away at last.

"Yes," Porker says. "About that. How are you sure we

won't be caught? I know we've gone through the whole thing before, but...can we really keep the NCA, MI6, and the FBI at bay? I've got a lot riding on this, Lawrence."

"So do I," replies Lawrence, "which is why we'll be fine. Our expert hackers have assured me we won't be located, not anytime soon anyway."

"No, not through our online activities, perhaps," Stephen interrupted. "But what about the live feed? A continuous live stream using a satellite link is easily traceable by the NSA and MI6; they'll be all over it."

"We have Alen Tusk in our consortium, though," Lawrence replied. "We're using his company's satellites, and he's assured us that won't be an issue. And let's play devil's advocate, even if we are located, we are in international waters, which complicates everything. The United Nations would have to get involved, they would have to follow guidelines from the UNCLOS treaty, and that involves cooperation between countries, which is never quick and straightforward. They'd have to rely on the ships' flag state jurisdiction, the country each ship belongs to, which, for us, is Russia." He smirks. "Seeing as we're showcasing British and American prisoners, I believe the Russian government is very happy to let us operate freely and to turn a blind eye."

"What about Port State jurisdiction?" Stephen asks. "Even if a ship operates outside the law on the high seas, it eventually needs to dock at a port. The port state can then detain the ship and take legal action against the organisation based on their laws."

"Who said I was planning to dock? We're staying in international waters, forever, even once we abandon ship. Unless we get clearance from Russia. We'll use the helicopter and tenders to leave. And if by some miracle all these political entities were to find us and act in agreement, in sixty days this will all be over and my work here will be done. That is a scarily short deadline. After these sixty days, we'll see."

"Wait a minute," Stephen says, eyes bulging, and for once I share his sentiment. "So we're at risk of being found out after these sixty days?"

"No, don't worry, everything is solely in my name. Your names do not feature anywhere, none of your names," he adds, looking at me, "I've made sure of that."

"It better be the case," Stephen says, wiping his forehead with a tissue. "I'm not going down with this ship, you can be sure of that."

Stephen may have the means to ensure he doesn't go down if all goes to hell, but I don't. But as long as Lawrence is right and the sixty days will go uninterrupted, I, too, will get what I'm here for.

That is all that matters.

7

ANONYMOUS UPC RANKINGS

Day 2 of the Ultimate Psycho Championships (UPC)

Rocky Bardeaux

The first morning was a significant change for everyone. Even though no one managed to sleep in later than 6 AM, everyone seized the possibility of just staying in bed and choosing when to get up. It was a luxury, not having a bell ring in your ears or a correctional officer banging on the door and shouting. Rocky stayed in bed, daydreaming and listening to Teddy's snoring, arms resting behind his head, until 7.30 – and he felt naughty for doing so.

He heard someone get up and put the kettle on in the kitchenette, so he put on his silly squirrel socks and followed suit after a pit stop to the bathroom. Someone hadn't flushed their piss, but Rocky was beyond caring. Glenys was stirring her coffee when he arrived into the dining area.

"A kettle," she said as she nodded to Rocky. "Can you believe it? They really must trust us, but I ain't complaining."

Rocky rubbed his hands together. "A nice cuppa to start the day. I could get used to this. Breakfast tea?" he asked to no one in particular as he looked for the teabags.

"Or Earl Grey," came Francopan's voice.

Rocky jumped. Francopan was sat at the other end of the dining table, immobile, his foot resting on his knee and his hands on his foot.

"Hadn't seen you there," Rocky said. "Earl Grey too, very posh. But I'm a breakfast tea kinda guy."

"Did you notice?" Francopan said, staring at his cup of tea on the table. "It sways. Earlier, the coffee's surface was left-leaning. Now it's right-leaning."

Slowly, the remaining four participants made their way to the common area. They all politely waited their turn to prepare themselves a drink – except Jan who chose to have nothing – but as Teddy was pouring one spoonful of sugar after another into his coffee, steps resounded above their heads.

It was like they'd rehearsed it; silence fell instantly. All eyes went up, staring at the ceiling as if they expected it to crash over their heads. The steps moved around, left, right, travelled to the opposite side of the room, came back above them. They all stood frozen in space, like predators listening to their prey, waiting for the first opportunity to pounce.

"Is that the plague barrister and his cronies, you reckon?" Teddy whispered.

"If we can hear them this clearly," Edmond said, holding

a steaming cup of coffee in his hands, "there must be a way to cut through. Can't be that thick."

"Why do you want to put an end to this?" Glenys said, pointing at her mug. "This is lovely. Don't ruin it for us."

"If it isn't our captors," Teddy went on, still staring at the ceiling, "then should we do something? Shout something so they hear us?"

"Don't be so silly," Francopan said. "They wouldn't be so careless as to allow anyone not related to this operation to go about their business this close to us. What does confuse me, however, is why cover the walls with soundproofing mats if they're going to leave the ceiling untouched, and clearly not soundproofed?"

Everyone's thoughts were interrupted by the apartment's PA system, and the plague barrister's voice emerged: "Participants, we trust you've had a pleasant night's sleep. We will now bring you breakfast. Please stand away from the hatch, and come get your plate one at a time."

A door opened behind the wall and the hatch opened. A large plate with a silver bell lid, just like in the movies, materialised. Glenys stepped forward and picked it up. They repeated the dance, with Teddy next ("Oh yeah, the smell, makes my tummy rumble"), and when Rocky's turn came, he couldn't help but share Teddy's excitement.

They all took a seat around the dining table, and Rocky removed the lid. It was a full English breakfast, and not prison quality either. Did the man-bird have a chef? Hash browns, sausages, crispy bacon, runny fried eggs, sweet baked beans, juicy tomatoes, and buttery mushrooms. Even the toast was still lukewarm.

"This is the Ritz," Francopan said. "My appreciation for this barrister keeps going up."

"He's a stand-up bloke, he is," Teddy said, his mouth full of baked beans and sausage. The edges of his red and black bandana bobbed up and down as he exaggerated the chewing, and it somehow took the attention away from his tattoos.

"The bamboo cutlery is slightly anti-climactic," Quentin said, sat next to Rocky, "but I suppose we haven't yet proved ourselves trustworthy of real forks and knives."

"Not that we couldn't make this work, if we needed to," Francopan said, winking, and it sent a chill down Rocky's spine, even though he himself had made it 'work' before.

When they finished their meal, each participant returned the plates and their silver lid under the hatch, where it was retrieved by silent male hands. Rocky was impressed, and not a little surprised, by his inmates' – well, teammates, he supposed – good orderly behaviour. They left the dining table spotless, without a single fork or crumb left behind. Had Francopan's show of force achieved something?

The PA system came on again: "Rocky Bardeaux," the plague barrister's voice said, "after hearing about your experience yesterday, we will allow you to choose another personal item. What is your request?"

He paused for a moment, but only because he was taken aback by the offer. He knew instantly what he wanted. "A harmonica, please."

"Your own?"

Rocky shrugged. "No, doesn't need to be. Any will do."

"It will be with you shortly," followed by the characteristic click of the PA system turning off.

"A fellow musician," Francopan said.

"What do you play?" Rocky asked.

"Wait," Teddy said, "let us guess. The mandolin? Or the harp?" He made himself laugh, but no one joined in.

"No, the violin."

"Nice one," Rocky said, nodding. "I wish I could play the violin. I love classical music; until the man-bird got me out, I actually hoped one day they'd allow me to do an Open University degree in music theory from my cell."

"A worthy pursuit," Francopan said. "Maybe you can do something about it when you're released. They did say they'd support us in pursuing a new profession."

Rocky mulled it over, but Francopan spoke again without waiting for a reply. He stood up from his chair and turned to address everyone.

"Now that our bellies our full and we are in the best mood we might ever be in the next fifty-nine days," he said, raising his voice, "I would like to suggest a plan of action. We, all seven of us, have a common objective: to survive this together, and not harm each other. But we are locked in a relatively tight space, and even though it is significantly more comfortable than what we are used to, trust me, it will get harder. We will get on each other's nerves, we will get triggered by each other's actions and mannerisms, and one thing we all have in common is *issues*. Mental ones. So we are the best candidates to lose it and prove the plague barrister wrong, and everyone else right. So," he clapped his hands together and left them glued to one another, "let's use my expertise to our advantage. I am a professional consultant psychiatrist, with all the letters after my name, and have helped countless people improve their mental health. I even have access to medication, as long as our masters and their own psychiatrist agree with my assessments."

This, more than anything, caught everyone's attention. Rocky didn't see much value in it, other than potential currency, but he ventured Francopan must have gone up in everyone else's esteem.

"I suggest we have regular private sessions to work on bettering ourselves. It will do you a world of good to open up, to share with me your deepest fears, to understand where your triggers come from, to talk about yourselves and let me help identify potential sources of pain. It will make it a lot easier to make it through our stay here without losing our temper."

"Mate," Teddy said, "no one will ever trust you enough to open up to you."

"Not to mention, you know, cameras," Glenys said. "We're not just opening up to you, but to everyone out there. Anyone who'll tune in."

"We will use one of the bedrooms and close the door, so we can create as intimate a space as possible. The plague barrister mentioned only this lounge is on a continuous stream, everything else will only be included in a video mash-up if it makes it past our masters' editing, so it's likely very little, if any, of our conversations will show up. And remember, you want the public to like you. If they do, they will put less pressure on authorities to hound you to the death, and public affection comes with many unforeseen benefits. And there is no better way to get people to express sympathy than to know more about you, where you come from, and to understand why you are the way you are."

"Dude," Edmond said, "are you being serious right now? There's no way, *no way*, I'm letting you psychoanalyse me, or telling you anything personal. You do you, but I'm out."

"No offence, Francopan," Rocky said, "but I can't trust you with personal details about my past. You, of all people. I can't believe you'll actually refrain from crafting saddles out of our skins before the fifty-nine days are up, let alone trust you with intimate information."

"Why are you all targeting me?" Francopan asked the room. "You're all murderers too, how am I worse than you?"

"Except me," cut in Teddy.

"No one here killed indiscriminately like you did," Rocky said, "and no one here has your murder count."

"Hang on," Glenys said, "are we comparing numbers? I don't know the details of his crimes, but I don't think I should be ignored here. Not often I get to blow my own horn."

"Yeah," Edmond agreed, "Glenys must be up there."

"My point being," Rocky said, "we all have clear-cut reasons for killing – or not killing, I know, Teddy – and specific types of victims. I just killed paedophiles. Glenys only male perverts, right?"

He didn't mention the other inmates out loud, but he didn't think he needed to; Edmond had only killed by setting fires; Jan had been psychotic during his killing spree and Rocky hoped he was now better; Quentin only killed once and sure, it was random, but he didn't have that dark side Francopan had, no thirst for violence, or blood, or sadism.

"Your victims are random," he went on, "because it has nothing to do with them, other than their perceived weakness. It's all about you, and your twisted psychopathic mind. So we're all prey for you, whereas you're no one's prey here."

"Rocky, in a different context you'd be absolutely right," Virgil said slowly, "but here you couldn't be more wrong. What do I have to do to show you that I genuinely want to get out of here? That I do want us to be a team and be successful?"

"As far as I understood," Rocky replied, "you can kill one

of us, or more, and still get out of here at the end. Right? If you're high enough in the ranking, they'll release you and they'll only let the authorities know later where they released you. I'm sure that'll be plenty of time for you to disappear. So you wanting to get out is no reassurance you have our best interest at heart."

"And how would that work, pray?" Fancopan said, crossing his arms in front of him and placing a hand on his chin in a theatrical position. "If I kill someone, I'm fairly sure I'll get the most points deducted of everyone, which means I'll either be returned to the authorities in a gift bag, or I'll be executed. I do not intend to die here, or to go back to prison."

"With that twisted mind of yours, who knows what you've got in store? You could get someone to kill themselves, like you did with that nurse, and if no one cottons on, you won't get points deducted. Or..." Rocky threw his hands up. "I don't know, I don't, but I know you're fucking clever, and there is no bloody way trusting you will end well for any of us."

"You give me too much credit," Francopan said, then turned to everyone else. "You all do. I won't say I'm stupid, but I am human. I got caught, didn't I? If I was as clever as you make me out to be, I'd still be out there. We are observed 24/7, and in here I am only one against six. Even if you were right about me, I physically can't commit any harm without failing or getting killed myself, and do any of you doubt that I place survival and freedom above *anything* else?"

He marked a pause, during which some glances were exchanged, and Rocky mentally rolled his eyes.

"Listen," Glenys said, "I don't know much about you, and maybe that's why I seem to be in the minority, but I'm willing to give it a go. If you're a psychiatrist, and you're not trying to get me sectioned, where's the harm? It's just a chat. I do have issues to figure out, like all of us. And hell, it's free."

"Thank you, Glenys," Francopan said, bringing his joined hands to his mouth. "Let me help you, team. Let me help us."

But that was the extent of the agreements. Edmond repeated his refusal, Jan just shook his head, Quentin and Teddy said they'd pass, and Rocky didn't budge either.

The plague barrister's voice came from the speakers: "We find Virgil's idea insightful, and potentially helpful. We will be mindful of your privacy when collating the daily highlights, and if there is something in particular you'd like to keep offline, you can tell us and we will abide. Anyone who participates will receive rewards of their choosing. Examples could be fine cheese, beer, wine – in moderation –, specific films, or music albums, like classical music, which currently isn't in your sound system's selection."

The bastards, Rocky thought. Of course, they didn't want to be deprived of juicy tidbits. It would, doubtless, provide fascinating content. He wouldn't mind Vivaldi's Four Seasons or a bit of Bach, though.

"There is no better time than the present," Francopan said, grinning his twisted grin. "Who wants to start us off?"

"I'll go," Glenys said.

Francopan nodded. "I know you will, but I'd like to make a statement, to have a reluctant teammate change their mind. Quentin?"

"Not a chance, pal."

"I'll talk to you," Teddy said. "Wouldn't mind some vino, if I'm honest. This could turn into the best holiday ever."

Rocky was surprised Teddy hadn't volunteered earlier;

he thought he'd jump at the opportunity to talk about himself at length.

"Rocky?" Francopan said, ignoring Teddy. "Come on, old chap. For old times' sake."

Rocky gave an audible sigh, then shrugged. "Fine."

It didn't mean he'd give him anything, though.

8

ANNA KIMPER

The shifts are draining. Not because they're boring, quite the opposite. I don't want to miss a single second, a single shot, and juggling the cameras to get the best angle of Virgil at all times doesn't come easy to me. I'm no IT wizard.

Is Lawrence's offer really going to sway them into talking to Virgil? I thought Rocky Bardeaux was the most sensible of the lot, but even he appears to sway under the temptation. They need to steer clear of Virgil as much as they can, or it will end in a bloodbath. But if they don't know him well, I can't blame them. I once trusted him too. There is something about him, this aura of intelligence, competence, medical authority, as if you're in safe hands because he's so clearly brilliant. Yet still, they know he's a serial killer. Murder and intelligence make for a bad combination when it comes to trusting someone. Lawrence should not throw them into the dragon's maw, but then again, does he know what he's doing? Few people know Virgil quite as well as I do. Maybe he does, and he knows the footage needs to be click-baity to increase the notoriety of our operation and therefore please the investors.

At the end of my shift I go down to my cabin to freshen up. On the way up to the sun deck, I bump into a deckhand, holding a notepad and checking deck supplies and equipment are properly stored and maintained. When he sees me, his face drops, then immediately brightens up.

"Mrs Kimper," he says with reverence, "finally I meet you." He has a foreign accent, maybe German. He wears a white polo shirt and brown cargo shorts. Tall and strong, hair light brown, skin tanned to bronze by the Atlantic sun, probably twenty years younger than me, and when he smiles he drops a few more years. "I am a fan. I used to be a junior tennis player, in Switzerland, in the top two hundred juniors in the world. I grew up watching you."

Nothing better to make me feel my age. "Nice to meet you...?"

"Stanislas, ma'am."

"Don't ma'am me, Anna is just fine. We're on the same boat, after all."

"Your first Wimbledon title," he raises his eyebrows and grins, "I became a fellow Brit for the duration of that match. I could feel the crowd's joy, their support, your pure happiness. One of my best tennis memories."

Yes, mine too. I am grateful to him for plunging me back all those years ago, when my life was easier, simpler, happier, oblivious to what would follow. When my only concern was putting a yellow ball out of my opponent's reach.

"That's when I knew I wanted to play tennis," he goes on, "to become a professional. It never worked out for me, but tennis is still a big part of my life, thanks to you."

I bring my hand to my heart. "Thank you for your kind

words. Though your junior days aren't that far behind you, surely?"

He gives me a sheepish smile. "You flatter me, Mrs Ki–Anna. I am twenty-six."

Slightly older than he looks, then. "Why didn't you make it to the ATP tour?"

"Injury," he winces, "probably not enough talent, and money. My parents are not rich, trying to make it on the tour without sponsors is very expensive, and I was not good enough to ask them for this sacrifice. Too much risk of failure." His eye catches my gloved forearm; he changes the subject. "I was very excited when I heard you were going to be on Mr. Lawrence's boat. I was wondering what you had become since your retirement, I have not seen you in the news for a long time."

Awkward subject, given the purpose of our presence on this boat. "Oh you know, fundraisers, helping the new generation of tennis players," breaking dangerous criminals out of jail. "It's a shame there isn't a tennis court on this yacht, or we could hit a few balls."

"Oh no, I have not touched a tennis racket in years, it would be embarrassing."

"Me neither, actually. I had a child since I last touched a racket."

I laugh, and he returns my laugh, but a bit too much. He overdoes it, which strikes me as odd.

"If you need anything, Anna, please let me know. I will be more than happy to assist you."

"Thank you, Stanislas. I will."

You can never have too many friends.

9

ANONYMOUS UPC RANKINGS

Day 2 of the Ultimate Psycho Championships (UPC)

Rocky Bardeaux

Francopan set up his little 'office', or therapy room, in his bedroom, placing one of the lounge's chairs in a corner and sitting himself on the bed, his back against the wall. The room was simple; one bed, complete with white sheet and brown felt blanket, one side table bolted to the floor, and a wall-mounted lamp. It felt a bit claustrophobic, but then again with no windows or doors the entire apartment felt claustrophobic. Francopan closed the door, and Rocky felt uneasy. Being a bigger man than him helped calm his nerves, but that hadn't stopped Francopan from overpowering his victims before.

Rocky glanced at the room's corners and found a camera

up against the ceiling, to his right hand side. He wondered where the other ones were, if any. Having a camera watching him in a small room was unpleasantly familiar, and he already couldn't wait to get out of there.

"Simple surroundings," Francopan said, gesturing, "nothing like my office, back in the day, but it will do. Do you know the painting 'The Red Leather Armchair' by René Magritte?"

Rocky shook his head.

"Just a surrealist painting of a red armchair in a vast desert, Magritte's way of contrasting comfort and opulence with isolation and emptiness, the idea that material comfort does not necessarily hold the answer to everything. My way of saying the room we're in does not matter one iota for the quality of therapy you could receive."

Rocky stared on, making a point of looking bored.

"Rocky," Francopan continued unperturbed, a twinkle in his eye, "did you know that you are the reason I agreed to go along with our captors, before I knew anything about their experiment? I took a liking to you during our time in Wakefield, and found it such a shame you decided to stop speaking to me."

When Francopan looked at you, he didn't really look *at* you; he stared at an imaginary point about one inch to the side of your head. But then, sometimes, rarely, he actually looked you in the eye, and it was beyond unsettling. He did so now.

"I hope we can pick up where we left off, and thaw this frost which came over our relationship."

Rocky sighed. "If I'm going to talk to you, it will have to go both ways. You're going to have to open up too, or we'll have a very boring time in here."

Francopan smiled, but didn't say anything. He waited a

good fifteen seconds before saying, "Fair. What do you want to know?"

"That nurse, there is no way to know if he killed himself because of you or not. We don't know what he was going through at that time in his life, could just have been a coincidence. Putting the blame on you is the kind of story people love, so it grew legs."

"Absolutely," Francopan said, nodding. "It is impossible to know for certain. Nobody truly knows. All we do know is the facts, and those are that he looked after me for three days, and my intention *was* for him to commit suicide."

A chill ran down Rocky's spine. "Why?"

Francopan gave a loud sigh, and looked away. He didn't answer for a while, then he fixed his eyes on that imaginary point next to Rocky's head. "My entire body was restrained, down to my head, wrists, and ankles. I was ill, physically weak. I was powerless, I *felt* powerless, and I hate feeling powerless. The only freedoms which remained to me were my toes, fingers, eyes, and mouth. So I used whatever I could to prove to myself I was not truly powerless. I challenged myself, in a way. I defied the authorities, too. I wanted to show them they could never fully restrain me, not against my will. I'm afraid I can be petty, when provoked."

It was Rocky's turn to mark a pause. "You realise this isn't encouraging me to talk to you, don't you?"

"Oh, that isn't fair. You asked me to open up to you, and I did. I've never revealed what I just told you to anyone else. I've been honest, told you exactly what went through my mind. I wouldn't do it for anyone else. Not in this flat, anyway."

"Fine, what do you want to know?"

"Nothing as deep and penetrating as you asked me, don't you worry. Just tell me about your childhood."

As if it was easy as that, to just open his mouth and talk about the most traumatic time of his life. He didn't know where to start, his headspace was a right mess. The small room didn't help, nor did the chair. It was too small for his frame, and it was like the room was closing in on him. He couldn't put any order in his thoughts, the glimmer of one memory leading to another and another until he shut it down. Like when you force quit an application on a computer.

"Go on," Francopan said, "your parents, your siblings, where did you grow up, which city?"

Rocky shook his head. "No." He would not, could not, give up any of this information, not to him. He simply couldn't bring his mouth to utter the words. "No, can't."

"Fine, then allow me to guess, to make deductions based on what I already know about you. Please?"

Rocky shrugged, then nodded.

Francopan brought his legs onto the bed and straightened them in front of him, then pushed his bottom against the wall to make himself comfortable. "You only killed paedophiles, so that alone tells me a lot. You suffered abuse yourself, as a young boy, probably at the hand of a man close to you. An uncle? A priest? A father figure? The violence you showed your victims betrays emotion, passion. You flew into a frenzy, especially that first kill, the one which landed you in prison in the first place. Not only did it mark you, scar you, change you to the core, but it murdered the person you once were. You became someone with nothing to lose, because you were already dead. You only reflected onto your victims the violence you suffered yourself, so you weren't subjected only to sexual abuse, but physical abuse too. And that is usually at the hand of a parent, perhaps both parents. Your household was violent, that was the norm. Spill a glass of milk, and you received a beating to make professional boxers look like wimps. You had siblings, and they were abused too. You developed a bond with them, a bond which went beyond siblinghood. You survived together, faced the world together, took the brunt of your parents' brutality only to fantasise together about returning the favour."

Francopan marked a pause, and only then did Rocky realise his own cheeks were wet. And he was gasping for breath. Trigger after trigger, flashback after flashback. Francopan paused, but not to give Rocky a rest. Perhaps to admire his work?

"You were poor, your parents could scarcely afford the worthless mash they put in your tummy. So when you left your house, maybe you ran away, you were on the streets, looking for ways to make a penny, any way. Things you're ashamed of, but things you had to do to survive. You were dealt a bad hand, Rocky Bardeaux, and you are a clever man. In different circumstances, you might've become a respectable person, one of those people the average Joe Bloggs uses as countersignatory to renew his passport. A doctor, a solicitor, an accountant, a police officer. Easy. But with your background, your lot, your starting point, you could only end up in here."

Rocky used his jumpsuit's sleeves to dry his eyes and cheeks. He swallowed a few times to get rid of his sticky saliva, then met Francopan's gaze, holding his head high. He wanted to feel sorry for himself, couldn't help doing so after what Francopan had just said, but he refused to show it.

"How did I do?" Francopan asked.

"Not bad, yeah." His voice was hoarse, so he raked his throat a couple of times to get rid of the phlegm. "All I remember from my childhood is the beatings. Once he locked me in my room for six months, and he only opened the door to beat me three to five times a day. And to feed me, I suppose, though I don't remember it. He'd beat me with gloved fists, or hit me with a stick, or any hard object he could put his hands on. He'd also rape me."

"Ouch," Francopan said. "Are we talking about your father?"

Rocky nodded. He felt like he could talk about it now without collapsing, as if he'd shed all his tears and now he was dry, and numb. "He didn't touch my sister, but he did rape both my little brother and me. Funny that, isn't it?"

Some friendly shouts rose in the lounge, someone – Teddy, by the sounds of it – ran in the hallway and past the door, but Rocky blocked it out. He stared in emptiness, plunged back in the darkness of his childhood bedroom, the smell of wood varnish still prickling his nostrils. He forgot he was talking to Francopan, or he no longer cared. He just needed to say these things out loud, as if putting them out in the open would stop it festering inside.

"I could stay quiet during the beatings, that was no problem, but when he pulled my pants down and...did the rest, I couldn't. So when he knew the neighbours were about, he'd turn on the only thing which made noise in my bedroom and which I was allowed to keep, a plastic snail which he needed to wind-up, and it would play Rock-a-Bye Baby. Sometimes he had to stop and wind it up again. I don't know if it actually muffled anything. I doubt it, because one day social services took me away, and then I was placed in a series of foster homes. Never long enough to forge any bonds with anyone. My father told my brother and sister I'd died, so they never visited after I left. Not until they learned of my arrest, and that I was alive after all."

"How did that make you feel?"

Rocky snapped out of his trance, as if Francopan's question had reminded him of where he was and who he was talking to. "How do you think it made me feel? Just one more reason to curse him. Like I was worth less than the dirt stuck in the grooves of my shoes."

"Of course. What happened when you turned eighteen, and you could no longer stay in foster homes?"

Rocky scoffed. "It was England in the early eighties. I ended up in the streets, didn't I? You know what, I'm done with this." He stood up. "You can move on to your next victim now."

"Rocky, it will help you to talk more about it."

"Fuck off." Rocky walked to the door, then paused, and turned his head in the camera's direction. "You can keep the things he said, his guessing, but don't show what I said after. Please. And I'll have Johann Sebastian Bach's French Suites."

10

ANONYMOUS UPC RANKINGS

Day 3 of the Ultimate Psycho Championships (UPC)

Virgil Francopan

The plague barrister's voice came on the speaker system, and Virgil welcomed it. That morning the others discovered Command of Duty on the gaming console, and they were like heroin addicts glued to their needle, unable to get away. Virgil had no interest.

"Delivery for Virgil Francopan," said the plague barrister.

Amid the loud gunshots, bomb explosions, and inane shouts from his fellow participants, the hatch opened and Virgil picked up a small stack of three neatly folded and ironed indigo jumpsuits. They paused the game, and silence fell. Virgil felt the six pairs of eyes fall on him, but he walked back to his seat at the dining table as if he hadn't noticed.

"What's that?" Glenys asked.

"Hm?" Virgil said, looking up and faking surprise. "Oh, that's just the jumpsuits I ordered, to be ironed and tailored to my dimensions."

"And why do *you* get that?" Teddy asked.

"Because I asked."

"Oy," Teddy shouted up to the speakers, "I want ironed suits too. And with a nice smell to them too, please. Lavender or something like that."

"Yeah, me too," said Glenys.

"And me," added Edmond.

"Your request is denied," came the plague barrister's voice.

Virgil grinned. "There is a time, and a way, to make demands. You got both wrong."

"Excuse me, Mr. Plague Barrister, sir," Teddy said with a funny voice, "may I please get your lovely purple jumpsuits ironed, and may they please, possibly, be washed using a fragranced softener?"

"It's too late now," Virgil said. "You had to do it when you had a bit of leverage, now you're stuck and at their complete mercy."

"I don't get why they love him so much up there," Edmond said. "He's just some creepy old dude."

"Now that you've paused your little game," Virgil said, "shall we get started on another chat in my room?"

"Yeah go on," Teddy said, handing the controller to Rocky. "I've got to wait for this lot to die before I can have a go anyway."

"After you."

They settled in Virgil's room, Teddy looking around him intently, as if this room was any different from his. "Nice and intimate," he said, finally fixing his gaze on Virgil.

"I have a feeling this will go differently from the previous session," Virgil said, more to himself than to Teddy. "How are you feeling, Teddy? How is your experience here going?"

"Honestly? I'm fucking loving it. It's like being in a hotel for free, innit? Don't have to cook and the food is better than I've ever had. We get to watch films, play games, listen to music, lockable bathrooms, private bedrooms, and we're even paid in kind to get free therapy! I keep pinching myself."

"Yes, it's not a bad place to be in. So, tell me who Teddy Brandt is. Though that isn't the name you were born with, is it?"

"Nah, became too infamous with my old name, felt like it hurt my parole chances. And I never liked it anyway, made sense to change."

"Why didn't you like it?"

"Well, it's a family name, and I was never...how should I put it...attached to my family. Except my big brother."

"Yes, well, given your history of violence, I imagine your household was considerably violent. Nothing surprising here, I believe that is the case for all of us here. Go ahead then, give me your life story. Tell me about your childhood, the good and the bad."

Teddy gave a dramatic sigh and stretched his arms above his head before bringing his left foot up onto his knee. "Grew up in Stevenage, on the streets mostly, raised by my mates, heh. R and B!" he shouted, raising a fist to the ceiling, then chuckled and pointed to his red and black bandana. "Dad was on disability benefits, mum part-time cleaner part-time carer for Dad. I had a dad, so that in itself was something, more than some. Though it wasn't all good. Didn't have much patience, my dad didn't. Gave me a few beatings here and there, whenever he drank or we annoyed him in some way. He fractured my arm when I was only a babe, or so my mum told me. Because I wouldn't stop crying. But I didn't get beaten more than my mates who also had a dad, and personally, it's my mum who marked me most, even though she never beat me."

"How so?"

"Well, you know. She wasn't very nice."

Virgil paused, but Teddy didn't offer anything else. "You're going to have to go more into details here, Teddy. I can help you, if you wish. You like attention, you crave it, which is partly why you're loving it here. It doesn't matter what people say, you want them to talk about you. The fact that thousands of people are watching you, talking about you, is stroking your ego, making you purr. You don't want to be forgotten, or worse, for people to not notice you. Your worse case scenario isn't to be hated, or to be viewed as the scum of society. It is to be ignored, for no one to talk about you, or know who you are. And that comes down to your parents, and more specifically your mother. She never gave you the attention you asked for, even when you acted out, though that's the only way you ever got any. You oscillated between a violent father and an indifferent mother."

Teddy mulled it over, shaping his mouth into a reversed U, then nodded. "If I weren't a bigger man I'd be offended. Lucky for you, I'm a big boy. Sounds about right. But mocking too," he added, lifting a finger. "An indifferent and mocking mother. She liked to make fun of me, she did. Here's a story for you."

He removed his bandana and pointed to one of his tattoos at the right side of his bald head, above his ear. It depicted a creepy, disturbing figure with jagged cracks and missing pieces. "The story behind this one. I must've been seven or eight, we were going some place, can't remember, a shop or something. I was with my mum and both my big brothers, and it started raining. Proper pissing it down. I don't have a coat, I didn't bring one and my mum didn't remind me. She starts getting angry with me for not having my coat. Looks in her bag and for some reason my big brother's raincoat's in there, a spare one. But it's massive, so I don't want it on me. I'll look like I have a dress on, no thank you. So I refuse, hold my ground, let her insults slide off my back, I won't wear that bloody coat, no matter what. We're on the street, yeah, and it's quite busy, it's a Saturday, loads of people around. A mother with two kids walks by and I notice my mum spot them, and I see she's embarrassed. I'm old enough to recognise this. So she doubles down, forces me to wear the bloody coat. And then, catch this, she glances at the other mother, starts chuckling to herself, nudges her chin in my direction, and says, 'Doesn't he look like Humpty Dumpty.' I go bright red. The woman gives me a sorry look, then grabs her kids and walks away without a word. Reggie, my big brother, the eldest, not the good one, finds it hilarious and calls me Humpty Dumpty for the entire week at school. It stayed with me, caught on like wildfire, until I left school. Well, until I got expelled because of it. Beat up a kid who called me that. Fucking hate that nickname. My mum never called me it again, was just a passing comment for her, but it plagued me my entire life. It kind of sent me to prison too. A bastard called me Mr. Potato Head in a night club and I lost it. Came close to killing him."

"Very telling," Virgil said, nodding, and unable to take

his eyes off the broken Humpty Dumpty figure inked on his skull. "Very telling indeed."

"The tattoo is my own way to reclaim the nickname in my own terms. Wearing it like an armour. I've been broken, but I'm still here."

"It's actually a healthy thing to have done, for your mental health. I'm impressed. What about the other tattoos? What made you decide to cover your entire head in them? Because it's a relatively recent thing, if I'm not mistaken."

"Yeah, I've had them for about ten years now. I had none before, believe it or not. Not a drop of ink. But then I thought, why not? I knew I wasn't getting out of prison, or if I did I wouldn't be getting a job at the local Tesco doing customer service, was I? And I wanted to send a message, to discourage anyone from mocking me. It intimidates people, you know. Only a crazy person would do this. It's a statement, 'Don't fuck with a man who's happy to brand every inch of his head.' That's definitely where *this* came from."

He pointed to his blacked-out eyes, a filled-in circle of black ink which gave them a hollow feel, as if the white of his eyes came from far inside his skull.

"Dehumanises me, doesn't it? As if I'm wearing a mask, I can hide behind them, and people are never sure about me. I like that. And I suppose somewhere it's also a way to... disconnect from who I used to be, and maybe even from society as a whole. Because I can never be a normal member of society again, can I?"

"Thanks for sharing, Teddy. I know you branded yourself in order to send messages so you want the message out there, but I also know it's personal and not always easy to put into words. How about your brothers? What role did they, do they, play in your life? You mentioned you didn't have the best of relationships with Reggie."

"Nah, he's a jerk. Haven't spoken to him in years. He was Mum's favourite, could do nothing wrong. And he abused it, always picked on me and Bobby."

"Were you close to Bobby?"

Teddy marked a pause, chewing his lip. Uncharacteristic of him. Then he nodded, avoiding Virgil's eyes. "He was a true brother. My best friend. Three years older than me, I looked up to him and we always stuck by each other. Two fingers of the same hand. I knew that when Mum and Reggie bullied me, I could always go back to our room and talk to him, and he'd comfort me. Never made me feel small, quite the opposite. Always lifted me, gave me any shred of confidence I have. He's the only family member who gave even the tiniest shit about me. But..." He fought the tears. They came anyway. "But he was taken away from me. Murdered, at eighteen. Stabbed in a pub over a game of pool." He rushed the last few words to get them out before he collapsed.

He buried his face in his hands and his body shook.

"I'm sorry, Teddy," Virgil said. "I don't see a tattoo which could be attributed to Bobby."

Teddy wiped his nose. "It's somewhere else, private. Between me and him."

A moment passed while Virgil allowed him to process all this.

"This...this is stupid," Teddy managed to say at last, in between sobs. "He's been gone over thirty-five years now, nothing new, why does it still feel so raw."

"I'm going to go out on a limb here and suggest you probably never navigated the grieving process in a healthy manner. You landed yourself in prison, closed yourself off from friends, never had a caring family, deprived from any kind of support you could've had, and your pain has festered and manifested through violence. You probably never allowed yourself to feel the pain, instead suppressing your emotions as soon as you felt them coming. And whenever you were out of prison, you probably resorted to harmful coping mechanisms, like drugs and alcohol."

"You're an expert, right?" Teddy met Virgil's gaze, wiping his eyes dry and creating shiny streaks on his black shading. "What am I meant to do then, to get over it?"

"You'll never get over it, but you can learn to be at peace with it. We can work towards this together, in our sessions, if you wish. You will need patience, because progress takes time. I'll help you identify your emotions, recognise the stages you go through – denial, anger, bargaining, depression, acceptance – and we'll talk about him, because sharing stories and memories can help keep the connection alive. We'll find ways you can express your grief; we're all different, so it varies for everyone. But it could be in a creative way, like writing, art, music, or through journaling. Writing down your thoughts and feelings helps process your emotions. We'll get there, don't worry. We don't have much time, fifty-seven days, but it's enough to build a solid foundation, and give you healthy routines and practices you can carry with you out of here."

Teddy removed the dirt from under his finger nails for a while. "You're catching me off guard, mate. Didn't expect you to be...actually helpful. Not many people have wanted to help me, you know."

"I know."

"It's...it's quite nice. Yeah, alright, let's do this. Let's work on processing my grief, heh. At fifty-one, never too late, eh?"

"Absolutely. Let's meet again tomorrow to start the work."

Teddy got up to leave.

"Aren't you going to ask the plague barrister for your reward?" Virgil asked.

Teddy glanced at the camera in the corner of the ceiling. "I don't know. Maybe later."

He opened the door, then muttered: "Maybe not."

11

ANONYMOUS UPC RANKINGS

Day 4 of the Ultimate Psycho Championships (UPC)

Virgil Francopan

Today's lunch consisted of smoked meat sandwiches – halloumi and grilled pepper sandwich for Quentin, the group's only vegetarian – and triple-fried chips, along with some ice-cold cola. Full and sleepy, lying about the lounge, the participants expressed yet again their gratitude for the plague barrister's unexpected culinary taste, and just as Teddy turned the gaming console on, the plague barrister's voice emerged from the speakers.

"As a gesture of encouragement, we would like to have flowers delivered. Glenys, do you have a preference for the type of flowers?"

"Why me, because I'm a woman?" Glenys said, looking up at one of the speakers. "Fuck me, do gender stereotypes never die?"

"Er, no, er," the plague barrister's voice muttered. "You requested a plant as your only allowable item, so we– er, I thought you'd appreciate flowers."

Virgil found it very amusing.

"I hate flowers," Glenys said, unwavering. "Give me a few pints of cider and you'll have one happy woman."

"I– er, I apologise."

"I'll have the flowers," Edmond said, lifting a hand. "I love tulips, if you don't mind. Or dahlias. They're my favourites."

Virgil stared at Edmond, the palest of them all and the one in here who looked the most unwell. He had a chronic cough and all the signs of oral thrush. The arsonist was rough on the edges and didn't strike Virgil as the type to appreciate the finer things in life. And setting fires was the most destructive practice one could engage against nature. Of all the people in here, Edmond was the last Virgil would have expected to enjoy flowers – and that made him all the more fascinating. Virgil was a sucker for contradictions.

The plague barrister settled on tulips and logged out, probably turned a bright shade of red under his mask.

"Glenys," Virgil said, "shall we have our first session?"

He would have asked Edmond, but he sensed now wasn't the right time. He preferred not to get his head bitten off just yet.

"Right now?" she said, holding a controller. "Let me have a game first."

Virgil reluctantly agreed, and left to get his 'therapy room' ready.

"Right, you and me," Glenys said after a while, darkening his doorway. "Thought you'd never ask me in here," she added with a cheeky grin.

"Saving the best for third. Please have a seat."

She closed the door and sat in the room's only chair. "So how does this work?"

"You've never had therapy?"

"Well, I've talked to psychiatrists, you know, I've been assessed, multiple times. But that's not the same, is it? Never sat down in a relaxing environment, where the purpose of the conversation is only to help me."

"It's just a normal conversation, where we focus on you and where I get to know you so I can better guide you in your healing journey."

Glenys gave out a nasal laugh. "Those words don't sound like they should come out of your mouth, and I don't even know you. But anyway, yeah, a normal conversation. Where do we start?"

"I don't know much about you, I'll be honest," Virgil said. "I gather, from what you've said before and the plague barrister's introduction for you, that you focused your crimes on men? Is there a particular reason for it?"

"Ha, *is there a particular reason for it*. You bet there is. Men are sex-obsessed pigs who don't take no for an answer, and I thought I'd make them understand what 'no' actually meant."

Virgil gave her a perfunctory smile. "So you only attacked men who tried to sexually assault you?"

"Oh, no, obviously not. I'm quite good at sensing what kind of person men are, and which ones are predatory, or the type to take a woman whether she likes it or not. And when I come across one, I get triggered."

"Do you know why you get triggered?"

"I have an inkling, yeah." She grinned.

"Do you want to share it with me?"

"Is that how this is going to work, then? I get vulnerable, you prod the wound, make me cry, tell me I need to process my trauma in order to feel better, to accept my lot and move on?"

Virgil waited a moment before replying. "Mostly, yes. You will need to talk about your past if you want to be at peace."

"I don't know, man. I don't think I'm ready to talk about this, not straight in, and not with you. No offence, but it's very private stuff." She glanced at the camera. "And you're freaking me out, with your gloves. It's like you're an assassin."

Virgil slowly removed his leather gloves, pulling one finger at a time. Then he stuffed them under his pillow. "Is that better?" he asked.

"Yes, thank you."

"Glenys, it's only you and me here – and our masters. The public will not know what you don't want them to know. Rocky asked the plague barrister not to include a snippet of our conversation, and as far as I know, the plague barrister complied. I can sense you are a conflicted woman, very much suffering from your past trauma – as we all are, certainly, but you are particularly affected by it. And being surrounded by men, dangerous men, cannot help in easing your nerves. I've heard you suffer panic attacks in your room. Not that I spy on you, but my room is next to yours, and we're all close together anyway. You don't always close your door. I believe you are the one who stands to gain the most from these sessions."

Glenys fixed her eyes on Virgil when he mentioned the panic attacks. It might be his imagination, but he felt her softening towards him.

"You need to identify the pain," he went on, speaking slowly, "to know it intimately, digest it, own it, absorb it. Recognise it as the living thing it is. Feed it, stroke it, love it, look after it, let it grow, let it thrive, and only then will you be able to shed it."

A silence settled between them, where Virgil gave her the space she needed to process things. At last she looked up at Virgil, and nodded, but didn't say a word. So he spoke to help her along. "So you killed men, many murderers in prison have, but that alone isn't enough to put them in the hole."

"The what?"

"The hole, the segregation unit, the colloquial term for solitary confinement? Maybe it's a British thing."

"Oh. Yeah, at first I wasn't in solitary. What happened is…a bit of a long story, I'll try to keep it short. My husband was abusive, you know, in every way you can think of. So after a while, when I couldn't take it anymore, I killed him, and that's what got me in prison to start with. There was a trial, yada yada yada, I was found guilty of first degree murder and sentenced to life in prison. I appeal the decision, don't believe I deserve a first degree murder conviction for killing my alcoholic and very violent husband, but it's dismissed. Two days later, I hear of another trial of a man who killed his alcoholic wife. I enquire about the case a bit more and turns out that woman, although she's a bitch and clearly abusive, she wasn't half as bad as my ex. But get this, the judge released the man from custody to serve a *community* sentence, and he expressed sympathy for him and commented that his wife would have tried the patience of a saint." She breathed loudly a few times, like a train letting out steam. "I lashed out. Killed a male guard with a smuggled shank.

Nine stab wounds before they pulled me off. Never had a cell mate since."

"Right, that'll do it."

"He was a bastard, I'll add. I didn't just pick any male guard, or the first one I saw. He was a classic perv, he'd cop a feel here and there, make inappropriate comments, offer better food in return for a blow job. He had it coming." She chuckled. "Boy, did he have it coming."

"Did he remind you of anyone in your past?" Virgil asked. "Perhaps your ex-husband?"

"Sure, and my step-father, and about three hundred and thirty-two other men I've met in my life."

"Your step-father," Virgil repeated.

Glenys gave Virgil a knowing look, then she sighed. A loud, extended sigh, where her shoulders dropped as she exhaled. "I guess it'll come out sooner or later." She glanced at the camera in the corner of the room. "Don't show what we'll talk about from now on, please."

She took a deep breath, fidgeted with her fingers, then started talking. "Ma' left my dad when I was eight, and she got full custody. I stayed with Dad on weekends."

"How is your relationship with your father?" Virgil interrupted.

Glenys smiled. "He's no longer with us, but he's the one person who's never hurt me. He's always been my rock."

"That's lovely."

"He was gentle, the opposite of me, and Ma'. I could see in his eyes how much he loved me, when I'd catch him watching me as I sang while drawing, or how he'd listen to my nonsense with a grin, arranging my hair at the same time. We just understood each other in a way that goes beyond words."

"So would you say he was the pillar in your life, the one

person keeping you grounded and safe from all external threats?"

"Yeah. Yeah, I guess he was."

"He's the one who made the most sense in your life, and helped you make sense of life in general, who showed you, through his love, that you had a place in this world. Without him, you may have turned out worse, perhaps even utterly alone. Is that a fair depiction?"

She took a moment to reflect. "I guess so, in a way. I can't really imagine my life, my past, or my childhood, without him."

Virgil nodded, then allowed a silence to settle before saying, "Please, pick up where you left off before I rudely interrupted you."

"Ma' quickly got with another man, within a year they were married. And he...he was an asshole. I mean, pure filth. He'd sneak into my room at night, when Ma' was asleep, or during her night shifts at the hospital. She's a nurse. At first he covered my mouth while he did what he did, and I hated it. Always tasted the tangy leather from his work gloves. Then when he knew I wouldn't make any noise, he stopped covering my mouth. He told me not to tell anyone, or he'd make my life hell, and no one would believe me anyway. He was liked and respected in the community. A firefighter, so he was everyone's hero. I knew he was right. But...I still told Ma'. Told her everything, and I expected her to throw him out. Maybe even go to the police. Instead she ripped into me for making things up and trying to ruin a good man who tried his best to be a father figure to me. Lucky for me she didn't tell him, or I would've paid for it. I never felt so betrayed, so alone, so powerless."

"Did you mention it to your father?"

Glenys shook her head. "I was too ashamed. Didn't want

him to think less of me. Valued his opinion too much. So one day, when I was thirteen and I'd had enough, I ran away. Didn't last long, they found me but I didn't want to go back in. I told the police why I ran away, what he did, how I couldn't stand the sight of him. Nobody believed me. I overheard someone say that if anything had happened, I'd asked for it because of my breasts and how I dressed, and my bubbly personality."

"That's harsh."

"I didn't let down, I didn't want the fucker to be off the hook. But there wasn't any evidence, couldn't prove anything. At least it stopped him coming to me at night, he probably knew I'd try to catch him out somehow, but I paid in other ways. He turned my whole family and everyone else against me, spreading lies, saying I was a slut and a junkie. It didn't matter that it wasn't true, and couldn't be true, people wanted to believe it. Even my school teachers didn't want anything to do with me. He made Ma' paranoid about everything I did, so she listened on all my phone calls, didn't let me see friends she didn't approve of, barely let me out of the house."

"Do you think your step-father's abuse is the reason you committed crimes later?"

"No it's not, you dumbfuck, and you call yourself a psychiatrist?"

Virgil smiled, as if he enjoyed the rebuke. "And your father?" he asked. "What did he say about all this?"

"He never knew about my step-father, about what he did before I ran away. But he never believed the fucker's lies, or anything else they said about me. He knew it was all bullshit, he trusted me."

"Do you really believe this?"

"Believe what?"

"That your father didn't know about your allegations about your step-father?"

"Well he didn't, I never told him, and he and Ma' didn't speak."

"Glenys, when you told the police, they would've been obliged to contact your father, and explain the situation. Whether they believed you or not, they would've informed him of your claims, of the reason for which you claim to have run away. And at the very least, he would've heard from other people. This type of thing doesn't remain confidential long, especially when it isn't taken seriously by the authorities. Did he fight for full custody after this incident?"

Glenys shook her head. "Not that I know of."

"Not even to try and get you away from that house half the time, at the very least? He

knew you hated your step-father more than anything, that he made your life miserable, that he was emotionally and verbally abusive. And he never tried to use this to see you more than just weekends?"

Glenys gave an imperceptible shake of the head, and looked down at her hands.

Virgil tut-tutted. "How I see it, he's just as guilty as your mother."

A single drop fell out of Glenys' eye and landed on the back of her hand.

12

ANNA KIMPER

"I feel liberated, now that Porker Stephen is gone," I say. I am alone on the sun deck, enjoying the sun and the cool sea breeze, my arm hidden under a shawl. My phone is resting on the table in front of me.

"Replaced with Harry," Ollie says.

I wave the mention away. "I don't mind him. He's harmless. Actually has interesting conversation." I run my hand over my arm, softly, barely touching the fabric. "My arm's been flaring up, lately. Ever since I arrived on the boat."

"Can it sense Virgil, or react to his voice?" Ollie asks, half joking.

I take a sip from my fresh orange juice, deep in my thoughts. "Something bothers me about Virgil's therapy session with Glenys. I can't quite put my finger on it, but I have a feeling he's up to something. He's generally acting too much out of character with these sessions. He knows he's being watched so he can't be himself, but still."

"Was he very different with you, then?"

Memories flood in. He'd started out as reassuring, sprinkling words of comfort in between questions, assuring me I wasn't going crazy. What I imagine a normal psychiatrist to be like. Then it spiralled out of control... As if in response, my skin sends a wave of pain through my arm and into my spine. He forever marked me as different.

"I suppose not, not at first. But that's how he lulls his victims into a false sense of security. I don't see how he'll be able to trap anyone here, with us watching him and able to intervene at any point, but he'll find a way."

"Did he ever...you know...sexually assault you?"

"No," I reply quickly, "not at all." I don't know what bothers me more, my son bringing sex into this, or the thought of Virgil doing anything sexual. "That's not the type of sicko he is."

"Oh, right. He's just the baby-killing type of sicko, then."

My eyes shoot up, hurt by the reference, the way it forces me to think about something I do not want in my head. But he's right; Virgil is the pain-seeking type, addicted to destruction, much worse than a sexual predator. "He's a monster," I say at last. "That's all we need to remember."

"And did Lawrence tell you where he plans to release him, if he makes it?"

"Still not."

"Well, how are we to prepare properly if we don't even know where in the world we'll have to go?"

"I don't know, Ollie. We'll just have to see. I'm not pushing Lawrence unnecessarily, not yet."

"We can't do all this for nothing, Mum."

A surge of red hot anger rises through my whole being. *"Don't you think I know that.* I am on it. He will not get away, do not worry."

"Sorry, I trust you. It's just, seeing him on the screen...he doesn't deserve to be there, eating like a king, plying his trade in the open, so smug with himself."

Before I can say anything, I hear footsteps on the stairs and swipe on my phone's screen, then I turn it over on the table. It's Lawrence.

"Ah," he says, looking around, "I thought I heard a voice. Am I interrupting?"

I shake my head. "Just hung up."

He drops a pile of paper next to my phone. I glimpse the writing on the document at the top.

"Gosh," I say, smiling, "you're going over the requests they made for their personal item?"

"No, I was just using the paper to write something down." He takes a seat two chairs down from me. "They did ask for a lot of silly things, though."

"I could've wagered my house that Teddy would try his luck with a request for some kind of weapon," I say, "just didn't see the crossbow coming."

"Or Edmond Van Helmont requesting a lighter. I was actually offended."

"Does he think us so stupid? Or do you think it was a poor attempt at a joke?"

"I hope the latter," Lawrence says. "Maybe it's a Van Helmont thing; Jan filled an entire page with nonsensical requests."

"Gosh, I'd forgotten. He wanted a whole menagerie's worth of animals, didn't he?"

"I suppose he's not quite over his thirst for blood, which Harry will need to keep an eye on."

"Has he determined yet if he's a risk to the others?"

"He can't assess him in person so it's tricky, but from what he's gathered, including the medical notes from his penitentiary, Jan has been stable. I'm looking forward to seeing what Virgil thinks, though. He hasn't had a session with him yet."

I mark a pause, hesitating. "Be careful with Virgil," I say at last. "Take everything he says with about twenty pinches of salt. He does not value freedom and survival above anything else, as he claims."

"Now *you're* offending me," Lawrence says, giving me a side look. "After all our time together, do you believe me so naive?"

I shake my head. "Of course not." And yet, why is he giving him such an important role, so much freedom?

"And since when do you know so much about Virgil Francopan?" Lawrence adds, arranging the pile of documents in front of him.

"I've read up on him. He's a savage." I hope it's enough. I need to scale back now, or he'll start suspecting something.

"A highly intelligent savage, but we have the upper hand. I have a trick up my sleeve, for emergencies, which should give us complete control over him, and he's aware of the many benefits freedom would bring. Only a fool would trade that for a few kills which would bring him certain death. And it's very useful to Harry to have Virgil conduct therapy sessions for him."

I fight to keep my mouth shut. It's difficult, but I manage it. I allow a passing shearwater bird to drag my attention away.

"Anyway," Lawrence resumes, "I came up here to share what I wrote on this sheet of paper. I've received the ratings. Do you want to guess?"

"Did we reach the million mark?"

"Yes."

"Really?"

"And more."

"More? How much more?"

"About fifteen times."

I stare. I want to say my jaw drops, that's how I feel, but it doesn't. "You have got to be joking."

A slight, smug smile appears on Lawrence's lipless mouth, and he shakes his head. "That's what they sent me. Fifteen million and six hundred thousand viewers."

"That's insane. I told you, it's big, maybe too big."

"Let's hope not, because it keeps growing. To put it in perspective, Croatia vs England in the world cup semi final was watched by twenty million people in the UK. Our numbers are worldwide, and we are gaining traction. We will soon surpass that."

It seems to thrill him, but I can't share in the excitement.

It terrifies me.

13

ANONYMOUS UPC RANKINGS

Day 5 of the Ultimate Psycho Championships (UPC)

Virgil Francopan

"Tell me about you," Virgil said. "Tell me about your childhood, where you grew up, how life was like in your corner of America."

As expected, Edmond simply stared with droopy eyes, as if his mind were elsewhere. Virgil adjusted his position on the bed, pulled on his leather gloves, and gave Edmond an inviting smile.

But the Van Helmont twin fixed his gaze on a speck on the wall. With his short, spiky, blond hair, pale complexion, and dark eyes, he could easily be mistaken for a wax statue. Faint cracks at the corners of the mouth betrayed he didn't have a clean bill of health.

"What are you going to request in exchange for your presence in this room with me?" Virgil asked.

Edmond shrugged, and Virgil took this as a win. The silence continued. Therapy wasn't just about talking; it was about providing a safe space, a containing environment, and most communication was non-verbal. Virgil opened his mouth, then closed it. He had to resist the urge to fill the void by talking. Talking would not encourage Edmond to open up; in the few days they'd spent together, Virgil had learned that Edmond was nothing but stubborn. Despite every single fellow participant's insistence that he stop looking for an exit or escape route, he was still at it.

By just sitting there and sharing the silence, he hoped to communicate something else, that he was happy to sit together like this, that Edmond could trust him. Therapy never went very far without trust, and it usually took time. Normally, Virgil was happy to let it grow gradually, over weeks, months, sometimes years. In here, however, time was in short supply, and it would make his life difficult. Fortunately, he had a few tricks up his sleeve to accelerate the process. But in the first session, maybe the first few sessions, rushing things would work against him.

So they sat like this for half an hour, listening to each other's breathing and the others' distant conversations, away in the lounge. Once, someone flushed the chain. Someone else showered. Edmond briefly glanced towards the door anytime a louder noise reached them, the only sign betraying he wasn't actually a wax statue. In a way, Virgil admired his patience. He expected the blunt American to ask to leave repeatedly, or to complain about being made to sit there in silence.

"I know," Virgil said suddenly, and gave him another friendly smile. "How about we talk about your brother?"

Edmond straightened his back and met Virgil's gaze. It felt like he'd finally snapped out of his trance-like state. He crossed his arms in front of him, but both hands rested on his biceps, as opposed to being buried inside his armpits. "I don't know, man," he said, wincing. "It's not because I won't tell you anything about me that I'll help you psychoanalyse my brother."

Virgil shook his head. "No need for that, I'm more than happy to only talk about what is already public knowledge. We don't have access to Google in here, so I can't just look up what everybody else with a laptop can read about him. Just tell me what you're comfortable saying."

Edmond considered this, then he unfolded his arms and placed his hands on his lap. "Fine."

"Wonderful," Virgil said, grinning. "When did you first notice Jan was different? Or that his illness was taking hold?"

He thought about it for a moment. "Not too sure. He was a normal kid for all of his childhood, even reasonably popular in school. He played on the baseball team, and he had a girlfriend in high school, so I guess he wasn't sick then?"

"How did it end with this girlfriend?"

"She went to college and he didn't, so they broke up. I guess he started acting differently not long after. He got into medicine – not to study at school or to become a doctor, he just started reading a lot about different medical shit, medical encyclopaedias. He started hunting animals in the neighbourhood, like birds and shit. I caught him in his room drinking a bird's blood once, straight from its chest. And then one day we found our dog, the family dog, Rusty, on our doorstep. Dismembered. Stomach wide open, and a human bite mark out of his liver. And Jan came down the stairs with dried blood around his mouth."

Virgil raised his eyebrows at that. Edmond chuckled. "Yeah, mad shit," he said. "Our parents lost it, and they threw him out of the house. That's when I knew there was something seriously wrong with him, but I had my own shit to deal with, you know? Dad couldn't stand the sight of Jan for a while, and it's Mom who gave him money so he could afford his rent. He found a job, though. Stacked shelves in town. Didn't last long. I went to his apartment a couple of times to see how he was doing and share a beer, but the place was scary. It smelled of...bad farts. He had rabbits in cages, a guinea pig too. Once I had to throw a little rabbit ear onto the floor before I sat down on his couch. And his orange juice press was out, it was caked with black stuff, and I didn't see a single orange around."

"How was he acting then? Could you see he was ill in the way he was behaving?"

Edmond shrugged. "He was quieter, I guess. Didn't talk much, but he'd never been much of a talker anyways. A few years down the line it escalated and he started wanting human blood and he ended up in jail. That's my brother's story."

He started pushing on his knees as if to get up, but Virgil interrupted him.

"So your parents never tried to get him some help? For his psychosis?"

"Yeah, Mom did, and he spent some time in a mental hospital. He was doing better, but then I guess he stopped taking his meds? I don't know, you'll have to ask him."

"Is he still taking medications now?"

Edmond shrugged. "I ain't his nurse. But he's better now, he just had an illness, right? He's cured now."

Virgil pursed his lips. "He's showing signs he may be about to relapse. He's closing in on himself, isn't he? He's not been talkative, shuts himself in his room most of the day, looking at his map of the human body."

"That's just my brother for you."

"Keep an eye on him, will you? We don't want him ruining our chances of liberation. One accident and we're all in a much worse situation."

Edmond nodded, and got up at last.

14

ANONYMOUS UPC RANKINGS

Day 6 of the Ultimate Psycho Championships (UPC)

Rocky Bardeaux

With every passing day, Rocky's impression of this experiment improved. How could it not? The apartment gave them a semblance of a normal life, like any flat they might find in London, better than many he'd lived in. Most pieces of furniture weren't bolted to the floor, as everything was in prison, especially in solitary cells. They were regularly supplied with snacks to which they had free access. Unlimited cups of tea, a tap to wash your cup, even the bamboo cutlery didn't bother him; he wouldn't trust Teddy Brandt with a metal fork either. He enjoyed the option to bolt the door shut in the bathroom. He wasn't so naive as to believe a camera wasn't hidden somewhere, but at least the man-bird had had the decency to conceal it. And the food was out of this world. He'd honestly never eaten such quality meals before.

It was the right approach, no doubt about it. Good meals mean you want to slide the plates back into the hatch in good order, and patiently wait your turn, and do everything as the masters want, because you don't want to rock the boat. You want to keep that good food coming.

But the one thing which convinced Rocky the man-bird and his people were genuine, well-intentioned individuals who believed in their project, was the increasing contact they had with the staff. By the end of the fourth day, they stopped using the hatch, and instead a door opened. A man of average height wearing a white ironed shirt and black trousers started delivering the meals under the silver bell lids directly to the dining table. At first they merely stared as he went back and forth, balancing two plates on one arm and opening and closing the door with the other, shocked to be allowed in the presence of an ordinary human. Then Teddy struck a conversation, and Glenys and Virgil joined in. Not that the man replied or gave anything other than bland greetings and perfunctory smiles, but it was a step Rocky had never thought the man-bird would take.

It was a sign of how appreciated the trust was, that none of the inmates attempted anything silly while the man was around. Not even Edmond, who would nevertheless inspect the door from up close for hours at a time following the delivery of the last meal.

Then on Day 6, the man-bird's voice came out of the speakers just as Rocky was about to blow someone's head off in the video game. He paused it, and listened as the man-bird asked them to stay out of their bedrooms while the cleaning staff cleaned and changed the linen and towels.

The door opened once more, and six men walked in. They were nothing compared to the food delivery bloke, whom Rocky considered a hero, but he still thought them brave, to walk inside a flat full of dangerous psychos. One of them was old, maybe in his seventies, and looked like he belonged more in a corporate office than in the cleaning crew of an illegal operation.

However respectful their treatment and comfortable the conditions, tensions started to arise, as they were wont to do. The day before, they'd argued over which DVD to watch – Glenys wanted *Fracture*, Teddy only had insults for Ryan Gosling and insisted on *Fast and Furious* instead, Edmond had been asking to watch *Marley and Me* for days and everyone was still ignoring him, so he became grumpy – and the situation was only diffused when Rocky suggested picking a DVD at random. He'd remembered exactly where *The Pursuit of Happyness* had been and managed to pick it out with his eyes closed, but nobody needed to know that.

And now, while Edmond was busy scratching away at a wall in his room, another argument was taking shape in the bathroom.

"Oh come on, mates," came Quentin's voice from a distance, one of the rare times he'd actually raised his voice since arriving here. "Who pissed all over the seat and floor?"

Rocky made his way over, preceded by Teddy and Francopan and followed by Glenys. Yellow blobs of urine covered the toilet seat and floor around the cistern.

"I don't want to wipe your filthy piss, mates," Quentin went on. "And just after the cleaners made everything nice. It was you, wasn't it?" He stared at Teddy.

"Why me?" Teddy said, throwing his hands up in the air. "Could be anyone. That's offensive, that is."

"Only Virgil and Rocky also use this bathroom, and I

can't imagine them pissing all over the floor without a care in the world."

"Same in the other bathroom," Glenys cut in. "Fucking pubes everywhere. It's not hard to wipe the shower tray and screen after your shower, guys."

Nobody met her gaze, including Rocky, for it had never occurred to him that he may leave pubes behind, or that it'd be a problem.

"And the toothpaste," Glenys added, "while you're at it. Not a huge effort to wipe it off the sink. We've been here less than a week and it's already looking like a pig sty."

"I'm not a bloody maid, am I?" Teddy said. "Tell the plague barrister to bring in their cleaners more often, if you're unhappy with the place's hygiene."

"Oh, is being a maid worse than being a career convict and rapist?" Glenys replied.

"It's definitely better than being a murderer," Teddy shouted. "If you love maids so much, why don't you become one for us?"

Rocky expected Glenys to explode at this, but she merely pressed her lips together and shot Teddy a murderous glare.

"Okay," Francopan intervened, placing himself in between so as to break their eye contact. "Let's all calm down and return to the lounge, shall we?"

Teddy's gaze shifted to Francopan, and Rocky could tell he considered directing his wrath at him, but after Francopan's move to neutralise him on the first day, Teddy hadn't yet come close to provoking him again.

"We will make sure we wipe the urine if we happen to spill," Francopan said, directing everyone to move away from the bathroom and hallway, "and we will do our best to keep the bathrooms clean from now on."

Rocky found himself next to Glenys, and he leaned towards her. "Sorry about the hair, I'll make sure I don't leave any behind next time."

"Appreciate it," she said without looking his way.

Then a shout rang out from one of the bedrooms. "I've done it!" It was Edmond. "I've broken the wall. It's a window, I'm outside!"

They all rushed over and found Edmond hanging off a circular window, barely balancing with his legs pressed against the wall. The matting had been torn off the wall and the board behind it broken using a chair.

"Is he for real?" Glenys asked, coming in behind Rocky.

"Is he escaping?" asked Teddy, still in the hallway. "Are *we* escaping?"

"He's finally done it?" Jan asked, emerging from his room.

Then Rocky realised it wasn't just any ordinary circular window; it was a porthole. And a porthole meant…

"Oh fuck," they heard Edmond swear from beyond the wall. "We're on a boat, fellas."

15

ANNA KIMPER

"I haven't had a chance to ask you how the cleaning went," Harry tells Lawrence.

We are on the sun deck, clouds are gathering. I wonder if this will end our spell of good weather and calm seas. Harry is a boring-looking man, with small round glasses and a wreath of light brown hair from ear to ear. He is exactly what I would imagine a psychiatrist to look like.

"Very well," Lawrence says, "and most glad we didn't find any makeshift knife or weapon of any kind. Reinforces my belief that with good treatment comes trust."

"Was it filthy?" Harry asks.

Lawrence winces. "Generally dusty and a few unsavoury surprises, but nothing we didn't expect."

"Not that I cast shadow over your beliefs," Harry says, "but the absence of makeshift weapons doesn't necessarily mean they do not intend to harm each other. There are plenty of objects that can be used as weapons in there."

"But nobody has done so, and we are creatures of habit. They are used to resorting to shanks and concealing things from the authorities, and the fact they haven't done so – yet – is a good sign, in my book."

"They're definitely surprising me," I say, but think more specifically of Virgil. I don't trust him to be genuine, or to remain as inoffensive as he's been for much longer, but I had expected him to show his true colours by now. "After that first day, when Teddy snatched the map from Jan, I didn't think they'd last the week."

"It's silly but I am growing fond of them," says Lawrence, and he has a look on his face which confirms this, as if he's looking back on photos of his children as babies. "I know they've committed atrocities, but I can't help but see them as wounded humans who've been through more than most of us, and afflicted by biological factors which reacted badly with their trauma."

"I don't think it's silly," Harry says. "I've seen my fair share of people society would consider 'bad', but as soon as you dig through the layers, and understand them, they appear in a new light. Even those who are beyond saving and rehabilitating, their conditions can be explained, and ultimately, it's down to how their brains are wired, whether they were born with it or it developed as a result of their experiences, or both. I've always believed that if you or I were placed in their shoes, with their brains and everything else that comes with it, we would not have done anything differently. After all, some learned people who know more about this than I do, claim that there is no free will, that everything is a result of biochemical reactions in our brains."

"You must have some pretty fascinating stories," I say.

He shrugs. "One marked me, and he wasn't even one of my patients. He was in a documentary I watched. He was a political campaign operative, a very effective one. He'd dig up dirt on political opponents, using unethical methods and sometimes inventing false narratives that would hurt candidates even once disproved. It would ruin their lives, or at least their career. When you look only at his actions then you think of him as the scum of society, a man who has no qualms destroying other people's lives for his own profit. But then they went over his background, his childhood, and we learned that he was physically and emotionally abused by his mother and step-father. They'd feed him dog food and dog meat sandwiches, make him stand outside in the garden naked in winter, until he was taken away and put in the foster care system, where he was further mistreated by his foster families. He was a tall and chubby kid, awkward, and he'd be routinely bullied in school, even by his teachers. His PE teacher once made him stand in front of his classmates wearing girls' clothing which were way too small, just because he'd forgotten his PE kit. He was mocked for years afterwards for it. His parents told him every day that he was worthless, that he shouldn't have been born. The boy grew up in a world filled with cruel, mean people who were gratuitously violent towards him, how could he develop a conventional moral compass? I would say it was biologically impossible for him to develop any other way. As far as I'm concerned, turning out to have no morals and financially and professionally profiting from it, all in a legal way, is not only understandable and justified, but a good outcome, compared to committing crimes."

Lawrence nods with his eyes closed, which is as fervent as it gets for him. "That is partly why I am against the death penalty. Some of our participants would be eligible for the death penalty in some American states, but I wouldn't want any of them on the electric chair. They are all capable of being rehabilitated, and just because our current system is unable to do so, it doesn't mean it can't be done."

"But they could potentially be killed within our experiment," I point out with a smile.

"No." He lifts a finger. "It's a deterrent. Just like governments do with nuclear power; we just want them to avoid unleashing the beast inside, thinking they've got nothing to lose. This way they run the risk of suffering a horrible death. I hope the threat will be enough; I have no intention to act on it."

"Right," says Harry, and he gets up. "It's time for me to return to my station."

When he's gone, I catch Lawrence staring at me with a twinkle in his eye.

"What?" I ask.

He shrugs. "I'm just wondering, as I often do, why you are a part of this. I know everyone else's reasons – we've just heard Harry's, and you know mine – but I can't figure out what yours is. It's been plaguing me since we joined forces." His eye flicks to my elbow-high glove, then settles back on me. "Anna Kimper, why are you here?"

I hadn't expected him to ask in so many words; it's uncharacteristic of him, and so very un-British. I get a flashback of our first encounter. I hear Ollie's voice, as he's told me so often, to tell the truth to no one or we will fail.

I meet Lawrence's gaze. "It is in both our interest that I keep my reasons to myself. *A simple security procedure, it would go against protocol,*" I add in a deeper voice, repeating his own words he had used against Porker Stephen.

He smiles, I smile, then Harry's voice comes crackling through to Lawrence's walkie-talkie, which we are only meant to use in case of emergency.

"They've broken through a wall, and one of them is hurt."

"It was bound to happen sooner or later," Lawrence tells me, and then into the walkie-talkie: "Send in the nurse."

16

ANONYMOUS UPC RANKINGS

Day 6 of the Ultimate Psycho Championships (UPC)

Virgil Francopan

Edmond came back inside and everyone else was quick to stand in the window to have a look at the sky and take in a breath of fresh air. Virgil could see, from the back of Edmond's room, the wide expanse of deep blue sea, reflecting a sky made of a brighter shade of blue. He, too, would have liked to stand at the porthole window and take in the scenery, but his eye caught Edmond, sat on his bed, holding his fist but keeping his eyes closed, and he saw an opportunity.

As he got closer, his suspicions were confirmed; Edmond was bleeding. He kept his injured fist against his stomach, as if to protect it from further harm – or to conceal it from everyone else.

"Come with me," Virgil said, laying a hand on Edmond's shoulder.

The twin lifted his pale face towards Virgil and gave him a confused look.

"Trust me," Virgil added.

Edmond stood up and Virgil wrapped an arm around him. Rocky noticed their behaviour. "He injured himself," Virgil said, "I'm taking him to a different room, make sure no one bothers us." When Rocky's stare became suspicious, Virgil added: "I'm going to contact the plague barrister, he needs treatment."

They settled on the lounge's sofa, hoping the others would find the outside world too interesting to come back in. Virgil couldn't help but notice Edmond had gone paler, and he was still trying to hide his hand. A blood stain had now formed in the centre of his indigo jumpsuit.

"I know you're bleeding, I've seen your hand," he said.

"It's...it's not that," Edmond said, his voice quivering. "I'm not good with blood. Even if it's my own."

Virgil found this ironic, and couldn't hide the smirk on his lips. He lifted his head towards one of the lounge's cameras and spoke loudly. "We have an injury here, could you please send in someone, or the required equipment and I'll tend to him myself? And I assume you know about his condition?"

Edmond's eyes shot up to Virgil. "What condition?"

Virgil's eyes softened. "I know all about it, and don't worry about contaminating the others, I'll keep them at bay until your hand has been dressed."

Edmond stood gaping, his eyes searching Virgil's. "Did they tell you?"

"No, don't be silly. But I've noticed the signs. Chronic fatigue, the cracking and redness at the corners of your mouth, which suggests oral thrush. I know you have night sweats and there is no other obvious cause for it. Not to mention your persistent diarrhoea."

Edmond looked terrified. He glanced behind them, worried someone might have overheard, then his gaze slowly floated towards the camera.

"It will stay between you and me," Virgil hastened to say. "I will not tell anyone else, and I will not say it out loud in here, in case our masters decide to make this footage public. No need for unnecessary stigma."

Edmond held Virgil's stare, and his eyes seemed to glow from the inside. Then he moved his uninjured hand, as if to lay it on Virgil's shoulder or to shake his hand in a gesture of appreciation, but Virgil hurried to tap his shoulder before he could; he spotted some blood spatter on his uninjured hand and he had no intention of risking contracting HIV any more than he already had.

Edmond nodded. "Thanks, man."

"I told you you could trust me."

Distant voices made their way to them from above. "Stay here," Virgil said. "I'll go and see what the others are doing."

To his surprise, Edmond's bedroom was empty. Virgil looked out of the porthole and heard voices coming from above, and saw a clear climbing path to the top. He scanned the endless expanse of sea, the gigantic sheet of blue only broken by sporadic white flashes of sea foam, and he revelled in the sweet scent of salt in the air.

He'd figured out they must be on a boat or other moving structure almost from the beginning; he'd first noticed it with the tea and coffee in the cups moving with the sea swell. The sea must have been calm this entire time, or it would have given it away earlier. It also explained the mats fitted all over the walls. The way he saw it, they served two purposes: first, it was an efficient way to block all windows and doors without drawing attention to specific weak spots, and second, it blocked any noise which might betray their location, like sea birds and waves crashing against the boat.

He followed suit and climbed out of the window, hoisting himself up until he reached a series of cleats and railings. There was a floor in between the one they lived in and the sun deck – the bridge deck, if Virgil's knowledge of yachts was up to scratch – but the windows had been boarded shut, and that provided some extra gripping points and footholds. Once he arrived close enough to the sun deck, Quentin gave him a hand and helped him up.

The sun deck was spacious for the six of them, and it had a bimini top to provide some shade, a fabric canopy supported by a metal frame.

"I don't know if we're allowed here," Quentin said, "and I don't care. This is brilliant."

"We just got an upgrade, boys!" shouted Teddy. "And girl," he added sheepishly.

Virgil still squinted from the sun's brightness, but the others had already adapted. This new event would make their survival to the end easier, and more likely. He had a good look around. "And did you notice?" he said, grinning. "There are no cameras here."

"Oh bloody hell," Teddy said, "now that is sweet. Think I might sleep here."

"Which makes me think it won't be long before we're forbidden from coming here," Rocky said.

"Not necessarily," came a voice no one recognised as their own. "No camera, you're right, but there is a microphone." It was the plague barrister. Virgil couldn't see the speaker, but it didn't matter. "As you can see, we are quite isolated, and we trust you not to abuse your newfound privilege. Sunlight is essential to good health, so it is important you make the most of this sun deck. And in case one of you develops some ideas, the bridge is locked and deactivated; the command centre is non-functional and everything on your yacht is controlled remotely from our own yacht, not too far away. Our nurse is on the way to you to tend to Edmond."

"What's wrong with him?" Glenys asked.

"He cut his hand open when he broke the board behind the matting," replied Virgil. "He'll be fine; I would've dressed it myself, but we have no medical equipment here."

A distant buzz came from far away, and soon enough they spotted a growing yellow spot to the east.

"Do you think it will be an actual nurse?" Rocky asked.

"I would hope so," Virgil said. "They must have a medical person onboard, if not more than one."

"Imagine that," Teddy said, staring at the spot on the horizon, "a woman in here. Haven't had one yet."

Glenys cleared her throat.

"You know what I mean," Teddy said, "all the staff we've seen so far are men." He looked away from Glenys and gave Virgil a guilty look. The rare bits of visible skin amidst his tattoos had turned a light shade of pink.

"Whoever it is, we must all behave," Virgil said. "No one attempts to steal the tender. We're likely in the middle of a sea, or ocean, and no one here knows how to navigate a boat or establish our location, so it would be a suicide mission."

"Not to mention eroding the man-bird's trust would only come back to bite us in the arse later," added Rocky. "We need them to feel like they can send medical help whenever we need it without worrying about safety."

"No need to tell us," Teddy said, "it's Edmond who should hear this, and he's not here. I have no intention to leave this paradise." As he said this, he lay down on one of the built-in booths and placed his hands behind his head.

The closer the tender got, the clearer it became that it was a yellow Zodiac, and only one person manned it.

"That's a bit risky of them, isn't it?" Glenys said. "It's good to see they trust us, but does it also mean they're a bit...foolish?"

Sometimes Virgil wondered if they forgot that the plague barrister and his people were continuously listening.

The reason there was only one person quickly became obvious. As the inflatable boat approached the yacht, the inmates gathered at the front of the sun deck and watched it float slowly towards the stern. The person manning it was a six foot five black hulk of a man, likely weighing well over a two hundred and fifty pounds. His arms were as thick as Edmond's thighs, and he wore a white, tight-fitting outfit. Virgil didn't remember seeing him as part of the cleaning crew.

"Are you the nurse?" shouted Jan.

The man waved, and nodded. He jumped onto the stern, about five metres below, and tied a rope around a cleat. The bridge deck blocked some of the angles but the nurse stood in a visible spot and looked up at the gathered inmates.

"Where's our wounded man?" he asked, his voice as deep as his appearance suggested.

"In the lounge," Virgil replied.

"I'm going to go through the main door, as all other staff did before me."

"Are you really the nurse?" Teddy shouted with a note of derision in his voice.

The man gave a small pause, and his lips stretched into

an amused grin. "Just as much as you're a convict, mate. I've got to give it to you, though, I may not look the part, but you definitely do."

He got a few laughs. "I like this guy," Glenys said.

"Now," the nurse said, lifting a hand, "there's no point trying to take my boat. There's just enough fuel to get back to the main boat, and you don't know where it is, so you'd only get lost at sea. I trust you to not be stupid; I don't feel like spending too much extra time with you lot."

"Hold on a minute," Jan said before the nurse left. "I'm not a fan of climbing down to get back to our rooms. Can't you open the door to some stairs or something?"

"I don't have any other keys with me, but our boss said he'd give you access to all your bedrooms' windows, and one of them is next to a ladder which will take you almost all the way to the sun deck. Patience, lads."

And he disappeared downstairs.

17

ANONYMOUS UPC RANKINGS

Day 11 of the Ultimate Psycho Championships (UPC)

Rocky Bardeaux

The nurse was as good as his word. The next day, the cleaning crew returned to the boat and removed the panels blocking each cabin's porthole. Quentin's window was the one positioned next to a ladder, so his bedroom became a busy pathway to the sun deck.

The discovery of being on a boat changed everything; not only did they now have natural sunlight inside their living quarters, but to be free to go outside whenever they wanted, and be witnesses to such a freeing and gobsmacking panoramic view of the ocean, were things of beauty. They now only stayed indoors to sleep, use the bathrooms, eat, and use the telly, but anytime it wasn't raining, you could find someone on the sun deck. Even when the gaming console was on, Francopan or Jan were upstairs, as they were the only ones who had no interest for games.

Although it improved everyone's mood and day-to-day life, tensions continued to rise. Quentin, understandably, started getting frustrated by the constant coming and going in and out of his bedroom, especially when someone knocked on his door to ask to go up early in the morning. Once, just before going to bed, he closed the window knowing Jan was still outside. Jan lost it, screaming and kicking the window as hard as he could, and Quentin didn't budge until Rocky asked him to end his torment. Rocky didn't know if Quentin would have allowed Jan back in at all, had he not intervened; he could be stubborn.

Usual co-living conflicts couldn't be avoided. Glenys and Quentin frequently complained about people leaving dirty mugs in the kitchenette's sink. Teddy and Edmond had a go at Rocky and Glenys for taking more of their fair share of a communal meal, when the man-bird provided a large pot of excellent chilli con carne. On several occasions they argued about the living quarters' room temperature. Glenys liked it hot, Jan and Edmond preferred it cooler. Teddy changed his mind, sometimes siding with Glenys, sometimes with the twins. The controls shouldn't have been left to them, Rocky thought, but the man-bird couldn't get everything right.

On day 11, one of the most heated arguments yet broke out. They'd spent the entire day inside, as it had been raining all day. Teddy had come out of his morning session with Francopan in a bad mood and seemed to be looking for arguments everywhere he looked. Glenys had had a bad night, screaming everyone awake because of a nightmare, and as a result had no patience for anyone.

Rocky enjoyed Command of Duty so much that as long as he could get his daily dose, his mood remained steady. He'd dreamed of having a gaming console in his solitary cell for years, and the bastard guards had never allowed him one. Purely out of spite, knowing full well how much he wanted one, so he was making up for lost time. Glenys, Teddy, and Edmond joined him, and seeing as there were only two controllers, they paired up and took turns attempting to take over a battle ship. Francopan was reading a book with a coffee at the dining table while Quentin peeled an orange, visibly bored. During Glenys and Teddy's game, however, things took a turn for the worse.

Teddy got killed, Glenys did not, and he placed the blame on her.

"I was looking for another weapon and ammo," Glenys said defensively.

"There was an ammo box right there," Teddy replied, red in his tattooed face.

"It was the wrong box."

"I was getting shot at! You should've picked the first box you saw and backed me up, you just wasted time. I was just about to kill him, a few shots from you and it would've been enough."

"I needed a weapon too, you moron," Glenys said. "It was the wrong type of ammo for my rifle, so I had to find another weapon, any weapon."

"Hey, you two, calm down."

"Oh go on," Teddy went on, ignoring Rocky, "you were on the same floor as me and there were loads of weapons everywhere, if you'd just looked for them. I saw you go up the stairs instead for some daft reason."

Glenys took a deep breath, then she enunciated every word that followed slowly and carefully. The tension could be felt in every syllable. "I could not see any, so I went looking for them. What else did you want me to do?"

Teddy threw the controller in the air. "Don't use incompetence as a valid excuse for failing, mate. Just be better."

She pounced on him, he shoved her away. Rocky tried to get in between, but they were stronger than he gave them credit, not to mention it was awkward to move over the sofa's plushy cushions. Glenys' thumbs found their way to Teddy's eyes, but then something happened which grabbed their attention.

Moans and grunts reached them from the dining table.

Francopan had turned his chair around and was facing the room's corner, where both walls met, turning his back to the lounge, and a wet noise became clearly audible. His hands were joined in front of his crotch and he was shaking furiously.

"Oh yeah," he groaned softly, "just like that."

Teddy and Glenys stepped away from each other, eyes glued to Francopan.

He threw his head back, gave some guttural, primeval grunts, his whole body shook, and then a slow release as he gradually relaxed.

Glenys and Rocky exchanged a look.

"No way did he just do that," Edmond said.

"Mate..." Teddy said, disgust written all over his face.

"Ahhh," they heard Francopan exclaim, "frothy milk."

Then he started shaking again, but this time it sounded like laughter. When he turned around to face them, he was holding a plastic lidded coffee cup, full of white bubbly milk, with his thumb pressed over the drinking hole to keep it from spilling.

He appeared surprised by the attention. "What did you all think I was doing?" He laughed again. "Just thought you needed something stronger than violence to quell the situation. Please continue playing, but may I suggest those two not be paired again?"

The atmosphere became awkward, as if on the verge of either taking further offence, or simply laughing at the absurdity of the situation, but Rocky had to give it to Francopan; he had achieved his purpose.

Day after day, Francopan kept proving his priority was, indeed, to keep the peace.

18

ANONYMOUS UPC RANKINGS

Day 12 of the Ultimate Psycho Championships (UPC)

Virgil Francopan

Quentin McQueen was an enigma, a locked box and no keys in sight. Virgil's challenge was to locate the right key, and he relished it. A common misconception was that a silent patient, one who wouldn't open up and talk to his therapist, was a problem. And perhaps for most therapists it was, but Virgil enjoyed sinking his teeth into a worthy test.

"Pretty boy McQueen," he said, repeating Glenys' sobriquet for Quentin with pleasantry in his eyes.

Quentin merely stared back at him, not exactly expressionless, but enigmatically. Those eyes of his were a pit of meaning, where conflicting emotions dwelled; boredom, amusement, irritation, interest. But not impatience; he seemed rather happy to sit with Virgil, so long as he didn't have to give him anything.

"I understand you're reluctant to join in these sessions," Virgil said, fiddling with his leather gloves. "I'm glad you're giving me a chance at last, twelve days in. Why the change of heart?"

The corners of Quentin's mouth went down. "I fancied some whiskey."

Virgil nodded. "Of course. To earn that whiskey, then, would you like to tell me about yourself? How are you feeling about this experiment?"

Quentin gave him a thin smile, and no words. He appeared to enjoy himself.

"No?" Virgil went on. "Not even something as innocent as your feelings around our predicament? Are you this scared of showing me your true self?"

"I don't remember the plague barrister requiring us to open up in order to receive our reward. So I'm quite happy to sit here, and wait for you to dismiss me. I'm not against idle chatter, though. As long as it's very...idle."

Virgil allowed several minutes to pass, while he mounted a plan of attack. He took his time to observe Quentin, and glean any information he could gain. Not the easiest thing when they all wore the same jumpsuit. Despite limited equipment on the boat, Quentin managed to keep his salt-and-pepper hair styled, and his cheeks were clean-shaven. In fact, Virgil had not yet seen him with stubble, so he paid particular attention to daily shaving. He'd chosen an ordinary watch as his personal item, which was an indication of his punctual and disciplined nature. He was a patient man who would have no issues waiting the required sixty days without violence, but strangely, Virgil didn't sense any strong yearning for freedom in him, as opposed to everyone else on this boat. He must desire freedom, as opposed to being returned to his solitary cell, who wouldn't? But he had not once mentioned how necessary it was to pass the test, and he'd not yet moved a finger to try and prevent any violence within the boat. He just seemed to find it all... amusing, for want of a better word.

"You are the opposite of art," Virgil said at last.

"Come again?" Quentin asked, bored.

"René Magritte, a famous surrealist painter, once said, 'The mind loves the unknown. It loves images whose meaning is unknown, since the meaning of the mind itself is unknown.' Nobody wants the depths of *your* mind to remain unknown, or secret. It will not work in your favour, ultimately, if it does. You could use these sessions with me as an opportunity to explain to the world why you did what you did, how you ended up in solitary. You could provide the reasons which justify, or at least explain, your actions."

"Why would I do that?"

"To get people to like you, to gain public affection, which I'm sure you already have, to a certain extent, thanks to your looks. The human mind is a wondrous and puzzling thing. Our ability for empathy is boundless. Unless they're psychopaths – which is probably a majority of us in here, but out there they're practically non-existent, statistically speaking – then I believe people can feel empathy for almost anyone. How many times have we seen parents forgive the killers of their children? Given the right circumstances, the right explanations for motives, and a true understanding of the killer's mind, people will, if not forgive, at least understand. And of all of us here, I think you're the one with the most potential for receiving public forgiveness." He counted on his gloved fingers. "You're handsome, not a serial killer, you have complete control over your emotions, you're a widower, and you have a fun name. Five reasons in your favour. So invite the public into your mind, and they won't see you as just another criminal. They will see you as Quentin McQueen, the man who used to be a respectable project manager with no criminal past before the death which changed his life – and trust me, nothing elicits sympathy more than the untimely loss of a loved one. We can all relate to that."

Quentin closed his eyes and shook his head. "You're assuming I give a toss about what people think."

Virgil raised a thumb on his second hand, now holding six fingers up. "Another reason why people will warm to you. Nobody likes a man who craves people's affection."

"I hate to break it to you, but being seen as a better man than those creeps and freaks–" he motioned to the entire boat and included Virgil in his gesture "–means nothing to me, I already know this and people can like me or not, it won't change anything for me."

Virgil nodded slowly. "You are distancing yourself from us."

"You said it yourself, you're all psychos. Except maybe Rocky."

"I accept you're most likely not a psychopath, though I can't know for certain unless I conduct a complete assessment, but you *are* nevertheless in the same boat as us, however superior you believe yourself to be. You are a murderer too, which to society marks you as a fellow 'psycho' in its colloquial use. And you've been violent while in prison, which landed you in solitary, so in some respects, you're not too different from, say, Teddy."

Perhaps for the first time, Virgil saw Quentin lose

control over himself. He sat up straight and pointed a finger at Virgil.

"I am nothing like Teddy Brandt. Yeah, I'm a convict too, and I accept what I did. But..." He squinted, intensifying his gaze. "There's a difference."

"Please, elaborate."

He sat back on his chair, crossed his arms, and the fire in his eyes dimmed. "I'm not saying anything else."

19

ANNA KIMPER

(just over two years ago)

This is a first for me; I'm actually enjoying myself at an event organised by the All England Lawn Tennis Club.

Ever since my retirement, I've seen coming to the site where tennis dreams come to die – or for the rare few like me, come to life – as a chore. Everybody sees the automatic full membership as a huge privilege, something a great many people would spend a fortune to have, and of course it is a privilege, but I've never asked for it, and if it weren't for my fundraising activities, I doubt I'd ever set foot here again – except during Wimbledon, naturally. Watching the finals from the royal box will never get old.

This time around, however, I've been looking forward to the Easter banquet. Mainly for distraction; over the last year I've opened to Ollie about...many things, and it's stirred memories, brought back nightmares I'd blocked out. My mutilated arm has been flaring too, and I don't think it's a coincidence. So I've loaded up on painkillers, put on my prettiest elbow-high glove so I can show it off as opposed to being ashamed, and walked up to the legendary club ready to embrace the small talk and distraction.

People are a lot nicer when you approach them in a good mood, I've found. I suppose they can sense you have time for them, and they reciprocate the feeling. Even talking to this old man, sitting across from me at the immensely long dinner table, doesn't fill me with boredom, as it has before. Perhaps it's because he doesn't talk to me about my past performances, my victory here twenty years ago, or anything tennis-related. It's so refreshing to speak of other things, like politics; this man is knowledgeable about England's political history, but he wants to know what I think, and he values my opinion, even though he's well aware I'm clueless. Then something in his gaze changes, and something comes over me. I realise he's not just a random encounter, I suddenly know he was meant to strike up a conversation with me, that originally he wasn't meant to sit across from me, but he made it happen.

"Mrs Kimper," he says, leaning forwards over his truffle mousse on a biscotte, "I believe you are a friend of Michelle Gardner."

He adds nothing else, but he doesn't need to. Everything falls into place.

Michelle told me about this renowned judge who has a crazy plan to shake the prison world to its core. She tested the waters, subtly trying to sense if I would be interested in investing in such a project, bearing in mind it would be highly confidential, because illegal. I accepted in an instant, and pushed her to tell me the judge's name, and to arrange a meeting as quickly as possible. She fell silent, and I thought

I'd screwed it up, that I'd appeared too eager and would perhaps be seen as a liability.

I haven't heard from her since.

"Are you...?" I say, unsure what to say next.

He nods, and then, against all expectations: "I am Judge Lawrence Claret."

I am speechless for a brief moment. Michelle emphasised how private he is, and how, given the sensitive nature of his project, he is extremely careful about divulging his name. It can only mean he trusts me, and has taken a liking to me, because he's no fool.

"Michelle mentioned you were interested in taking part in my project."

I look around, slightly self-conscious. Does he really want to talk about this now, hemmed in by all these posh people?

To my horror, Lawrence turns to the lady to his right and tilts his head in my direction. "Mrs Kimper may partake in the exhibition I am organising as a fundraiser for my charity."

The lady raises her head and nods gravely.

"Oh, how silly of me," Lawrence adds, "I haven't done the introductions. Mrs Kimper, this is Susan Parker, a full member of the All England Lawn Tennis Club, and the reason I am here today, as her guest."

"He's a complete tennis noob," the lady says, giving me a conspiratorial look. "I'm astonished he knew who you were as soon as he saw you."

"Mrs Kimper extended her fame beyond the tennis world when she won Wimbledon," Lawrence says. "Within England, at any rate."

"You're too kind," I say, and resent the familiar direction this conversation is taking. "Yes, I'd be more than happy to join in your fundraiser. In fact," I add, leaning forwards in my turn, "I would love to join you in organising it."

Lawrence sits back in his chair, and eyes me intently. I can tell he's not sure about me, or perhaps he's just taken by surprise.

"Do you mean...you'd like to help fund the event?" he asks.

"No." My voice is firm. He needs to know I am serious. "I will help finance it too, but what I mean is, I want to be your partner and organise everything alongside you. I am passionate about your cause, and want to make a difference."

Susan Parker glances from Lawrence to myself, as if watching a tennis match.

Lawrence comfortably holds my gaze. "We can discuss the details in a more intimate setting, but I am open to it. If you are sure."

"I am."

I've never been more sure of anything in my life. It's the only way I will ever have access to Virgil again, and I will make damn sure he's a part of it. Or I'm out.

Except I can't tell him this, so I'll have to be more subtle about it.

After dinner he calls me to a corner of the dining hall, far enough away from anyone else to eavesdrop, and away from Susan.

"Why do you want to be my partner in this?" he asks over his glass of sherry.

I take a sip of my own drink, Bailey's, and meet his stare. "I could lie to you and make up a reason why I'm passionate about giving second chances and everyone, even criminals, can be rehabilitated, or I could be honest and tell you that

I'm going to keep my reasons to myself. I think you know which one I'm going to opt for, don't you?"

His barely visible lips remain flat as the horizon, but his eyes give me a smile of appreciation. "I will invite you to mine later this week to have a proper discussion, and go over the details, but in the meantime, perhaps you can already start working in the background. We are still very much in the planning stage, where gathering funds is our priority. This project is very money-hungry, and I have my contacts, but your own network will be most welcome. It's all about convincing wealthy individuals and getting them to bring their friends in, and when prospective investors know their trusted friends are in, it becomes a doddle. They'll want to know who else is investing, but they won't know until they've already committed some funds, and then it's up to us to play them against each other, to appeal to their competitive side, their ego, because the amount each invests quickly becomes known. Once they've invested a small amount, something clicks in their mind; they're in, and they want to outdo their peers. So please, talk to people you know."

I nod. Begging for money is not my cup of tea, but I'll do anything for Virgil.

20

ANONYMOUS UPC RANKINGS

Day 16 of the Ultimate Psycho Championships (UPC)

Rocky Bardeaux

Bringing the harmonica to his lips transported Rocky to a different place and time. Arguably, this different place and time was worse than his current circumstances; he had never before been able to relax on a sun deck, or any terrace of any kind, in the blazing sun with nothing to do with his day but stare out at the sea, with no fear of abuse or need for drugs or threat of creditors coming for him. But the harmonica, in a time of pain and misery, had been a liberation for him. He'd found one in a pile of rubbish in his teens, and had taught himself how to play, alone in the morning which, in his lifestyle at the time, was the only time of day he enjoyed some form of peace.

He remembered sitting on his springy bed in his cold bedsit in South London and trying out different sounds, until he hit on the desired notes and committed the sequence to memory. Getting something right, something he'd taught himself from scratch, provided a glow in his stomach he'd never felt before. He was proud of his harmonica-playing skills, even though in the grand scheme of things they were modest at best.

Today, perched on the boat's sun deck, sat sideways on the built-in booth and staring out at the grey horizon, he felt at the top of the world. Quentin watched him from the other booth, and having an audience fuelled him. He played 'When the Saints Go Marching In', and it may have been his best performance yet.

As he played, however, his mind drifted off to the absence of cameras on this part of the boat, and how free it made him feel. Being constantly watched was a humbling experience; it made you learn about your behaviour and how you came across to others. In a way, it was a good thing. He'd never felt this way in prison because he knew the feed was only used for security purposes, and watched by either no one, or one person at a time. Knowing thousands of people watched you for entertainment was a different experience entirely.

He noticed how grumpy a man he was, and how he never, or rarely, made a joke, or said something lighthearted. He felt that wasn't who he was, deep inside, yet that was how he came across. He decided he would try to change this. As much as he disliked Teddy and didn't want to be anything like him, he couldn't fault his general energy; when he wasn't getting into a fight or being offensive in some way, he exuded a happy, infectious vibe. His excitement for things around him was pure, and it was pleasant to have around. Rocky imagined his own mood never lifted people around him. And in a way, that might eventually contribute to their mission's failure. A dark general mood could result in the worst outcome.

The song came to an end, and Rocky's lips kept throbbing from the instrument's vibrations and his own thrill. He glanced at Quentin, sprawled over the other booth and staring at a bird nearby. "How did you like it?" Rocky asked.

"I'm not the biggest fan of harmonica, I can't lie," Quentin replied. "A bit of a grating sound, like rusty hinges. But I can tell you're good at it, so well done to you."

Rocky eyed him sideways, then chuckled to himself. "Is it true what the man-bird said, when he introduced you?"

Something changed in Quentin's eyes when he looked at him. "What do you mean?"

"That it all changed after your wife's suicide?"

"Oookay," Quentin said, sitting upright on the booth, "is this where we're going now?" He cleared his throat. "After her *death*. Yeah, pretty much."

"Sorry to hear it, mate."

Quentin nodded. "She had two daughters, not mine. Great girls. You can imagine how it affected them. I was so angry."

"You got along with their father?"

"Yeah, well enough. Not mates with the guy, obviously, but he was a good father, and that's all you can ask, isn't it? That's why I felt I could go off my mind and land in prison. The girls didn't need me."

Rocky wanted to ask why Quentin had felt going off his mind in that way was the answer to losing his wife, but it wasn't his place to prod, not at this stage of their friendship.

"No children of your own, then?" Rocky asked.

Quentin shook his head. "We were planning to, eventually. We'd been married two years, I thought we might start trying within a year. What about you?"

"No, course not. Been in prison most of my adult life. I have a niece and a nephew, though. Stevie, the nephew, is a football star, or going to be. He's the closest thing I'll ever have to a son."

"Think you might be able to see him when we get out?"

"I'll definitely try. Might be difficult, depending on where they release us. Probably won't be able to return to England, will we?"

"I'd rather be out of prison," Quentin said, "of course I would, but I'm not sure what I'll do with freedom. Can hardly project manage in Guatemala, can I? And I don't really have other skills. I suppose I'll have to think of something to learn."

"Anything you've always been passionate about?"

"Golf?" Quentin laughed. "Can't just become a pro golf player at forty-seven."

"No, but you could become an instructor. I doubt Guatemala have many of those."

Quentin raised his eyebrows. "Something to think about."

The sun deck's hidden speaker came on. "Participants," came the plague barrister's voice. "We will give you a cat. We will provide cat food and the litter, but it will be your job to look after it. Every day, when we deliver the meals, we will pick up the bag of dirty litter. The cat is already housetrained. If any harm comes to this cat, we will make a note and points will be deducted retroactively for the perpetrator or perpetrators. We haven't named her. Enjoy."

"Plague barrister," Quentin called loudly, "while you're here, I have a question."

A pause, then the speaker came back on. "Yes?"

"If there is violence before the sixty days run out, but no deaths, do we still all get freed?"

"It all depends on the degree of violence. The violence we've seen so far did not warrant point deductions, so minimal violence is acceptable. However, if you abuse this rule, well...we make up the rules, so we can change them as needed. Just behave, and you'll be fine."

The PA system turned off.

21

ANONYMOUS UPC RANKINGS

Day 16 of the Ultimate Psycho Championships (UPC)

Virgil Francopan

The cat was delivered immediately after they retrieved the dirty trays from lunch. It was a tortoiseshell cat, with mottled stripes of black, grey, and brown-orange, and a snow-white patch around its mouth. Edmond and Teddy fawned over it as soon as the dinner man released it inside the lounge. Teddy fetched a bowl and poured a pouch of food inside, then brought it to the cat and stroked its head admiringly while Edmond stroked its tail and hind legs.

"We'll look after you," Teddy said in a silly voice. "We will. You eat up, you look a bit skinny to me."

The masters had selected a good cat, for it was very

friendly. It welcomed human contact, and perhaps to a feline, Teddy's tattoos just looked like odd fur patterns, because it did not seem bothered in the slightest. Virgil, for one, would recoil at having Teddy Brandt's inked scalp in his face.

Edmond appeared just as smitten, but he didn't say a word. He couldn't keep his hands off the fur. He followed the cat around, squeezing around the coffee table and the sofa, as it started sniffing its surroundings and studying the rest of the inmates.

"Don't come to me, you hairy thing," Glenys said, lifting her hands and feet up in the air. "I don't want any of your hair on me. I know what cats are like."

Rocky gave it a stroke when it strolled by its feet, the cat arching its back under his hand. He shook his hand over the sofa and a cloud of hair floated down.

"Mr. Plague Barrister has just made his cleaners' job a lot more difficult," Quentin said.

Teddy emptied the bag of litter into the provided tray.

"Put the bag into the bin," Glenys said when Teddy discarded it carelessly.

Teddy rolled his eyes but obeyed without complaining, which was a testament to his affection for the furry pet.

"We have to name her," Edmond said, his eyes glued to the cat.

"What about Mrs. Whiskers?" Glenys suggested.

"Can you think of a more boring name?" Teddy said. "It's got to be something like Clawdia or Purrincess. Even Furball would be better."

"I don't know," Rocky said, "I've always liked human names for pets. Something like Karen, or Mary."

The cat came to Virgil. It rubbed against his leg, shedding its hair on his jumpsuit, and Virgil watched without moving. Then it sat on its hind legs next to Virgil's feet, and glanced around like a queen observing her queendom, slowly blinking.

"Or we could go down the Greek mythology route," Virgil said, and the cat briefly looked up at him. "You've all heard of the Minotaur, right? A monster housed in a labyrinth in Crete, and every nine years seven young men and seven young women are sent to the Minotaur as a tribute."

"What's that?" Teddy asked.

"A sort of punishment. The King of Crete waged war on Athens, and to end it, Athens was forced to send a regular tribute of fourteen young people as a form of submission. Until a young hero named Theseus volunteered to go with the intention of killing the Minotaur and ending the cycle of sacrifices. The king's daughter, Ariadne, gave him a ball of thread which he used to find his way out of the labyrinth easily, and he killed the Minotaur, putting an end to the tribute.

"I can see some similarities between our predicament and the Minotaur's story. We're seven in here, so it seems like a meaningful number. We're trying to get out of prison, which is a much more elaborate labyrinth than the Minotaur's, and we're striving to put an end to our punishment. This cat could help us make it to the end, pets are a known method for soothing our emotions and generally calming us. So if the cat's a female, Ariadne could suit her? With Ariadne's thread being a tool which helped Theseus."

"All sounds a bit complicated to me, mate," said Teddy. "I'm still in the Furball camp."

"What about Thesea?" Rocky said. "She could be our little heroine, and if we love her enough, she could become our mascot and lead us to success."

"Yeah, adding a female slant to a Greek hero," Glenys said, "I like that."

"Can we see a show of hands for Thesea?" Virgil asked the room. Rocky, Glenys, Virgil, and Edmond raised their hands, which was a majority.

"Thesea it is," Virgil said, "sorry Quentin, Jan, and Teddy. Democracy has spoken."

Quentin shrugged. "I wasn't against it. Just no general inclination for a name."

"Between her and me, she's Furball," Teddy said, and the love which coated his words made it impossible to tell him off.

The cat jumped onto Virgil's lap. It made him start so he raised his hands ever so slightly.

"Woh," Teddy shouted, standing up quickly. "Don't, Virgil."

Virgil waved him away. "Oh relax, I would never harm her. I'm not interested in cats." He stroked the fur in between her ears. "Now if you could talk, it would be a different story."

The skin at the tip of her ears was so soft, the fine hairs so delicate. She blinked slowly, gazing up at Virgil with overflowing affection. Virgil forgot about Teddy and Edmond fixing him with their eyes, more tense than a guitar's strings. Thesea raised her head behind his fingers, implicitly asking him to stroke her throat. He obliged, feeling her cold breath on his wrist. She contorted her neck and rubbed her cheek against his hand, her whiskers tickling him as they brushed against his skin. A wave of chills started in his shoulders and ran down his spine.

Something deep, fundamental shifted within him. He knew why he was the way he was. Why he was unusual and his brain had been wired the way it was. His background, coupled with quite a few personality disorders. What he was currently feeling simply did not fit with *him*, with everything he understood about himself. A desire to make this cat comfortable, to make her happy, compelled him to stroke her and continue to do what he could feel she enjoyed. He joined his legs together to try and make her 'bed' less gappy and more snuggly.

What was he doing?

He suddenly grabbed the cat – gently – and set it down on the floor. He nudged her back to Teddy. She looked back one last time, then solemnly sauntered over to her adopted father.

For the first time in his life, Virgil felt violated.

22

ANONYMOUS UPC RANKINGS

Day 20 of the Ultimate Psycho Championships (UPC)

Virgil Francopan

Virgil had done it, at last. He'd broken Edmond. As the Van Helmont twin talked about his early life, a part of Virgil's brain listened to every word while the other part rejoiced in having gained the man's trust at last.

"...because Mom had no patience for our whining," he was saying, "so she'd lock us up in our room for days on end. We quickly stopped whining after that, but then she'd always find a reason to lock us up again."

"Were you and Jan in the same room?"

"No, we each had our own."

That might explain why they didn't seem overly close,

for twin brothers, Virgil thought. "Do you have any memories involving fire from your childhood?"

Edmond seemed taken aback by the question. "Yeah," he said, slightly confused, "loads of them."

"Do you remember when you first played with fire for fun?"

He took a deep breath and thought for a moment. "I think I must have been eight, or nine. We had loads of candles out for Christmas, and I couldn't stop lighting matches and melting the wax and watching the flames. I'd cover all kinds of things with melted wax, watch it harden, then light it up again. I loved how the flame changed, the colours, the size. Made a mess too, Mom and Dad got mad at me so often."

"So it's the fire itself that fascinates you," Virgil said, "the mechanics of it, the visuals, the way in which you start it."

"Oh yeah, it's a thing of beauty. It's a form of art, if you ask me. I'll never get enough of it."

"Did your mother or father like fire too?"

"Nah, not really. Well, Dad liked having bonfires to get rid of things. He'd have them every month or so, in the garden. The smoky smell of bonfire was the smell of my childhood. He was the opposite of a hoarder, couldn't stand crap accumulating in the house, and reducing things to ashes is the best way to get rid of things. Saves a trip to the tip. Not just crap though, he'd throw our toys in there too, and our stuffed animals. Anything he didn't want to see anymore. Well, to him it probably was crap, but not to me. I think I was twelve when I found my baseball bat in there, it had been signed by a pro player. I remember going up to Dad in tears. He was standing by the flames, feeding branches into it, drunk out of his ass. 'You don't play baseball no more' he said, 'don't need a bat in the house.' I just stood there, little ol' me, bawling my eyes out. 'But just because I quit the team doesn't mean I don't like baseball no more. Gary Sheffield *signed* it.' But it was too late, so I don't know why I said anything. Pretty sure it was my only valuable possession left at that time."

"Have your parents ever been violent with you?"

Edmond shook his head. "We weren't a violent house. I'm not a violent person."

"Other than breaking walls?" Virgil asked with a smirk.

"You count that as violence?"

"I definitely count starting fires to hurt people as violence, don't you?"

"To me violence is what Teddy does, hitting people, getting mad and breaking shit. I don't do that; me breaking the wall was calculated, and it didn't put anyone else in danger."

"Teddy's is but one form of violence," Virgil said. "He's just an impulsive, violent-minded Humpty Dumpty due to his background and the violence he suffered in his household, as a child."

"Humpty Dumpty?" Edmond repeated, frowning.

"Yes, the nursery rhyme character? Maybe it's more British than I thought. He has a tattoo of it on his scalp, a version of the character that is rather worse for wear. There's a physical resemblance between them. To come back to you, your form of violence is different, but can be, and has been, more destructive. More destructive than Teddy's actions."

Edmond shut himself down, Virgil could detect it in his gaze. Perhaps he'd pushed a bit too far.

"I don't mean to offend," Virgil went on, "we're in a safe space here. It's important we identify everything about you, to help you move forward. If you believe not to be a violent person, but your actions say otherwise, it's a conflict which can lead to problems. It can be solved, though. You have started fires other than for your love of it, haven't you?"

"I feel like we're back in my trial. You sure you're meant to ask me questions like that?"

"Very sure, Edmond. The trial is over, whatever we say here does not matter. It's about you now, about helping you improve your mental health, to come to terms with who you are, and how you attain peace. You have a fascination for fire and fire-setting, but you've also used it to hurt people you saw as threats."

"Well," a guilty grin came over Edmond, "sometimes both purposes converge nicely, they serve one another, and that's a beautiful thing when it happens."

"Thank you," Virgil said. "You just took a big step forward. I am confident, from what I've learned about you, that you are both an arsonist and a pyromaniac. An arsonist deliberately sets fire to buildings, property, or objects, as part of a meticulous plan to achieve a specific outcome. Pyromania is a psychological condition which means a pyromaniac has an impulsive and uncontrollable urge to start fires. The pyromaniac doesn't have an ulterior motive to start a fire, he does it for the intense pleasure or relief he feels from setting the fire or watching things burn. You, Edmond Van Helmont, are both, and that is extremely rare."

Edmond beamed. "Thank you."

"Not sure it was a compliment, but rather a diagnosis which will help us move forward. I think we've made big strides today, it's probably best we end the session now so we can both reflect on what we've learned."

Edmond stood up, then glanced up at the camera. "It's not because I'm a willing participant now that I don't want to keep receiving my reward. Keep them lollipops coming."

23

ANNA KIMPER

I can finally rest in my cabin after a long twelve-hour shift in the surveillance room. Wu, our Chinese investor, cancelled his trip at the last minute, so I had to cover for him. Not that I mind, I enjoy having an excuse to observe the goings-on as much as possible, but it does take its toll on me. I kick my shoes, let my hair down, pour myself a glass of water, grab a dark chocolate bar, and jump on my bed. Talking to Ollie will help me decompress.

"What has been going on in the boat?" he asks.

"Virgil has gotten to Edmond. I think he's gained his trust now, which, outside this experiment, I would say is the beginning of the end for Edmond, but here I don't know."

I stroke the leather patches on my glove. It's soft, always soothes me.

"How do you know Edmond's fallen for his antics?"

"They just had a session, in Virgil's room. Edmond opened up, about his childhood, his feelings on the boat. Virgil gave him a diagnosis, said he's an arsonist and a pyromaniac."

Sixty Days of Virgil

"Are you going to show this session on the daily highlights?"

"Some of it, sure. But I've left the final say to Lawrence because I'm pooped. I've given him my notes, so we'll probably show the key moments of the conversation."

I move to lean against the bed's backrest, and I wince as my skin sends a flurry of shooting pains up my arm.

"What is it?"

"Nothing, just my arm."

"What about your arm?"

"It's been flaring ever since I've been on the boat. I've already told you."

"Why don't you remove your glove? You should let it breathe."

"It's a special kind of glove that already lets it breathe. I'd rather keep it protected from the sunlight, even when I'm indoors."

A pause, then: "You know," he says, and I can sense he's about to broach a delicate subject. "You never told me what actually happened to your arm."

I let out an annoyed sigh. "There are many things I haven't told you."

"*What?*"

"For your own good, Ollie. You're young, much too young to know what you already know."

He talks over me. "You can't keep things from me, not after everything you've already confided in me. And I'm not a child anymore, I can take it."

"You're nineteen, Ollie. Not even twenty years old!"

"Exactly, an adult. What did you not tell me? What did Virgil do to your arm?"

I just want to go to sleep. "I'd really rather not do this now. Let's talk again later."

"Well then you shouldn't have kept things from me before. What did he do to your arm?"

"He did what he does, Ollie. But that doesn't matter, it's just physical pain. It's what he did– what he did to your baby brother which matters."

"It all matters, Mum. I need to know everything that bastard did before we get to him. I don't want to learn of more atrocities after he's already gone, when I can no longer make him pay for it."

Oh, what have I done. I've ruined this boy's life. No nineteen year-old should ever have to say these things, to be this aggressive, this blood thirsty. I can't keep the tears from falling, however hard I try.

"What did that bastard do to you? When he held you captive for forty-eight hours, what did he do to you?"

"Stop it."

"What did he do to you?"

"I said stop, Ollie."

"What did he do to you?"

"Stop."

"WHAT DID HE DO TO YOU?"

"HE KILLED MY BABY BOY." Too loud, someone will hear me. "How does it matter what else he's done?" I can feel myself spiralling out of control, but I'm powerless to stop it. "He focused his sick hobby on my son, and then– then–" I collapse in a babble of sobs. "The notebook," I mutter. It's all I can see in front of my eyes. The leather-bound notebook which I used for months afterwards, with embossed letters on the front, a gift from the hospital staff as I was discharged, or so I thought. "The blasted notebook," I repeat in between sobs.

"What about the notebook?" Ollie asks as if I'm not a useless mess right now. "What notebook?"

"The notebook is my baby. Was my baby."

The letter will haunt me for the rest of my days. Blue ink on white parchment paper, in neat, slanted handwriting: *Your notebook's leather is prime quality. Doesn't it smell good?*

As soon as I learned the notebook was from Virgil I understood what had happened, and I still feel sick to my stomach to think about it today.

"His hobby..." Ollie mutters. "Oh no. It was a leather notebook?"

I don't reply, I don't have the strength.

"What a scummy, rotten bastard," Ollie says. "An absolute twisted fuck."

He falls silent for a while; it gives me enough time to pick myself up. Then a knock comes at the door.

It can't be Lawrence, he's busy putting the daily highlights together with the Anonymous team. Porker Stephen isn't here, and he's the only one who gets my hair up on this boat. I dry my cheeks, check myself in the mirror, and adjust my blouse. A good job I don't wear make up these days.

I open the door. It's Stanislas, in his white polo shirt and brown cargo shorts, holding a plastic bag in his hand.

"Sorry, am I disturbing you?" he asks in his German accent, studying me.

I shake my head. "What is it?"

He holds the bag up. "We received a delivery. The medications you ordered. Would you like me to come back later?"

"No, it's okay." I take the bag. "I'm sorry, I'm just a bit tired. Thank you for this, it's much appreciated."

"No problem." He looks to his left, then leans towards me. "Do you mind me asking... Why did you not ask Dr. Harry for these? He saw me take a bag of drugs and I felt a bit awkward."

"What did you tell him?"

"Nothing, he didn't say anything. I just went down to my cabin, as if I was taking supplies meant for me."

"Thank you, Stanislas. I just have my own doctor and I'd rather Harry not knew everything about my medical history."

He nods. He throws a furtive glance inside my cabin and I automatically close the door a bit more.

"Are you sure everything is okay?" he asks.

"Yes, of course." He knows I'm lying, but he's polite enough not to insist.

"You can come to me for anything, Mrs Kimper. I hope you know this."

"Anna."

"With respect, I would rather not. I have thought about it, and I hold too much respect for you. In German we address people we respect deeply using the pronoun 'Sie', and to me, even though such a thing does not exist in English, saying Mrs Kimper is the same, it preserves this deep respect and admiration I have for you."

"Fine." I am too tired to fight this battle.

"Thank you. Have a good night, Mrs Kimper."

"You too, Stanislas."

24

ANONYMOUS UPC RANKINGS

Day 23 of the Ultimate Psycho Championships (UPC)

Rocky Bardeaux

Thesea played a big role in uplifting everyone's mood. Rocky enjoyed having something to look after, and so did Teddy and Edmond. They almost fought over who got to feed her, and as soon as he had to set the cat down from his lap to get up, he could be sure one of them would be over in a jiffy to take over the stroking. Even Quentin enjoyed the occasional cuddle, and though Glenys made a point of staying away from Thesea most of the time, he'd caught her, one morning, stroking her under the chin while she waited for her water to boil. The one chore Rocky was glad to leave to Teddy and Edmond was the cleaning and replacement of the litter, so he couldn't truly claim the title of co-parent. He was just the fun uncle, which seemed to be his natural role in life.

Rain and dark clouds plagued their journey for several days, but on day 23 the sun poked through the thick layer of clouds and gradually dispersed them. The inmates seized the opportunity to climb up to the sun deck and gaze at the vast emptiness. The sea was not completely still, resembling the texture of a heavily oiled canvas, dark grey verging on deep blue in some patches. With the sun came the cry of birds travelling through, sometimes coming to perch on the bimini top. The cool breeze made Rocky think they must be somewhere in the northern hemisphere, but it was disconcerting to not have a clue of where in the world they were.

This was one of the rare occasions where all seven of them were out together on the sun deck. The Van Helmont twins looked out of place basked in the sunlight, but they appeared to be in a joyous mood; Jan was even smiling at something Edmond told him.

"D'you reckon they'd really execute us, if it came down to it?" asked Teddy, lying down on the booth with his head on an arm rest. "Like the plague barrister said in the beginning."

"They were bold enough to break us out of prison," Quentin said, standing up against the guardrail and staring into the horizon. "It's not such a stretch of the imagination that they could kill us too."

"They're already in serious trouble with the law," Glenys added, "I don't think they'd balk at it. It's not such a big step from breaking us out of jail to killing us, as it is from breaking us out of jail in the first place."

"Not to mention I imagine the public wouldn't be too outraged," Francopan said. "Our lives aren't viewed as worthy as everyone else's, they'd think the world is better off with us dead than with us potentially free, or free to harm others in prison."

"How many points do you even get taken off for murder?" Quentin asked. "We all have sixty points, right? And if we get down to twenty they kill us. How do we get down to twenty?"

"They're keeping a lot of information to themselves," replied Rocky. "Rightly so, I'd say. Because they can, so why not, and this way we can't plan anything."

"And yet, we can infer some of the information," said Francopan. "They said that if a death occurs, then the rankings kick in and only some of us will get out. That's not us getting executed, so one murder must not get us down to twenty points. I would imagine two would, or perhaps one murder and one act of severe violence."

"It's not just that they kill us, though, is it?" Teddy said. "The plague barrister said his psychiatrist would suss out what our worst nightmare is and kill us with that in mind. Can't understand how he's going about doing that, but I don't care to find out if he got it right or not."

"Guys," Glenys said, "you've been thinking about this way too much. We're not killing anyone, remember? It's simple, we go to the end together and we're free, start a new life. You're starting to make me think the plague barrister *is* a fool for thinking we'll make it."

Rocky was grateful for Glenys. "Too right," he said. "It doesn't matter if they would kill us or how many points we'd get docked. We keep behaving and we'll get the largest reward we could ever hope for. We've already come too close to risking failure for my liking." He gazed at Teddy as he said this.

"Mate," Teddy said, "I'm with you on this. We're just

talking here, right? Got fuck all else to do. I just said I don't care to find out, didn't I? I'm being a good boy."

"Well, mostly," Francopan said, giving Rocky a look.

"You're saying all the right things," Edmond said, looking at Glenys, "but I'm not sure you mean them. You been looking stressed, you lashed out at Teddy not that long ago, and you're a pro at killing. It comes more natural to you than any of us."

Rocky understood where Edmond came from – Glenys had woken up several times in the past week with nightmares, screaming the boat down, along with a string of panic attacks where only Francopan could calm her – but she was not at the top of his list of people who worried him most. Beyond Teddy and Francopan, Edmond was actually up there with his relentless efforts to find an escape.

"You can't be serious," Glenys said. "Of all these psychos, I'm the one you think will make us fail?"

Edmond shrugged. "It's not like you haven't killed fiercer men than us before."

"How many people have you killed?" Quentin asked, studying Glenys under a new light.

"Have you really never heard of Glenys Murphy the Manhunter?" Edmond asked the four British men, dumbfounded.

"I've heard of her," Rocky said, "but I don't know the details."

"I know her quite well now," Francopan said, "but before arriving here, no, like Rocky, I only knew the name."

"Wow," Edmond said. "She was everywhere at the time, the papers couldn't have enough of her."

"Why?" Quentin asked. "Surely she's not the first woman to kill men."

"Man, you have no idea. Do you want to tell them?" Edmond asked Glenys.

"Please, you go first," she said, smirking. "You sound like you're a fan."

"She got locked up for murdering her husband, but around what...five years in?"

"Four," Glenys said. "When my appeals dried up."

"Four years in, she called a journalist for an exclusive interview, and that's when her nickname was born and became a headline grabber worldwide. In that interview she said she killed fourteen men, all men who had assaulted her or she knew had assaulted other women. And she gave details of the location of those bodies. It came completely out of the blue; until then she was just another case of domestic violence gone wrong. You can imagine the total media frenzy."

"And were the bodies found?" Rocky asked.

"Oh yeah," Glenys said before Edmond could open his mouth. "I'm no liar. Last I heard they only found ten, but it was enough to show I was telling the truth."

"Might sound a bit...insulting," Teddy said, "but that's not how I intend it, I'm genuinely curious, and admirative, if that's a word. How did you manage to kill so many men?"

"Ha, I'm glad you asked. I used their weakness to get close to them, made them believe I was easy. Not hard to fool you bastards; as soon as you make 'em think you crave their dick, they'll follow you to their grave. But I studied human anatomy, learned where the vital organs and arteries were. I became a butcher and worked in a slaughterhouse for years, so I developed a familiarity with slicing through flesh, using knives, dealing deadly blows. Became second nature. So surprise was all I needed; by the time they realised I wasn't actually going to let them fuck me, it was too late. The knife had already sliced their carotid artery, or I'd drive a blade in the diaphragm area, where the rib cage kind of separates, that's the easiest way to reach the heart and the aorta."

"Fuck me," Teddy said. "And that's how you killed that correctional officer too?"

Glenys nodded. "I happily helped with drug smuggling in exchange for a shank, and once I had a blade, the rest was a walk in the park."

After this, Rocky couldn't help but share Edmond's concerns. Regardless of whether she seemed genuine about making it to the end, if her mental state became unstable enough, who was to say she wouldn't grab a weapon and use those skills to lash out? Following her nightmares, it took a good two minutes to neutralise and calm her down. She didn't seem in control at all. And there were plenty of items in this boat which could double up as weapons.

A slow clap came from Rocky's right. It was Francopan, with a quiet air of appreciation on his face. "Bravo," he said. "Masterful. There's a lot going on in between those two ears. I can't believe I never heard the details of your story before."

"What I can't wrap my head around," Quentin said, "is why you told the world about your murders? Sounds like you were getting away with it. You might've been out by now, if your only murder had been your husband."

"I was sentenced to sixty years in jail for my husband, honey. Without parole. I wasn't getting out even before I started talking."

"Still. Why bother?"

Glenys didn't reply right away. "I guess if you get to the bottom of it, it was pride? And guilt. I'm proud of how I managed to pull it off, to defeat all those strong men and make them pay, and then get away with it. If I'm the one who tells the police about it, then I still got away with it, didn't I? I wanted the world to know about all of it, didn't want to take my story to my grave. And I guess I felt a bit guilty about those men's families and the women in their lives who probably loved them. They didn't know where they were, what had happened to them. Now they can grieve properly. It's not their fault their brother or nephew or grandson was a swine. And I'm sure some of their parents did their best, and just couldn't turn them into decent human beings."

"Mate, what are you doing?" Rocky said, catching Edmond from the corner of his eye.

He had already unzipped and removed the top half of his jumpsuit, revealing a sickly pale and bone-thin torso with a handful of wispy brown hair in the dip of his chest. He was now removing his socks.

"Testing them," he said as he went on to step out of the jumpsuit. He stood against the guardrail in his grey boxer shorts.

"He's not about to attempt suicide, is he?" Quentin asked.

"I don't believe so," Francopan said. "Though he might kill himself by accident."

Edmond climbed onto the guardrail and crouched on top, holding onto the edge to keep his balance.

"Edmond," Francopan called out, "going for a swim in these cold waters is not your best idea. You could easily develop some serious health issues."

It sounded like Francopan was holding something back, as if he knew something Rocky and the others didn't. Edmond paused for a second, then he gave a small shrug and made the long jump to the sea.

His dive was elegant, Rocky had to give it to him. He

dived head first, arms above his head, hands brought together like a shark's fin so that he sliced through the water seamlessly. His head emerged back up and he started swimming away from the boat. He was a practised swimmer, this was obvious, but where was he going?

"Does he see something we don't?" Teddy asked.

"He just wants to see what happens," Francopan said. "I'm curious too, how quickly will our masters come? But he may pay the highest price."

"If he dies," Quentin said, "we won't be penalised, right? Not our fault he's that stupid."

All six of them stared at the little white dot making its way into the endless dark grey expanse. He was moving slowly, the sea so large around him that it looked like he was stationary. For a while, a long while, nothing happened. And soon, though it was hard to tell with the distance, it looked like Edmond was weakening.

"They're going to come, right?" Teddy asked.

"They have to," Rocky replied. "It's not in their interest for us to die so...unnecessarily. It's not even caught on camera."

Now he was barely moving. The cold water must have gotten to him, he could not go on much longer. They heard the Zodiac before they saw it. A distant buzz, the same as when the nurse had come, and the same as whenever the staff brought their meals. Just as Edmond started struggling to keep his head above water, the yellow Zodiac pulled up next to him and a man dragged him onto the tender.

"I'll go down to fetch him," Rocky said, studying the route to climb down to reach the stern.

"I'll come too," said Quentin.

It was not a straightforward climb down but they managed it. Shortly after they set foot on the stern, the

Zodiac reached the yacht. On it was the nurse they had seen once, and the plague barrister himself in his outfit, complete with his beaked mask and gavel. They pulled up against the stern, the nurse lifted a limp Edmond, and Rocky held him under his arms while Quentin grabbed his feet.

"I'll open the doors to the lounge for you," the big black man said as he stepped onto the stern, holding a bag in his hands, "so you can lay him down in a warm room straight away."

Edmond was ice-cold to the touch, and he'd turned blue.

"He's going to need some medical attention," Rocky said.

"Virgil will know what to do," the nurse said as he unlocked the door, "but you need to remove his boxers, wrap him in blankets and towels, give him some warm water to drink, and we're giving you an electric blanket." He threw the bag he was holding inside the lounge. "We'll have to see how it goes from there."

They carried Edmond to the door, but just as they reached it, the plague barrister spoke. "Albert Einstein once said, *Two things are infinite: the universe and human stupidity. And I'm not sure about the universe.*" He lowered his head and glanced at Rocky and Quentin as if looking at them over his glasses. "Please don't prove him right."

The nurse jumped back in the Zodiac and they took off.

25

ROCKY BARDEAUX

(Six years earlier)

The tray materialised through the hatch. The usual dinner of tough, dry chicken breast with polystyrene-like plain rice and a portion of rubbery boiled green beans. The only difference, this time, being that the guard delivering the meal lingered. Rocky could hear him behind the hatch, hovering, the rustling of his clothes as he scratched his nose or took something out of his pocket. He could also see the light shifting behind the door's small reinforced window, the only way to look inside the solitary cell other than the camera. Then the man's face appeared, close against the window, and their eyes met.

It wasn't Klein; Rocky had never seen this one before. "You new?" he asked.

The man nodded. It had happened before; sometimes new guards arrived with a sort of fascination for the monster who dwelled in Her Majesty's Prison's dungeon.

The fascination never lasted long; they soon joined Klein's ways and treated him worse than a feral dog.

"Sorry about the food," the guard said. He was young, must've been in his late twenties, but he already had thin hair and an advanced receding hair line. "Looks revolting."

"Not your fault." Rocky sat himself on the concrete slab which served as his bed, then he grabbed the plastic fork and plopped a piece of bone dry chicken into his mouth. He took a sip of water to wash down what felt like a mouthful of dust. "New to the job, or were you stationed somewhere else before?"

Rocky didn't want the guard to leave. Conversation, any conversation, was rarer than good food in his life. Regardless of the man's motive, his company was appreciated.

"I was in HMP Pentonville for four years, relocated here."

"Lucky you." Rocky could sense this one was different. No guard had ever been happy to engage in small talk before.

"Officer Klein doesn't like you."

Rocky half-suppressed a laugh. "That's putting it mildly. Don't worry, you'll come to agree with him soon enough, I'm sure."

"Don't think so," he said.

A moment of silence as Rocky took a few mouthfuls of tummy-fillers.

Then the guard asked: "How can you kill someone?"

Rocky ate a bit more as he reflected on how to best answer the question. He had no objection against veering away from small talk. "Your name?"

"Martin."

"Right, Martin. Your parents, or the average man's parents, didn't go to prison, no one in your family has gone to prison, you don't even know someone who has. Your parents may have emotionally abused you, shouted at you, called you names at times, grounded you, sent you to the naughty step, at worse they smacked you a couple of times, then felt terrible about it. But you also received some love and affirmation and support. Most people get this to varying degrees. Most people won't even have been smacked, and many won't have been emotionally abused. As a kid, if you ever stepped out of line, hit another kid, disrespected someone, you would be told off. Your punishment would be the end of your world. You'd be made to feel ashamed. As an adult, you wouldn't even consider committing a crime. Your family's never done that, your role models are straight people who would never come close to committing a crime, imagine what they'd think of you, if you did. You've got so much to lose. Your parents support you financially, or there is money waiting for you when they pass. Or you have a job to lose, friends who would immediately kick you out of their circle, or siblings who would never understand how you could possibly do something like this. Maybe you have a girlfriend, or a family of your own who looks up to you, children you wouldn't dare abandon."

Rocky marked a pause as he ate the last of his green beans.

"Your baseline," he resumed, "your default, is leading a normal life with a well-paying job, or enough to pay the bills anyway, a loving family to support you if the going gets tough, a partner or potential partner who you want to keep and impress, and when you're triggered, the few times when you step out of line, you'll shout, maybe throw out some insults, curse God, belittle someone, throw your phone, or God forbid punch a wall or break a piece of furniture. Instead of hitting someone who provoked you, you'll leave, huffing and puffing, because you know that's the better option. Your baseline is here." Rocky placed his hand around shoulder-height. "Stepping out of line, going beyond your baseline" he raised his hand to eye-level "means having some minor anger management issues – if you have any. You have a life to ruin, if you commit the unthinkable."

He shoved a forkful of rice into his mouth and washed it down with water.

"Now me, and people like me, we have an entirely different baseline." He placed his hand a foot above his head. "My father did time, so did my mother. I never met my uncle because his entire life he was either in prison or didn't give a fuck about meeting me. My father physically and sexually abused me, my mother beat me, and then I went into the care system, where the abuse didn't stop. When they released me into the wild at eighteen, I had no education, no money, nowhere to sleep, no one to help me out, and I knew no way to make money other than through crime. All the people around me were doing it. What appeared to you as unthinkable was mundane for me. 'Oh, Jony got caught, got slapped with two years," that's what I heard on an ordinary Wednesday morning. Prison is an integral part of our baseline. Too many of us look forward to prison as a twisted rite of passage. We've already been told since birth that we'll never amount to anything, at home, at school, society at large. So we choose the only path available to children who have been beaten down psychologically before we even had a chance to dream beyond our belittlement."

"Why did you kill, though?" Martin asked. "Before prison, and after."

Rocky sighed. "Because killing wasn't an impossibility for me. It wasn't out of my world. It had its place in my world, because I was already familiar with fates worse than death or prison. I had nothing to lose, no life to ruin. After years of violence on the streets and years of being locked up, you become immune to cruelty. Your world narrows and gets smaller and smaller and soon you are filled with so much hate that you hate absolutely everything in your life. The roommate, the clients, the cell bars, the food, the man in the cell next door who hums too loudly, and especially the guards. You explode thinking the hate will be expelled from your body."

He took his final bite of rice, and allowed it to tumble down his throat without washing it down.

"But it never leaves."

26

ANONYMOUS UPC RANKINGS

Day 26 of the Ultimate Psycho Championships (UPC)

Rocky Bardeaux

For the first time, Rocky actually asked Francopan for a talking session. Not that he wouldn't demand his reward at the end, but he had a question which, since it had come to his mind two weeks ago, would not stop nagging him. This self-awareness business induced by being watched was raising a lot of internal questions and he wasn't sure he liked it. If anything, he liked himself less and less.

"My good old friend Rocky," Francopan said, giving him a smile free of kindness, "what brings you to my room? I deeply enjoy not having to coax you into joining me here, for once."

Rocky couldn't bring himself to meet his gaze. He found

it harder and harder to be on the receiving end of Francopan's odd way of staring at an imaginary point a couple of inches off his face, instead of directly into his eyes.

"I've always been sort of a loner," Rocky said, looking down at his hands as they fidgeted, "preferred my own company to anyone else's. There have been exceptions, obviously, but I'd rather rely entirely on myself than have to deal with people. So when things happened to people around me, friends, it never affected me much. I've never thought of myself as part of a team, my goals have always been my own and nothing else mattered. And obviously, I've killed. And it's not like it keeps me awake at night. So, I suppose…"

He marked a pause. He'd only thought about it in his head, not yet mentioned it aloud. Would speaking it make it real?

"I suppose what I'm wondering is, is whether I'm a psychopath."

Francopan stared back at him, his gloved hands resting peacefully on his lap, legs extended in front of him on his bed and crossed. From this angle, he looked like he had dark patches around his eyes, a bit like Teddy's blackout eyes.

Realising Rocky wasn't going to add anything else, Francopan raised his eyebrows. "Are you asking me if you're a psychopath?"

"Yes."

"No, you are not. But I can double check, if you like. Do you care for anyone in your life? Anyone at all?"

"Well, yeah, my nephew, my niece, and my sister. And my brother, even though we've lost touch."

"Then I confirm, no, you are not a psychopath. Psychopaths have empathy for no one. It's not a pick-and-choose situation, where you love your mum but can't feel anything for the neighbour and your drug dealer. Psychopaths do not have the ability to express empathy, so if you *can* care for someone, then you aren't a psychopath. Simple, isn't it?"

Rocky nodded. It was like someone had been pressing on his chest with their foot, and they'd just stepped off.

"What makes you think you may be one," Francopan went on, "is your selfishness, your egocentrism, but humans are selfish, so nothing out of the ordinary there. And you are not the most selfish person I know, by far. In fact, you might be the least selfish person on this boat."

"Hardly a reference."

"No, indeed, but still. The mere fact that you are here, questioning yourself, proves you are a goodun'."

"Right, enough about me," Rocky said, crossing his arms in front of him and leaning back in his chair. "Tell me about your childhood, what made you what you are. Remember, with me it goes both ways." He gestured between himself and Francopan.

Francopan tut-tutted. "That won't happen. I will not talk about my childhood and all its intricacies. But–" he lifted a finger as Rocky opened his mouth to speak "but, I have a secret. A dark secret no one knows about. Not the media, not the police, not my fellow inmates, no one. And one day, when the time is right, I will tell you. Because of everyone on the boat, you are my favourite."

Rocky narrowed his eyes. "I find it hard to believe."

"You shouldn't. I've been open and honest with you so far, haven't I? No reason why it should change."

"Then tell me about your murders. How did you go about choosing your victims?"

Francopan took a deep breath and crossed his legs the other way around. "That's a complex question. To answer this, we need to establish *why* I killed people. I never felt pleasure in the actual act of killing, that was always just a practicality, a necessity if I wanted to keep operating in the shadows. I did find a good deal of pleasure before, and after. I suppose you can call me a product killer. Some victims came to me, as clients. Others I sought, like acquaintances, or people my clients talked about. Each victim was different, though. They awakened something different in me, all to do with exerting influence, power, manipulating the physical as well as the mind. Sometimes I'd make them trust me, especially if when we first met they mistrusted me, or wanted nothing to do with me. Then I'd invite them back to my house, and when their defences were down, when they were as comfortable as one can be, I'd pounce. Those would be the easiest to convert into art, since they were already in my workshop. Not long before my arrest I set up my office in my house, and that would have changed everything, had it not all gone pear-shaped. To the detriment of my sadly unfinished masterpiece."

He marked a pause, and Rocky allowed his confusion to show. Then he thought harder, and understanding dawned. "You see your leatherwork as art?"

"What else would it be? My entire life is based around my statement on life through my art, viewed through a surrealist lens."

Rocky's gaze was drawn to Francopan's gloves, and nausea rose from his belly. He'd already suspected, known even, where the leather had come from, but now it was real.

"With other people," Francopan resumed, "the fun lay in starting a chain of events. Causing someone to kill another person, or to commit some form of crime. So causing deaths indirectly, through words and actions."

Rocky thought about all the implications, and Francopan himself seemed plunged in his own thoughts.

"So what you're saying," Rocky said, "is that you committed more than the three murders they know about."

"Hmm?" Francopan asked, only just coming back to the present.

"The authorities only found three corpses, and you killed four people while incarcerated. But from what you're saying, it sounds like your murder count was much higher, before they arrested you."

"Oh yeah," Francopan said matter-of-factly. "Naturally."

Rocky was dumbfounded by his frankness. "Does the police know?"

"I don't believe they do. I've never said this out loud, other than to a victim."

"You realise there's a camera recording everything, right?"

In classic Francopan fashion, he waited fifteen seconds before moving his gaze from somewhere on the bed up to the imaginary point next to Rocky's head. "Yeah, yeah I know. I've got nothing to lose now. I'll either be free, or killed, or returned to prison, where I've got no hope of ever leaving solitary confinement, regardless of how many corpses they uncover." He turned his head towards the camera in the corner of the room and stared straight at it. "There are many more missing persons and unsolved mysteries that are attributable to me." Then he gave the camera an artificial, twisted grin, and he returned his attention to Rocky. "Your turn."

Rocky could not deny he'd received more than he'd bargained for. "Okay."

"Let's pick up where we left off," Francopan said. "What

happened when you were thrown onto the streets, at eighteen?"

"I became a rent boy, didn't I?" A ball formed in his throat, so he took a moment to swallow it back down. "I was homeless, surrounded by rent boys, druggies, thieves, and burglars. I needed money to support my drug habit and get a roof over my head – and mark my words, it was only a roof. I don't remember most of the men, the clients, because I was so high all the time. Thank fuck."

"Did the drugs play a role in your first murder, then?"

"Not directly, no. I was in a bad place. I attempted suicide three times, ended up in a psychiatric hospital. I was hearing voices in my head telling me I needed to go home and kill my parents. Even when I didn't hear the voices, I had a longing to kill my parents for what they did to me."

"But they weren't around, were they?"

Rocky shook his head. "Mother was dead, father locked up. Just as painful was not having the opportunity to get back at them. So when one of the clients started showing me videos of his own paedophilic activities, it triggered me. Reminded me of my past. All I could see was the pain and fear in the boys' faces, it was so familiar. I lost it."

He fidgeted some more with his hands. The ball in his throat returned and it took slightly longer to swallow it back down this time around. "It was my way of making up for losing the opportunity to make my parents pay. If I couldn't kill my father, I would kill others who had committed the same crime and got away with it."

"He went to prison, so he didn't really get away with it."

Rocky met Francopan's gaze. "Not for *this* crime. And to me, going to prison is, in fact, getting away with it."

"I imagine this is the story of your other murders?"

"Pretty much. All convicted paedophiles; just seeing them triggered me."

"Your first murder, he wasn't convicted."

"I saw the videos, and he bragged about it. I don't care what the law does or doesn't know, he was a paedophile and had it coming."

"Absolutely," Francopan said, raising his hands. "Millions of murders have been committed for far less. It's a good job none of us here are paedophiles." He giggled.

Rocky returned a deadpan stare.

"Right," Francopan said, straightening his face, "never mind. Are you happy to leave it here? I'd say we learned enough about each other to call it a day."

Rocky stood and looked up at the camera. "Chopin, please. Any composition will do."

27

ANNA KIMPER

It's raining, so we're in the surveillance room, with all the screens. There are only three of us from the consortium on the boat at the moment, so there's plenty of room. Lawrence called a meeting; he was preparing for his trip away from the boat – his first, to take care of some things back home and show his face in society – when Virgil requested to speak with him. He had to wake Harry up, so the psychiatrist still has sleep in his eyes.

"Mr. Francopan is talking medication," Lawrence says, handing a piece of paper to Harry. "I've written the names down, had him spell them out for me. Something for Glenys, he says she's struggling more and more with her nightmares, taking longer and longer to come back to reality. He's afraid she might spiral down because she's showing all the signs."

"Can we trust his concern to be genuine?" I ask. How can I tell them not to listen to any of his requests without sounding too invested in this, without betraying myself?

"Glenys is very anxious at the moment," Harry says, rubbing his eyes. "Especially at night, she's managing to cover it quite well during the day. And she's keeping it together during her sessions with Virgil, so I'm not too worried. Based on the medication Virgil is prescribing, he seems to think she's showing signs of early psychosis. I'm not sure about this, to me she's just showing anxiety, but it's not impossible. An event like this experiment, with all the stress and pressure it brings, can trigger psychosis in people predisposed for it. I don't remember seeing anything in her medical files indicating she ever had a psychotic episode, but she has spent some brief spells in psychiatric units, mainly because she had suicidal tendencies. Virgil is much closer to her than I am, so he may notice things I don't."

"But can we trust his judgement on things like this?" Lawrence asks, and I silently thank him for speaking up. "Do you think he could have an ulterior motive?"

Harry makes a face. "The medication he recommends wouldn't do her any harm, in the short term, and we can keep an eye on her to see how she reacts. I'll prescribe a small dose to start with, just to be safe."

"He also wanted to double check that Jan is prescribed antipsychotics?"

"Yes," Harry replies, "we deliver them every three days."

"And do we have any way of knowing if he actually takes them? He thought maybe with the cameras we'd have a better chance to know than him."

"The first week he took them, or he appeared to take them on screen. I can't know for sure unless I'm there, and even then we can never know for sure. Ultimately it's up to the patient."

"I suppose we can look back at the footage to see if he appears to take them. I'll assign someone to it. And lastly, he's asking for medication for himself, I've written it here, buspirone? I'm not sure how you pronounce that. To help with a bout of anxiety he's experiencing. He says he's feeling restless, irritable, and he has difficulty concentrating at times."

I give Harry a look. "Virgil? Anxious?"

Harry shrugs. "I haven't picked up on him being particularly anxious, but not only was I not looking for it, but psychiatry is not like other medical sciences where you can double check with machines; there is no way to know for certain that someone is experiencing a mental condition or not. Buspirone is a mild anti-anxiety medication which doesn't cause sedation or dependency so I see no harm in it; he's not pushing the limits of what he can ask for."

"Yet," I add. Perhaps that's what he's doing, starting small, gauging what he can get away with.

"Indeed," Harry says, "but I see no reason to alienate him right now, they all seem like reasonable enough requests."

"I'm just as wary as you are," Lawrence tells me, "I find this version of Virgil Francopan looking out for everyone, keeping the peace on the boat, slightly unsettling to say the least. But don't underestimate the lure of freedom, especially if it comes with financial means, which we will provide to some extent. The man was doomed to a life in a solitary cell. It's not just prison, it's complete solitude and horrendous treatment from staff until he gives his last breath. The pull of a life of freedom after having given up on it must be irresistible. I'm not surprised he's willing to do anything to gain this, including being his very antithesis: saving lives. Also," here his face darkens slightly as his eyes shift back and forth between Harry and myself, "I have reasons to believe he wants to get back to his house. Did you know that he hasn't sold it, and he still pays someone to maintain it, feed the plants, clean it monthly even though no one lives there?"

"He knows the house would be constantly monitored," Harry says, "if he were to be released into the wild, but that's the kind of challenge he loves, isn't it?"

The thought of his house makes me nauseous, so I keep my mouth shut.

"Are you okay?" Lawrence asks.

He's looking at me. Did I make an involuntary sound?

"Yes, why?"

"The medications you had delivered here recently," Harry says, "did that have anything to do with your arm?"

I subconsciously place a hand on my leather elbow-high glove, as if protecting it from a threat. "No, it didn't." My pulse quickens and I become all hot and bothered. He's been spying on me, the little rat. "But my medical history is none of your business."

Lawrence jumps in to defuse the tension and talks about his trip back to England, but it all goes in one ear and comes out the other. What was that about?

28

ANONYMOUS UPC RANKINGS

Day 28 of the Ultimate Psycho Championships (UPC)

Rocky Bardeaux

Rocky and Quentin had been enjoying the return of sunny weather alone on the sun deck, growing an unlikely friendship they both welcomed, when the rest of the crew joined them and dragged them into the collective conversation. On parenting, of all things.

Edmond was there, huddled in the electric blanket and his own woollen blanket from back home in the booth's corner, but he was still recovering from his cold swim. Francopan was confident he'd make a full recovery, and his currently redder nose and ears, due to frostnip, would gradually return to a normal colour, but in the meantime he felt tired and rarely talked, joining his twin brother in almost complete silence.

"Did you notice how when a parent mentions how terrible having a child is, or used to be," Teddy was saying, sat on the table with his feet on the booth, "they always precede it with 'oh now it's amazing, so worth it' or 'I love them so much that it was all worth it in the end,' and then they go on to list how much of a torture it is to have babies and kids. Ha, I'm not fooled." He tapped the side of his nose with a finger. "It's society's greatest scam. They can't possibly be heard saying how shit it is to be a parent, so they have to add that rubbish. I'm not falling for it."

"Just because you couldn't deal with having kids doesn't mean others can't," Quentin said. "Believe it or not, some parents actually find joy in watching their children grow."

"I've only got a niece and a nephew," Rocky said, "but I find a lot of joy in watching them grow, so I can't imagine what it's like when it's your own kids."

"It's much worse, is what it is," Teddy said. "When it's your kids, you have to deal with all the shit mate, and the few minutes of joy you may – *may* – get per day is not worth the entire day of chores and shite you have to deal with. I saw my sister raise her kids, no fun there. Don't go believing being an uncle has anything to do with being a parent."

Glenys stood up and left, climbing down the ladder to Quentin's room's window on the main deck.

"I think what Teddy means," Francopan said, "though he may not know it himself, is that when the parent has a difficult background, their childhood wasn't the happiest, then having children can trigger them significantly, and repeatedly. In those cases, having children is challenging and can be very painful, outweighing any potential reward. The ultimate sign of selflessness is a parent who, having been abused in their childhood, emotionally or else, takes it upon themselves to be a kind, caring parent to their children without passing on that abuse they suffered, despite every fibre of their being pushing them to lash out. Because the easiest thing to do is to give in to the dark voice inside you and replicate the only thing you know."

"Yeah, whatever he said." Teddy stood up and followed Glenys down the side of the boat.

Soon after, shouts arose from below, on the main deck.

29

ANNA KIMPER

I don't like being on the boat when Lawrence isn't here; he's the only one I know for certain will back me no matter what. I'm glad Stanislas is here, but I can't trust him as much as I trust Lawrence; I've only just met him. Harry is being odd, and the staff other than Stanislas are basically strangers. The man D. Card is sending to act on his behalf is arriving soon and I've never met him, so who knows what kind of man he is. Lawrence assured me our team has vetted him extensively, and Lawrence has met him once, so there's nothing to worry about, but I can't help it. I am not a fan of D. Card, generally; not his name (Dil Cardinal, was he high when he came up with that?), not his music, not his personality, and him investing in our experiment is reinforcing the idea I already had of him before. I am not familiar with American rappers, but I'm fairly sure I would've welcomed anyone other than him.

It doesn't help that Lawrence slipped in, just before leaving, that we'll start heading south as soon as he gets back. Now that the government agencies know we're at sea, we'll need to navigate to a safer spot, less overlooked by western agencies. But moving away means changing points of contact on land and using different supply spots. It means crossing busy shipping lanes and risking being spotted by aircrafts. Lawrence has planned for it so it's fine, he says, but I don't see it as fine. I see it as a can of worms, a source of endless potential problems. And it's my job to establish communication with the new people, so I can see a boatload of stress heading my way.

At least the inmates are firmly on the business-as-usual train, and they're all gathered on the sun deck, making it nice and easy to listen to just one feed and no need for screens. The hardest part of the job is when Virgil is holding a session in his room and some of them are in the lounge and someone else is on the sun deck. I don't want to miss a single word of Virgil's sessions but sometimes I have to in order to keep track of the rest of them.

Glenys leaves the sun deck to head back inside, and shortly after Teddy does the same. Everyone else is still outside, conversing nicely. I listen to their discussion all the while following the other two with my eyes. Glenys heads to the bathroom, Teddy crosses the hallway, then places his foot so that the bathroom door won't close.

They exchange a few words, then Teddy goes inside the bathroom, with Glenys still there, and lets the door close behind him.

I switch to the bathroom's camera, placed so that the inmates can keep their privacy but we can still see most of the angles.

Teddy grabs Glenys' arm, Glenys snatches it away.

Crap.

My immediate reaction is to call for help, but quickly remember this is the whole point of the experiment.

Trusting them not to be criminals for sixty days, and if they fail, they must pay the consequences.

I mute the sun deck and turn the bathroom's volume up.

"It's not going to happen, you moron," Glenys says.

"You know you want it, when's the last time you had a bit of a rummage?"

"A rummage? Did you just say 'a rummage'?" Glenys bursts out laughing.

Teddy pushes her against the wall, forcefully unzips her jumpsuit and turns her around. She resists but he's stronger, even though his head only reaches her nose.

And this is where we see their dark side... A side of me wants the experiment to succeed, for the inmates to make it to the end together without tragedies, but another just... doesn't give two pence. All I want is Virgil, and I'll get him whether the experiment is a success or not. But I've been conditioning myself to care for so long, so that I can lie more effectively to Lawrence, that it's hard to turn the auto-pilot off. And here I can only empathise with Glenys; I struggle not to at least try and stop Teddy somehow.

"Of course," Glenys says, "of course you're not going to take no for an answer and you're going to rape me. Or try, anyway."

"Try? Did you say *try*?" He cackled.

I can see Glenys' face on the screen. Even though her eyes are a window into hell, incredibly, she manages to etch a grin on her dry lips.

Teddy has his jumpsuit around his ankles, only the top of his head visible behind Glenys – the part of his tattoos with the broken Humpty Dumpty figure – but on the first thrust, he unleashes a screech coming from the bottom of his guts and he backs away as if his pants are on fire. He unloads a string of swear words as he looks down at his

Johnson. The angle and camera's quality prevent me from observing anything with clarity, but he's not happy.

Glenys pulls her jumpsuit back up and walks out of the bathroom, cackling away in her turn. She crosses Quentin's bedroom and climbs out of the porthole window to go back up to the sun deck.

As Teddy hobbles out of the bathroom, struggling to pull his jumpsuit back up, I glimpse a darker patch on the front of his underwear.

It looks like blood.

30

ANONYMOUS UPC RANKINGS

Day 28 of the Ultimate Psycho Championships (UPC)

Rocky Bardeaux

Rocky was on his way down the ladder when Glenys appeared at the porthole window.

"Go back up," she said. "All good here."

"Are you sure?" Rocky asked. She nodded.

She climbed out of the window and followed him up the ladder. Once on the sun deck, everybody gathered around Glenys, except the Van Helmont twins who remained seated on the booth, Edmond wrapped in his blanket.

"What happened?" Rocky asked.

"Where's Teddy?" Francopan asked.

"He'll be up soon enough, I'm sure," Glenys said. "You see, I decided to take action against rapey pervs, to make sure it never happened again. So instead of fitting a contraceptive coil, like many women do, I got my own kind of contraceptive. I had a spike fitted in my hoo-ha, small but sharp as all hell, ready to receive any uninvited cock."

"What about invited ones?" shouted Edmond from the booth, speaking up for the first time in a while.

"There are none," Glenys replied. "I get off in other ways."

The metallic clanging of someone using the ladder reached them, along with Teddy's grunting. "The bitch sends mixed signals," he shouted from the side of the boat. "And then she lets me tear my cock to shreds!"

He strained to lift a leg to climb onto the sun deck, visibly in pain.

"Mate," Quentin said, "we've been on the same boat this entire time, and in no way, shape or form has she ever come on to you."

"The spike is the only reason you're not dead, man," Glenys said. "And that I won't kill you until this whole thing is over. It calms me down. Because otherwise, you're exactly the type of asshole I eat for breakfast."

Seeing Teddy stand there, confrontational and unapologetic, Rocky shook from an urge to beat the crap out of him. Preying on the vulnerable, it was the lowest of the low. He managed to hold himself in check, but he walked up to Teddy anyway and stood a foot from his inked face, forcing him to look up. "Touch her again, and I'll kill you. I'll go back inside, I don't care, as long as I know I've rid the world of another lowlife."

"Don't, Rocky, please," Glenys said. "Not only is he not worth it, but don't ruin it for everyone else for my sake, especially since he can't do what he wants to do anyway."

Rocky backed off, and common sense took over his

senses. She was right, of course. He let himself go, and hadn't thought twice before speaking. "Yeah, sorry. I apologise, everyone. I won't ruin it for you all because of this shitbag." And he did care about not going back to his solitary cell. "But I won't let you get away scot free either." He added to Teddy.

Teddy, at last, dropped the arrogant glare, and looked subdued.

The PA system clicked, but the voice which came on was one they'd never heard before. A woman's. "Attention, participants. The crime committed was not severe enough to fail the experiment, especially since Glenys successfully defended herself, but as there *was* penetration, and the intent was there, if the ranking system should be triggered, Teddy Brandt will be docked points retroactively." The system clicked off, but then clicked back on immediately. "Oh, and Teddy, we're not sending the nurse in."

31

ANONYMOUS UPC RANKINGS

Day 29 of the Ultimate Psycho Championships (UPC)

Virgil Francopan

"I'm surprised Teddy and Edmond let you keep Thesea for our session," Virgil said.

The cat was comfortably sat on Quentin's lap, purring under his loving strokes.

"I gave Edmond my hashbrowns this morning," Quentin said, his eyes fixed on Thesea. "Besides, he's been hogging her ever since his swim, for *health* reasons, only fair I have her for a bit. And Teddy hasn't been saying much since yesterday, has he? He doesn't get a say anyway. She belongs to all of us."

Thesea looked at Virgil and blinked slowly. He looked away.

"So, ready to talk today?" he asked. Jan and Quentin were the only two who had remained clammed shut, and now they were running out of time.

Quentin shrugged. "No harm in talking a bit, I guess. A *bit*," he added, looking up at Virgil.

Virgil tried not to let his surprise show. "Wonderful. Tell me about yourself, then. Where you grew up, what challenges you faced, anything you think might be relevant to a therapist."

Quentin's attention returned to Thesea; the cat must have a role in Quentin agreeing to talk today, and for that alone Virgil was glad the masters had introduced it. "Never had therapy, so I wouldn't know what's relevant. I've had a pretty normal life, up until it wasn't anymore. I grew up in Hereford, then we moved to the Brecon Beacons in Wales for a bit. Father was a regional director for a building supplies company, Mother worked in admin, for a university and then for a doctor's surgery. I have a younger sister, we get along well enough, even now, she visits me in prison regularly. I talked to her the other day, when the plague barrister gave us a phone. She's watching me on their stream."

"Is she proud?"

Quentin shrugged. "Is there anything to be proud about? She's happy I made a mate in here, and she hopes I'll get out, though she doesn't trust Teddy or the twins."

"She trusts me?"

"She didn't say, but she liked that you're doing sessions."

Ah, there we are, Virgil thought. Perhaps it wasn't the cat after all.

"Any violence in your household growing up?" Virgil asked.

"No, our parents never even smacked us. I mean, we got

told off when we were naughty, but nothing other parents wouldn't do."

He stroked Thesea for a while, so when he didn't venture any additional information, Virgil spoke up. "What else can you tell me about your background? Did you go to university? When did you have your first girlfriend? Any incidents with the law?"

At this point Virgil would normally go on a monologue and make an educated guess at the reasons why his patient became who they were, but with Quentin he wouldn't be able to do a good enough job. He remained a mystery to him, unable to read him as well as someone like Teddy.

"Never had to do with the police until later. I went to uni in Reading, studied business management. Graduated with a 2:1. Then I got a job in Reading, worked my way up the ladder, became project manager. First proper girlfriend was in college, I was seventeen. Lasted a few months, then she broke up with me. Not sure why, she said she was searching herself, but not long after she got with someone else, so who knows. Then I dated a few women during and after uni, but nothing serious until Wendy, really."

"Wendy?"

Quentin looked up, as if checking whether Virgil was testing him. "My wife. Who died."

"Right, sorry. So you met in Reading?"

Quentin nodded, and returned his attention to Thesea. "She had just separated from her ex. She already had two young daughters but I quickly came to love them. We clicked right away, Wendy and me. She was bubbly, happy, always busy. I'm calmer, grumpier, so kind of opposites but it was perfect for us. We moved in together quite quickly, and then we got married. She'd never been married before, even though she had a serious relationship with her girls' dad, so I felt privileged. We had our issues, but nothing serious. We loved each other, we just felt right for one another. Then she went on a business trip, she was a sales rep for a software company, and she never came back."

"Any idea why she might have done what she did?"

Quentin shook his head. "It wasn't a suicide. It was a murder, I know it, just never been able to prove it."

That came as a shock to Virgil. "You believe she was killed?"

Quentin nodded but remained silent for a moment. "I was so angry. Still am. To make those girls motherless, ruin their lives, ruin my life, ruin her parents' life. It was just unfair. I didn't have any will to live after that, but I was too cowardly to take my life."

"Why do you think it was a murder?"

Quentin shook his head, still looking down at the cat. Virgil wished he could see his eyes. "I'm not going into that now, mate."

Fair enough. But one question still lingered in the back of Virgil's mind. Everybody else's presence on this boat made sense, given their background. But not him. He was not a violent person, no serious trauma in his childhood, no criminal history before his thirties, a life as normal as they come. He knew *how* he'd ended up in solitary; he'd been violent with staff, and it was only meant to be a short stay before he was returned to the normal wing.

But *why* was Quentin McQueen here, along with the world's most dangerous prisoners?

32

ANNA KIMPER

(Ten years earlier)

The room has everything to make me comfortable. Large windows which make it feel more open and calming, the walls are a light blue, and the soft furnishings are mustard-coloured, adding warmth without overwhelming the senses. The armchair is supportive yet cosy, he's even lit a sandalwood fragranced candle; I could easily fall asleep here.

The therapist has accepted I bring my newborn in, too, or I couldn't relax. He's currently sleeping in my arms; I would transfer him to the pram, but I don't want to risk waking him up.

"Thanks for meeting me here," the therapist says. "The hospital was a bit cramped, and it didn't feel as private as this will."

I nod and glance at my baby again. I love watching him

sleep. So peaceful, so harmless, so vulnerable. I would do anything to keep him safe. Anything.

"How are you feeling?"

I raise my head. This psychiatrist has this odd thing where he rarely, if ever, looks at me straight in the eye. I wonder if he has some type of lazy eye condition. "Baby's been sleeping in bouts of two hours at a time, so I've been trying to sleep then, with mixed results. But he's hungry and feeding well, so I can't complain."

"No," he says, "how are *you* feeling, Anna? Not the baby. I can see he's doing just fine."

I look back down at the baby, but I don't actually look at him. My eyes wander to the armchair's armrest next to his head. It's a nice red leather armchair, it feels heavy and lavish, but it has these odd patches of different shades of red, and in some places – I noticed before sitting down on it – there are patches missing. As if it's unfinished.

"I'm still feeling this presence," I say, tentatively looking at him, afraid he's going to mock me, even though he's been nothing but supportive so far. He gazes at me with loving eyes, which is odd and disturbing, seeing as I've only seen him twice before this, but I don't know how else to describe it. At least he's not laughing at me. "It started out as whispers, like static in the background, almost like a radio that isn't quite tuned in. Gradually, the volume and intensity built, and now, now..." I look back down at my baby, my throat closing. "It's like a storm of accusations, coming from all sides, telling me how worthless I am. I feel like I'm constantly watched, they're lurking in the shadows, and I must..." Protect my baby from them, but I stop myself before I say it out loud.

I'm okay with mentioning any threats against me, but I'm not telling Dr. Francopan that my baby is in the middle of this. That they're threatening him above anyone else, because they don't believe I can protect him, defend him. "But it's not all the time," I add, struggling to keep my voice even. "They come in waves. Nights are the worst."

I'm not going to reveal my deepest inner thoughts to a man who's effectively a stranger, regardless of how many letters come after his name.

Dr. Francopan nods slowly, and remains silent for a moment, staring blankly in front of him. Then his eyes fix on something next to my head. "Who's *they*?"

"The voices," I reply. "Those forces which are more powerful than anything else."

I hear the words I just said, and for an instant, it's like I'm outside my body. "It sounds ludicrous, doesn't it?" My pulse quickens, my mouth dries up; I'm suddenly very afraid. "Am I," I stare at the doctor as if my life depends on it, "am I going to be okay?"

"Anna," he says, and gets up from his chair. He crouches in front of me, and grabs my right hand. My only free hand, the other holding the baby. "Anna," he says again, and this time, startlingly, he's looking at me straight in the eyes. He has golden flecks in his brown irises, which I hadn't noticed before. "You aren't imagining things, they're very real, but it's okay, everything will be okay, because you are aware of them. We, you and me, are a team. You are lucky you met me, because I will not let you down. We will fight those forces, together, and we will fend them off."

The small gesture of holding my hand in his soft, moisturised hands, really gets to me. In a good way. It tells me he's not afraid of me, and he doesn't think me a lunatic. A bit longer and I'll be creeped out, but he takes his hand away just in time. Even my husband won't touch me, he thinks I'm crazy.

Dr. Francopan gives me a gentle smile, and I believe him, wholeheartedly, that we will make these voices go away. My baby and I will be fine; I've taken the first step in protecting him, getting the right help.

How lucky I am to have found him.

Over a year later

I STILL HAVE IT.

That's the first thought that comes to my mind as I finish a long rally with a top British junior. My forehand, my backhand, they're still there. Incredibly, even after two years of not touching a racket, it still feels as though the racket is an extension of my arm. The strings strike the ball smoothly, producing a satisfying *pop*, and I swing without thinking.

I hit for thirty minutes, and it's the first time my mind is clear and focused on anything other than the past year's events. Maybe that's what I needed, to get back out on court and distract myself with the only thing I know how to do with my eyes closed.

At the end of the session, I go back into the clubhouse and sit down on one of the armchairs. The telly is on, BBC News. I've only hit for thirty minutes, but it feels like I've played a tough match. My legs are wobbly, my skin is soaked, I'm still slightly out of breath. It doesn't come as a surprise, I've done no exercise in...two years? At least two years. I wave to my hitting partner as she walks past, heading to the restaurant for her lunch, and the telly catches my eye.

Virgil's face is on the screen. A mug shot, with the headline underneath, 'Psychiatrist Arrested After Human Remains Discovered at Home.'

My world stops. Everything blurs, my head spins, the noise becomes one continuous stream of white noise. I close my eyes and fall back in the armchair to give my brain a rest, hoping it will pass with time. Nausea rises in my stomach.

As I slowly regain my senses, the interviewee and news anchor's comments reach me. One of the corpses found has signs of flaying. They're speculating as to who the victims may be, and how many there are, but with those recent discoveries, they are certain they can get a conviction.

My right hand starts tingling. The scars he gave me come to life, suddenly awakening, some seeing the light for the first time. He is the reason for all my misfortune. How many other victims are there, who may never be accounted for because he let them live?

Now he's been arrested, I am crushed by the loss. The loss at never exacting my revenge, and letting him get away. He will have the privilege to end his days in prison, he will never see the light of day in the free world again, forever out of my reach.

My journey to peace is over before it started.

33

ANONYMOUS UPC RANKINGS

Day 30 of the Ultimate Psycho Championships (UPC)

Rocky Bardeaux

"They're late," Rocky said, glancing at the clock above the dining table. He meant it as a comment, an observation, but it came out as a complaint.

His remark went unnoticed. Francopan was reading a book on surrealism, Edmond, Glenys, and Quentin were playing Command of Duty, Teddy was off in a corner listening to music, and Jan was either in his bedroom or up on the sun deck. As had become their daily routine, from twelve they all gathered in the lounge and dining area, keeping themselves busy until lunch was served. Rocky was hungry, he didn't feel like playing video games again, and there was only one pair of headphones to listen to music and Teddy had them. It was now 12.45, and still no sign of food.

Rocky went over to the sofa and lifted Thesea off the armrest. Edmond was in the middle of a battle, but he still gave him a hurt look as Rocky gathered the ball of fur in his arms and walked back to his chair at the dining table. Then the plague barrister's voice came on the speaker system.

"Participants, today marks Day 30, the halfway mark. Congratulations. I wish I could say you've had a perfect course so far, but Mr. Brandt put a dent into this. Still, you're on the right track. Another thirty days and you will be able to live as normal a life as it can get for you. Can you smell the freedom? To reward you for making it this far, you will receive restaurant treatment for your lunch, with an *A la Carte* menu. You will have a choice of a starter, main dish, and dessert. Bon appétit."

Just as the system turned off, steps resounded above them, the ultimate sign that the staff had arrived and were starting preparations. Although they couldn't see into the upper deck because of the boarded windows, Rocky was certain it had a kitchen.

When the food delivery man, as they called him – though Rocky didn't know why he couldn't just be the waiter – arrived, he covered the dining table with a white tablecloth and set the table with bamboo plates, cups, and cutlery. Then he politely asked for everyone to take a seat, and he distributed the menus.

It felt nice to be treated like important people, with the respect owed to free, upstanding members of society. The menu was made of thick, quality card paper, and the writing was in a special font, like a proper restaurant might have, though it wasn't like Rocky had extensive experience in that area.

"Seared scallops with lemon butter," Teddy read from the menu's starters. "Wild mushroom soup with truffle oil, and burrata salad with heirloom tomatoes," he looked up, "or burrataaa? How the hell do you pronounce that? And what in the world is it?"

Teddy had been quieter than usual since his assault on Glenys, sensing the group's hostility towards him, but he was gradually opening up again.

"Burrata," Francopan pronounced correctly, "it's a soft Italian cheese, with an outer layer of fresh mozzarella and a creamy interior."

"Oh, sign me up for that one," said Quentin.

The man-bird had been careful to cater to Quentin, as he'd done the entire time so far, so he was happy to choose all the vegetarian options. Rocky chose the scallops for starters, the grilled ribeye for his main, and the panna cotta for pudding. The meal took considerably longer than usual to be served, primarily because there were three courses as opposed to one bell dish, but Rocky couldn't complain as they were provided with a regular supply of garlic bread until the main dish was served.

When the meal was over and the table cleared, Rocky claimed the headphones, plugged them into the old fashioned built-in hi-fi system, and sat himself on the sofa. He now had something resembling a collection of classical music, and these moments of peace made his uncomfortable talks with Francopan more than worth it. Most of his roommates had gone up to the sun deck, and only Francopan had remained behind, still reading his book at the dining table. Almost ideal conditions to lose himself in the music.

But just as Bach's Brandenburg Concerto No. 3 in G major was getting underway, a faint smell of burn reached his nostrils. He glanced around; only him and Francopan were around, and the lunatic psychiatrist was just reading his book peacefully at the other end of the dining table. The air did look a bit hazy, so Rocky removed his headphones and stood up. As he walked towards the hallway leading to the cabins, the smell became stronger and stronger, until it started stinging his eyes. He followed the source, and was unsurprised when it led to Edmond's room.

He stormed in, and found flames licking a woollen blanket. Edmond's woollen blanket, the one he'd requested as his personal item at the very beginning.

Rocky took everything in in less than a second. The electric blanket the man-bird and the nurse had given the twin following his swim lay on his bed, and next to it were the blanket's batteries. A ball of steel wool was on the batteries, and next to them were the burnt remains of the lollipop sticks Edmond had asked as rewards for his sessions with Francopan. Now the blanket was aflame and Edmond was attempting to place it on the bedside table in an attempt to make it catch fire.

Rocky leapt onto the bed, grabbed the duvet he knew to be fire-retardant, barged Edmond out of the way and threw the duvet onto the blazing blanket. But Edmond came back immediately and tackled Rocky. They rolled onto the mattress, Edmond snatching the duvet with a flying hand just before they fell onto the floor. Edmond landed on top of Rocky and was about to land a punch when he was pulled off by Francopan. As Francopan executed a few expert-looking manoeuvres to neutralise a furious Edmond, Rocky rushed to place the duvet back over the blanket, and within seconds the flames were starved and a thick, suffocating smoke filled the bedroom.

He opened the porthole window and ran out of the room, closing the door behind him. Francopan had already dragged Edmond into the lounge.

Everybody climbed down from the sun deck and came to see what had caused the commotion. Edmond was lying on the couch, half moaning half cursing, and the stench of smoke was overwhelming.

"What was that?" Rocky asked Francopan. "Those moves you pulled."

"Krav Maga," Francopan replied. "I'm an Expert Level 5."

"Bloody hell, mate," Teddy said, "is there anything you haven't done? You were a bloody psychiatrist, where did you find the time to work, become an expert in Krav Maga, *and* murder people?"

"Well, in my line of work, martial arts can prove quite useful, can't they? So it made sense to take the time to master one. And as my line of work, I don't mean psychiatry." Followed by his best impression of an evil, disturbed grin.

"So, what happened here?" Glenys asked, glancing at Edmond and peering at the smoking room.

"Edmond tried to set the bloody boat on fire," Rocky said.

"He scavenged a battery from his electric blanket and a piece of steel wool from our cleaning supplies," Francopan explained, "and he created a short circuit by touching the steel wool to the battery terminals. He then used the sparks to set his shredded lollipop sticks on fire, and then ignite his very flammable wool blanket. If I weren't so irritated by his relentlessness to make us fail and potentially kill us," he grabbed Edmond's chin and gave him a few hard shakes, "I would be impressed by the amount of forethought which went into this."

"I thought you might want Edmond to succeed and seize the opportunity to escape?" Quentin asked, a glint of amusement in his eyes.

"How would that work, exactly?" Glenys said. "We're on a fucking boat in the middle of the ocean, in case you'd forgotten."

"The consortium wouldn't let us burn and sink, so they'd come and rescue us," Quentin replied. "They wouldn't have time to plan anything, so they could make mistakes, and we could capitalise on some opportunities. They might have to accommodate us on their own boat, and who knows what would happen next?"

"Exactly," exclaimed Edmond, lifting his hands, "why wouldn't you want to seize your chance?"

"They'd call everything off and send our arses back to prison, is what would happen next," Rocky said.

Francopan shook his head. "Our masters have broken seven of the most securely held prisoners in the world in the space of what, two? Three days? Without a single failed rescue. They are not stupid. They have resources, more than we can imagine. We are not getting out of here other than their way, I'm afraid. All other efforts are futile – and a waste of time and sweat," he added, glaring at Edmond.

"Guys," Rocky said, trying to make eye contact with everyone, "we can do this. We can make it to the end and earn our freedom. We've already done half the work, can you believe it? Personally, it doesn't feel like we've been here for an entire month. We just have to do it again, and we can be free men and women, but *you have to stay put and behave*, for fuck's sake. Let's work as a team and show everyone out there that we aren't senseless monsters who can't help but shoot themselves in the foot, even when they're handed freedom on a platter. You with me?"

He got nods from Quentin, Glenys, and even Teddy. That was enough for him, he knew not to ask for the moon, but he hoped he'd planted a seed in Edmond's mind. They could not self-destruct out of sheer stupidity; he would never forgive Edmond, and himself, if they went back to the shithole because Edmond Van fucking Helmont pissed off the consortium or got someone killed with his antics.

And this was the first motivational talk Rocky had ever given, in his fifty-four years on this planet.

34

ANONYMOUS UPC RANKINGS

Day 33 of the Ultimate Psycho Championships (UPC)

Rocky Bardeaux

"Who left the window open?" boomed Edmond's voice.

"Which window?" replied Teddy's voice from his room.

"Quentin's. How often do I need to remind you all to keep the damned window closed when you go up to the sun deck? What if Thesea balances on it, the boat shudders, and she falls into the water? No one wants to jump in after her, trust me. I would know."

Rocky found it endearing how Edmond's fatherly side came out thanks to the cat. And he much preferred him stressing about the cat instead of looking for ways to kill them all in another failed escape.

"Don't worry," came Glenys' voice from the kitchenette, "I won't be jumping after her."

Rocky flushed, washed his hands, and came out of the bathroom just as the man-bird's voice echoed throughout the boat.

"Can all the participants please gather in the lounge," it said. "In the next few hours," the man-bird resumed once everybody was there, "we will run into a tropical storm. Once it starts, it will be uncomfortable for the next twelve to twenty-four hours. Our yachts are equipped with a sea anchor, which acts like an underwater parachute. It holds the boat facing into the wind and waves, reducing the risk of capsizing, and it provides more stability. Our captain will steer your boat remotely and has extensive experience with storm navigation. There are several things you must do if you want to make it through the storm unharmed.

"Secure all loose items. Tie-down points are built into the deck, and all loose pieces of furniture have straps to hold them firmly in place. Please go over every piece of furniture which is not already bolted down and attach them to the tie-down points.

"The main deck has dedicated stowage spaces where smaller loose items can be placed, keeping them out of harm's way during the storm. You can find some in your cabins, in the area in between the kitchenette and the dining table, and under the sofa's cushions."

Francopan asked Rocky and Quentin to stand up from the sofa, and he lifted the wooden plank supporting the cushions. A large empty space revealed itself.

"You could hide a body or two in there," Francopan said.

"Virgil, please," admonished the man-bird. "Close all

portholes to prevent water from entering. The stowage space next to the kitchenette has all the safety gear, like life vests and emergency flares, in case you need them."

"What about the lifeboats?" Rocky asked. "Where are they?"

"Yes," Edmond said, nodding, "I'd like to know that."

The man-bird marked a pause; Rocky thought it might be due to embarrassment. "There are none," he said at last. "For obvious reasons. But we will never be far from you, so we can always intervene if need be. We will cut the live feed for the duration of the storm in order to limit the information authorities can gather on our location. If you have questions at any time, speak up. One of us will answer. Good luck, and...brace yourselves."

The system turned off.

A moment of silence imposed itself, heavy with apprehension. Rocky was not sure what to expect, and he suspected it was the case for everyone else. None of them had ever spent any time on a boat before, let alone ridden out a storm.

"Fuck me," Teddy said at last. "A tropical storm."

"And no lifeboats," Rocky said. "We're pretty much on our own, if it all goes tits up."

"It's not in our masters' interest to let us drown," Francopan said, "so I don't think there's any need to worry about that. No need to worry at all, really; boats survive storms at sea all the time."

"Let's get to work," Glenys said, "and then we'll have less time to worry. I'll place all the kitchenware in the stowage spaces, and if we want anything to eat or drink, we'll just need to fish things out one by one and put them back after."

"I'll tie the loose pieces of furniture down," Rocky said.

Within three hours, the boat started rocking and the

wind howling against the side of the boat, hurling large raindrops against each cabin's porthole. Five hours after the man-bird's warning, the storm started proper. The boat swayed violently as it rode the waves, and series of sudden, jerky movements shook them as the yacht rose steeply on a wave and then dropped sharply on the other side. The pitching and rolling made it feel as though the ground beneath their feet was constantly shifting. It didn't matter where they stood, or sat, or lay down, they couldn't get a moment's rest without thinking they might be thrown onto the floor.

Then the nausea started. Nobody was spared, save Francopan. Two toilets weren't enough. Jan was about to open his cabin's porthole to unload when Rocky reminded him they couldn't let any water in – not to mention the risk of Jan falling overboard – so he ran to the kitchenette's sink, and that became a regularly used outlet.

Around dinner time Quentin took some bread out with the intention of slapping some butter on it and handing out slices, but a wave knocked the plate off his hand and he retched over the kitchenette sink. He met Rocky's gaze and they silently agreed there was no point; their stomachs couldn't take anything.

Keeping their balance was a struggle, so they tried to hold onto something at all times; Rocky was grateful the yacht designers had built handles into the walls to move around. Even so, they were thrown from side to side if seated, and knocked into walls and furniture if standing. The howling wind and roaring of the waves crashing against the hull created an unnerving background noise, adding to the already terrifying creaking and groaning as the yacht flexed with the force of the storm.

When night came, they attempted to sleep but unsurprisingly failed. Even if it hadn't been for the frequent vomiting and the stench which came with it, made worse by the almost airtight space, Rocky was too anxious to close his eyes. The lack of visual confirmation of the storm made it feel like he was stuck in a nightmare, and he couldn't wake up. He was fully aware of the chaos outside, but couldn't be sure of exactly what was happening. Surely it would end soon? But anytime he looked at the clock, disappointment engulfed him as he realised it had only been five, six, seven hours since the start of the storm, and the man-bird had said it would last twelve hours minimum. And knowing there were no lifeboats did not help matters.

He felt powerless, at the complete mercy of nature's wrath. Thrown around like a puppet tied around a hyperactive child's ankle. Even if the boat made it through the storm, would he die of an accidental knock on the head against a sharp corner? That would be his luck; well on his way to gaining a miraculous freedom, but knocked out just before the finish line by a stupid accident. He realised, then, that he didn't want to die, or go back to prison. He may have had a miserable life so far, but he still had time to make the rest of his time here enjoyable. This promised freedom meant more to him than he realised. Didn't he deserve to build himself a peaceful life in his old age, on his terms, and make an honest living like everyone else? Fifty-four years of misery made for a harsh enough sentence, didn't it? Please, God, let me live out the rest of my days in relative comfort and peace, he prayed, though he was a confirmed atheist.

It seemed the other inmates experienced a similar time in bed, for when he got up at last at three in the morning and made his way to the lounge, Francopan, Quentin, Teddy, and Jan were already there, and Glenys and Edmond soon joined them.

"I'm knackered," Teddy said, sat on the floor, his back against the wall under the television and one hand holding on to a built-in handle. "Absolutely washed out. The type of exhaustion that penetrates inside my bones."

"Me too," Quentin said. "It's the mental strain of remaining alert, isn't it?"

"And the stress," Edmond added. "Not knowing when it will end, if the boat will make it. And I have nothing left in me. Nada. Threw it all up. No energy to feed my body."

"I'm sure the lack of sleep has a part to play too," Rocky said. "It's the middle of the night."

"Satan's hour," Francopan said with a faint grin, a blank stare on his face.

The air felt stuffy, and there still lingered a faint whiff of vomit.

"Come on," Glenys said with unexpected energy, "we've gone through worse shit than this. We've all of us here had to suffer worse nights than this storm on a boat in the high seas. In case you need reminding, I'll tell you about a night I would definitely *not* choose over what we're going through right now. Who here has been four-pointed?"

All three Americans raised their hand. Glenys glanced at the Brits.

"Is that not a thing in England?"

Rocky, Quentin, Teddy, and Francopan looked at each other. "Don't think so," Rocky said, shrugging.

"Well," Glenys went on, "in the States, it's very much a thing. The first time was just after I killed the guard, and the second time was when I refused to take my meds. That second time was the worst spell by far. Each of my limbs was chained to a hook, and they left me like that for twenty-three days. They freed one of my hands three times a day to eat a peanut butter and jelly sandwich, and that's it."

"That's it?" repeated Rocky. "What about when you needed a piss?"

Glenys and Edmond laughed at the same time. "Man, you have no idea," said Edmond.

"I was chained on the block," Glenys said, "couldn't scratch an itch, or swat at the insects. Because they know, they're not stupid, those insects. They know they're free to crawl, to slither all over your most vulnerable body parts, up your nose, in your ears, down your mouth, in your eyes, anus, vagina. You're unable to protect yourself, left alone with fucking cockroaches and the occasional rat that emerges from a toilet, sensing a helpless soul who can only watch as it ravages through the cell, eating whatever it wants, while you lie powerless, terrified it might choose your love handles rather than a stale crust of bread hidden under a pillow."

"Or your balls," added Edmond, nodding slowly.

"Like a pig," Glenys went on, "you're made to piss and shit where you're chained, because it would be a *threat to security* to allow you to relieve yourself humanly. And then they dared say it's for my own good, because I was suicidal."

The boat shuddered, and a bamboo cup which hadn't been locked away flew across the dining area and came to rest in a corner.

"All that because you refused to take your pills?" Quentin asked.

Glenys nodded. "There was no pretending by the guards when it came to me, a killer of one of their own. They waited outside my cell like vultures, eager for any excuse to four-point me. They enjoyed it, they taunted me, organised extra humiliation, all for fun. I was never believed when I complained, because I lost all credibility when they threw me in solitary. I was no different from a wild animal. After that second stint, I made sure not to give them any reason to make it happen again. And it didn't, until the plague barrister got me out. But if I go back..."

"You're all hearing this now," Edmond said, "and your imagination is on overdrive, but you can't know what it's like until you've lived it. No way to accurately describe what it's like to be buck naked and stretched out on a cold slab of concrete for hours, causing bad blood circulation, numbing the fingers until a painful pins and needles sensation starts to burn. Slowly but surely turning your digits into burnt marshmallows. And it's not just a feeling, the damage is real. Serious lasting nerve damage, all in the name of security and staff safety."

"I'm glad I'm English," Francopan said, "because my friends would have had a whale of a time four-pointing me, I'm sure. Several times. The worst I got, when they really wanted to punish me, was the body belts. But I was clothed for that, and I was allowed to use a toilet. While they watched me, and sometimes helped me, which was humiliating enough, but nothing like what you said. None of that savagery."

"Well, hold your horses," Rocky said. "We don't have it as bad, but it's not a piece of cake either."

"Yeah, I was going to say," said Teddy.

"They moved me to a different solitary cell once," Rocky said, "just for one night, because they were about to move me to a hospital for a planned surgery. It was a cold winter night, and the guard threw me a shredded blanket. Out of habit I thanked him, then took it back and started to go off, but I caught myself, knowing that's what they were waiting for. I didn't want to give them an excuse to cancel my surgery. The blanket reeked of piss, it was stiff in parts and had shit stains on it. It clearly hadn't been washed in years. I was so cold I held it anyway, but my eyes started to water and burn so I threw it into the farthest corner because it just stank too much. I sacrificed my feet to the cold and removed my shoes to use as a pillow on the bed slab. I felt like I was on an ice block because it was so cold and hard. I put my hand up to the vent and felt cold air blowing in, not warm. I kept my swearing silent because again, didn't want to give them any excuses.

"While I rubbed my hands together, blew warm breath into them, and walked in circles to get my blood circulating, I grew angrier, and sadder too, wondering how many other prisoners had suffered this nightmare, unable to leave this hell of a cell. I felt like a wuss for not being able to handle it. My nose started to run and I didn't have any toilet roll. I remember thinking, after this kind of treatment, can you blame someone taking it out on correctional officers?"

"I remember my first solitary cell," Jan said, and everybody's head turned in his direction. He rarely, if ever, spoke up in group settings. The vomiting had turned his skin paler than ever, and he had dark bags under his eyes. "I inspected the toilet and sink combination, and the toilet bowl was covered in some stranger's faeces that I had to remove with bare hands, without soap to wash afterward to kill the germs and stink off them. The shit was literally caked on and solidified. It reeked, the mere sight made me want to vomit, and I kept wondering how many dirty, diseased prisoners with AIDS, Hep C, had sat here before me and released a load."

"Fucking hell," Teddy said, "I'm glad my stomach has nothing left to hurl."

"Then I checked the shower," Jan continued.

"Oh no," Rocky and Quentin exclaimed together, and everybody else followed, laughing and making various expressions of disgust.

"The shower," Jan repeated when the others calmed down, "where some guys jerk off, blow their nose, spit, piss, but rarely clean, so the stainless steel was covered in months and years of fossilised slime."

"Mate, stop," Quentin said, bent over double and covering his face.

"Yeah," Jan said, oblivious to the effect he was having. "And the guy before me had thrown turds through the bars onto the cell's outer steel door. I couldn't reach the steel door to clean it off, so the stink was still there."

"People should make all this more known to the public in America," Teddy said, "might reduce crime."

"Doesn't work like that, man," Edmond said.

"But guards can really make our lives a nightmare when they want to," Teddy said. "No desserts on the food tray even though it was there when it left the kitchen, or some mornings breakfast comes at ten, then lunch between eleven and twelve, and dinner at three, so I'd get hunger pains at night."

"Yeah, all that," Rocky said, "and postcards and photos missing from letters, no pills for my blood pressure for a week and then I'd receive three or four at once. They kept the lights on 24/7, and some nights they rang a phone nearby every fifteen fucking minutes, so impossible to fall asleep."

Glenys laughed out loud. "Guys, we've just told you about four-pointing and washing other people's shit with your bare hands and without soap, and you're moaning about no desserts and a postcard missing from your mail?"

The lounge erupted in laughter. Even Rocky and Teddy joined in; it helped release the tension.

"Alright alright," Rocky said, raising his hands. "Not as bad as the four-pointing, but when it's been going on for thirty years, making every single day of them miserable, a photo missing from a letter about people you love means the end of the world."

"Shit, thirty years," Glenys said. "I can't imagine doing this for thirty years. How are you still standing?"

"That's a question I often ask myself. I've tried to end it, though. A few times."

"I bet you did," she replied. "I would've been out of this world by now."

"Well I, for one, am glad you didn't," Quentin said, laying a hand on Rocky's shoulder. "And aren't you glad you didn't? You might be free now."

"I know," Rocky said before the emotion got to him. "Guys, we're a good team. Even though we're a bunch of misfits and damaged goods," he chuckled, "we're good together. We'll make it through this storm, and we'll make it out of this boat alive and free."

Rocky looked around, and noticed that every single head bobbed up and down. He knew, in that moment, that they all shared that same glowing feeling of being part of something, of being useful, finding their role and place in a team, at last. All together working towards a common goal, like a football squad.

These people, sat around him in a boat in the middle of nowhere, were good people really, when you dug deep enough. They all had a fucked up life in common, all had been dealt a bad hand, but they all proved they had a caring side. Teddy had a question mark over him, with what he'd done to Glenys despite the context, and though it would never be enough, he'd apologised to Glenys, and he genuinely cared for the cat. Could there be hope? Even Francopan had proven he genuinely wanted them to succeed; in fact, if actions speak louder than words, he was the one who'd spoken the loudest in that regard. Edmond was irritating with his relentless search for an escape, but Rocky hoped he'd finally understood, and it didn't make him a bad person. His love for Thesea was evidence.

It gave him faith in humanity, something he'd lost a long time ago. Because if he could find goodness in these people, then he could find goodness in anyone, if not everyone.

"Is it me or the boat is not rocking quite as much anymore?" Francopan pointed out.

Rocky no longer had to hold onto his chair's armrest to keep from swaying, and the howling wind outside had quietened. "I think you're right," he said. "We've made it past the worst. Nothing can stop us now; the road to the end is clear. Let's stamp on that accelerator."

∽

BACK IN THE other yacht's surveillance room, Lawrence, Harry, and Anna celebrated over a glass of champagne.

"Whatever happens next," Lawrence said, raising the flute high, "this moment, right here, is proof that my method is working. It's already yielding results. To the Ultimate Psycho Championships!"

"To the Ultimate Psycho Championships!"

35

ANNA KIMPER

The landscape isn't any different, but the air is hotter and more humid; the main indication that we've travelled south. Birds, too, are different. Right now, for instance, a south polar skua, a grey bird that looks like a larger version of a sea gull, is perched on our bimini top, eying our bowls of olives and chorizo slices. Are all gull-looking birds of the thieving variety?

"Have you seen the reaction to our latest video?" Lawrence asks me.

It's only us on the sun deck, Harry is on duty in the surveillance room.

I give Lawrence a reproachful scowl worthy of a mother. "Yes, it's quite the talk, but I'm afraid the added attention it will bring will give away some clues as to our location."

"Oh come," he says, waving my concerns away, "we cut the visuals and edited out the bits where anyone mentions the storm. And we've triggered a conversation the country – nay, the world – needs to have."

"I won't disagree with that." I just...I can't even come

close to imagining my devastation if the authorities get to us before I've managed to end it with Virgil.

"I was listening to Jeremy Vine on Radio 2 yesterday," Lawrence says, "they did a segment on this, and I was fascinated by how much support we got. Both us, our operation – because people are feeling empathy for what our participants had to go through – and our cause. Of course you had the handful of heartless authoritarians who want the death penalty brought back and will never show compassion to criminals, but you could tell there are many more out there who are all for improving prisoners' human rights and their conditions in prison."

"From what I've seen," I say, "people in Britain are appalled at the conditions in America, but they're quite smug with their own prisons. Just by comparison, because they don't adopt the four-pointing approach."

"Well, regardless," Lawrence says, sipping on his Pimm's, "they're talking. That's all I ever wanted. If all else fails, we've forced a national conversation on those issues, that is how all significant societal changes begin, and I will die a happy man."

I wish I could say the same.

Lawrence's phone goes off. It's Harry. Lawrence hangs up, then stands up. "Our apéritif is over, for now. Dr. Virgil Francopan has requested an audience."

I had started getting up too, but as he says his name my knees buckle.

"You will join us, yes?" Lawrence asks before taking a last sip of his drink.

No, I don't want to, and I shouldn't. Is it going to be a video call? No it can't be, we've taken the phone back. Maybe I can be there, then, but I can't talk or he might recognise my voice; I already adopted a different accent when I had to announce Teddy's point deduction, but Harry and Lawrence weren't around. If I don't talk at all, won't Lawrence and Harry find that odd? He's already eying me with a frown, I need to say something.

"Yes, of course. Coming."

He disappears down the stairs, and I remain behind for a brief moment. Just to take a few deep breaths. It's okay, he won't be able to see me, and I won't say a thing. He'll never know I was there. I don't need to speak anyway, surely? What if they ask me a question directly, and call me by name? Oh fuck fuck fuck.

I can't make up an excuse now, they'll know something's up. They're already acting strangely sometimes, they don't need any additional encouragement.

When I enter the surveillance room, they're already talking and Lawrence silently gestures for me to sit down next to him.

Virgil is on the main screen, alone in his cabin with the door closed behind him. He's standing up and looking at the camera. It's odd to see him looking at me, though it's not straight *at* me; in fact, it's a similar feeling to when I used to be in the same room with him, and a wave of paralysing heat starts in my belly and spreads throughout the rest of my body.

"We must increase Jan's dosage," Virgil says. I'm not looking at the screen, I can't. Instead I fiddle with the leather seams on my glove. "He's not well, I fear he's going back to his old ways."

"He had been doing well for a long time before we broke him out," Harry says, "we were confident he was stable. What makes you think he's getting worse?"

Virgil looks behind him, as if double checking no one

can hear him, then he lowers his voice a smidgen. "I caught him looking for Glenys' dirty sanitary towel in the bathroom's bin, and...sniffing it."

I bring my hand to my mouth.

"Is it..." Harry starts, then glances uncomfortably at me, "her time of the month?"

"Yes, I believe so."

All three of us look at each other.

"Has he shown any more interest for blood so far?" Lawrence asks. "In any way?"

"Not that I've noticed," Virgil replies, "but this alone is enough to worry me. A lot. I watched him carefully when Edmond injured himself and bled, and he showed no interest. But then again, he might know of his brother's condition, and therefore has no interest in *his* blood. And it was some time ago."

"I know he hasn't said anything to you in your sessions," Harry says, "but has he said anything at any other time that we might have missed? Have you heard him say things that could indicate psychosis?"

"No, but that's mainly down to the fact he just doesn't talk. He spends a lot of time in his cabin studying his map of the human anatomy, and he's started spending more time outside, on the sun deck. Though as soon as someone else joins him, he leaves."

Harry glances at Lawrence, Lawrence glances at me. He nods with his eyebrows raised, I return the nod – what else am I to do, if I don't want to talk? – then he does the same with Harry but with his eyes closed.

"Right, we'll increase the dosage," Harry says.

"Anything else you wanted to address?" Lawrence asks.

"Yes, Glenys. Same as Jan, she's getting worse. She's

continuously fidgeting, unable to calm down and just sit to watch a film. We set out to watch a film all together last night, and she must have gotten up ten times to go to the toilet or else. She's short-tempered, her nightmares are still happening, and what is really making me think something's off, is she's getting paranoid. She's convinced the authorities are about to find us, and I heard her asking Edmond what his next plan to escape was."

"What did Edmond say?" Lawrence asks.

"I didn't hear, but he shook his head. It was yesterday morning, in the kitchenette, as they were washing the dishes. If you want to replay the footage."

"I did hear her worry about the police getting to them," Harry says, "when she was on the sun deck with Quentin. She was watching the horizon like a hawk and Quentin commented on it."

"As you will know," Virgil says, "it is a sign of early onset psychosis, perhaps schizophrenia. She's clearly going through an episode triggered by the change of environment and the added stress, the storm probably didn't help, and she wasn't known to be psychotic or paranoid before, so we need to act on it now before it gets worse."

Harry keeps silent for a moment. Both Lawrence and I stare at him; this is beyond our remit. "I've been thinking of Glenys," he says at last, "and I came to the conclusion it was just severe anxiety. But her showing signs of paranoia does throw a spanner in the works. I have to reflect longer on this, but I've taken your concerns on board, Virgil."

I expect Virgil to insist, a proof he has an agenda, but he doesn't say anything. From the corner of my eye, I think I see him nodding. That is surprisingly mild of him.

"Is that everything?" Lawrence asks.

"Yes."

"Thanks, Virgil. Keep up the good work with the sessions."

The audio feed turns off, and Virgil exits his cabin.

36

ANONYMOUS UPC RANKINGS

Day 35 of the Ultimate Psycho Championships (UPC)

Virgil Francopan

"Right," Quentin said, "I think I'm ready."

"For what?"

Virgil was fairly sure he knew what Quentin meant, but he didn't want to appear as though he was expecting it. They'd been chatting for a good fifteen minutes, a waste of time as far as Virgil was concerned, but he knew that was what Quentin needed. Virgil could sense he'd come to his cabin with a different energy, as everyone else had since the storm. And if engaging in small chat for fifteen minutes was what Pretty Boy McQueen needed to address the juicy stuff, then so be it. Virgil was all about foreplay, after all.

"To talk about Wendy's murder."

Virgil merely nodded. He didn't want to frighten him by rushing him with a question. Right now, Virgil felt like he was handing a squirrel a walnut and the squirrel was slowly inching closer, gradually trusting the situation enough to accept the gift, but any sudden movement – a twitch of the cheek, a clearing of the throat, a readjusting of his feet – and it would flee, never to return.

Quentin gave a long sigh, as he might do just before diving off a cliff. "Wendy was away on a business trip, which was normal for her. She was a sales rep for a software company, so she had to meet potential clients regularly. She booked an Airbnb – she was given a fixed budget for travel expenses so she was always on the lookout for good deals, and she often went for a standard apartment. She arrived on the Sunday night, messaged me to say she'd arrived safely. And then I never heard from her again. On the Monday, I thought it odd, but when she was away on business she was not always in the mood to chat, and she often had to dine with clients. Same on Tuesday, it was unusual but I wasn't worried enough to do anything about it. On Wednesday I thought I'd check with her office, and when they said they hadn't heard from her since the previous week, and in fact they were a bit grumpy with her because she'd never met with the client, that's when I knew something was wrong. By the time I found the Airbnb, contacted the host to gain access, and got in, it was Wednesday evening."

He marked a pause. He just looked down at his hands on his lap, an indication that the juicy stuff was imminent.

"As soon as we got in we were met with a wave of heat, like walking into an oven. The central heating had been turned up, and it was the middle of summer. We found her dead in the bath, in a suicide position, naked, with deep slits on both wrists, and a strange knife in the bath. And...as I said, it was really hot in there, so her body had already...you know..."

Virgil nodded. "Started the decomposition process."

"Yeah." Quentin's voice was shaking now, and though he fought them, the tears started coming through. "And because the death fluids just flowed down the bath's drain, it didn't smell strongly in the flat. No one could have known she'd been there all this time. We called the police and everything, no DNA examination could be performed on the corpse because of the state it was in. No DNA was found in the flat anywhere, and no foreign DNA in the bathroom, including on the knife, except my wife's. A suicide note was next to the sink, some nonsense she would never have written. It was typed so we couldn't check the handwriting. We knew she was on antidepressants, there was an empty bottle of wine in the flat, her wrists were slit, no signs of a scuffle, she died from the loss of blood, so the police and coroner concluded it had been a suicide. Case shut."

"But you're convinced it wasn't."

"From what I've just told you," Quentin said, looking up at Virgil, "you don't pick up how nonsensical that is?"

"She was already on antidepressants, you said. She wasn't as happy as you made it sound, so the possibility of a suicide isn't nonsensical."

"Exactly, she was on antidepressants, so she wasn't feeling depressed right then. But anyway, *both* wrists were slit. I hired a lawyer, a good one who flayed my bank account, and both slits were deep, which requires some considerable strength. Go on, describe to me how you would go about slitting your second wrist just after you've slit the wrist of the hand holding the knife? And at the same time applying enough force to make a deep cut?"

"That's a valid point."

"And there's a whole host of other things that don't make sense. I've never seen that knife before, and it was quite unique, it had a lotus pod shaped blade, you don't forget seeing something like that. Several curves on it, with holes in the pattern of a honeycomb. There was *no* DNA in the flat? Not the Airbnb host's, the cleaner's, or my wife's? Did she go around wiping everything before jumping in the bath? Her suicide note, typed, with no personal information in it. No mention of her daughters, of me, of her parents. The most generic shit you can write, the only thing someone who doesn't really know her could write. And what about the heating. Is she meant to have cranked it way up before her bath, in the middle of summer, and placed herself in an unplugged bath to make sure her stench didn't warn anyone of her suicide?"

He shook his head.

"And what did the expensive lawyer do with all that information?" Virgil asked.

"We found the fucker who did this. We appealed, presented all the information to a judge, but it was deemed as insufficient evidence. A CCTV camera caught a man nearby around the time she was estimated to have passed away, some time on the Sunday night, and we found a connection between him and Wendy. But he got off the hook because he had a plausible alibi and reason to be there, there was no DNA evidence, and he was diagnosed with trypophobia, a fear of–"

"Irregular patterns and clusters of small holes, yes."

"Yeah, so he couldn't possibly hold the crime weapon, the weird knife, apparently. A bit convenient, isn't it?"

"I can certainly imagine how frustrating it would have been for you," Virgil said. "The sense of injustice is one of the most powerful catalysts for strong emotions. How did this injustice make you feel?"

"I went bonkers, didn't I? How else did you think I'd feel? You and your therapist questions."

"Is that why you're in prison? How do you think it impacted the rest of your life?"

Something changed in Quentin's eyes.

The picture of Quentin McQueen was becoming clearer and clearer. Virgil was beginning to get some insight into why he'd ended up in prison; everything was starting to come together. And just now, Virgil suspected Quentin sensed it as well. As if he knew what Virgil was doing, where he was going.

And Quentin did not want to go there. He put an end to their talk, requested a cheese board, and left the cabin.

Everything was starting to come together, yes, but one piece was still missing. One crucial piece.

37

ON THE CONSORTIUM'S YACHT

"Thanks for coming," Harry said.

"No problem," Lawrence replied. "You sounded ominous."

Lawrence took a seat at the surveillance room's table. Harry was sat in front of the screens, his stare focused on the only screen without a CCTV feed.

"I've looked into Anna's medical records," Harry said.

"That's not public information."

"No, no I had Joe from Anonymous hack into the records for me."

"I know we're not following the highest code of ethics here," Lawrence said, crossing his arms, "but I would appreciate it if you consulted me before doing something like this. Anna is my associate, I am protective of her."

Harry spun around on his swivel chair to glance at his boss, unsure if he was being gravely told off, or just told off. "Sorry."

"Well go on." Lawrence jerked his head at the monitor. "Now it's done, what did you find?"

Harry turned back to face the screen. "There is no trace

of the injury Anna sustained to her arm anywhere on here. Nothing could even come close, even by a stretch of the imagination."

"So she was never treated in hospital?"

"Nowhere records are kept. A grave injury like hers, it would have had to be treated by professionals."

"So it was done privately, under the radar?"

"It must have been," replied Harry. "But why? It brings up so many questions."

"I have an idea," replied Lawrence. "But I'm not quite ready to share it, yet."

"And look at this." Harry pointed to a box on the screen. "There was a superinjunction to prevent this from becoming public knowledge in any way."

Lawrence kept quiet for a moment, staring at the screen. "I had suspected something like this," he said at last. "This just...makes it all too real. Thanks for bringing it to my attention."

"Do we go on as if we didn't know?"

"Of course. You obtained that illegally, and she wants it kept confidential. We just have to keep it in mind."

Harry nodded.

38

ANONYMOUS UPC RANKINGS

Day 37 of the Ultimate Psycho Championships (UPC)

Rocky Bardeaux

As had become their tradition for the past fortnight or so – briefly interrupted by the storm – Rocky and Quentin were having their elevenses in Rocky's cabin. Quentin's cabin had never been an option, with the constant coming and going to climb up to the sun deck.

Rocky had a steaming cup of breakfast tea with milk, one sugar, and a buttered toast. Quentin a mug of instant coffee with milk, no sugar, and a strawberry jam toast. They would have gone to the sun deck, but Jan had gone up earlier and hadn't yet come back down, and some dark clouds were heading their way. Not to mention taking hot water up there required some challenging skills and logistics. They enjoyed their privacy and preferred not to be eavesdropped on – other than by the thousands of people watching on their screens.

"I've told Virgil now, so I might as well tell you too," Quentin said. "It actually felt good getting it off my chest."

"Getting what off your chest?"

"The story around Wendy's death."

Quentin went on recount the circumstances around her death, with Rocky agreeing with him on every single point.

"Trypophobia," Rocky repeated, making a face. "It just sounds made up, especially when you consider the coincidence. How could a judge not see how ridiculous that is?"

"I've been asking myself that every night for years."

"Have you talked to charities like The Innocence Project? I've read about them, they seem good."

"No one's been convicted wrongfully in Wendy's case, so it doesn't apply. It's only me, the lawyers I hired, and my debts. Too broke now to do anything about it. And now that I'm in prison, I've got no chance. They see me as scum, no judge is ever taking me seriously again."

"Tell me about it," Rocky said. "Once you get on their bad side, there's no coming back. They're only waiting for us to die to make space for other prisoners. Once, I came back to my cage after an hour of exercise, and there was a knife there, sitting on my concrete slab of a bed. A normal kitchen knife, six inches long, plastic handle, the type you'd use to chop your onions. Blade sharp as a scalpel. If that isn't evidence that the guards wanted me gone, I don't know what is. The temptation was...untenable. I reached for it, let my hand hover above it, but then...I pulled away. If I'd touched it, I would've grabbed it and ended it. I should have, probably, but I didn't want to give them what they wanted.

I'm that stubborn. Tell me I can't kill people, and I'll grab a plastic fork and fashion a knife out of it. Give me a knife and tell me to kill myself, and I'll hand you it back, handle first."

Quentin chuckled. "I'm a bit like that too. Right, I need some fresh air, and the sun is back," he added, looking through the porthole window. "I'll keep Jan company, if he's still there. Are you coming?"

"I'll make myself another toast. I'll come up in a bit."

A quick glance around the lounge and the dining area and Rocky noticed Teddy and Glenys weren't there. Ever since the incident, he'd kept tabs on them; he took some responsibility for letting it happen in the first place. Francopan was sat in his usual spot at the dining table, staring blankly at the lounge, where Edmond was eating a bowl of cereal.

"Francopan, where's Teddy? Or Glenys?"

He didn't move, or acknowledge he'd heard Rocky.

"Francopan," Rocky repeated. "Virgil. Oy, Virgil." He wondered if he was doing it on purpose. He waved a hand in front of his eyes, then louder, "VIRGIL".

The mad psychiatrist finally turned his gaze on him. "Sorry," he said calmly, looking half asleep. "I just don't understand why Quentin is here. Why did he end up in solitary? He is mentally sound, no illness or personality disorder, he does not have violent tendencies, just boringly normal. The injustice is his fuel, but why choose to burn it this way? What is he doing here?"

Rocky raised his eyebrows. "Did you see Teddy or Glenys?"

"Teddy headed that way not long ago, haven't seen Glenys."

Rocky walked to Teddy's cabin, and there he was, napping with his door ajar. It came as a relief, but a second later the noise of glass shattering rang out behind him, and he knew it came from Glenys' cabin.

He rushed in and found her with bloodied hands, holding a jagged piece of thin glass in the air. The bedside table's lamp's lightbulb lay on the floor in a thousand pieces.

He leapt forward and held her arm up with one hand, then pried her hand open with the other, exerting force until she let the shard of glass go.

"Francopan," he shouted into the hallway. "Come *now*." Then he turned to Glenys, still holding her arms up. "Bloody hell, Glenys."

He glanced at her wrists; one had a scratch on it, where she'd clearly tried but failed to cut deeply. Her hands were covered in blood, coming from small scratches all over her fingers.

"This paper-thin glass is a bitch," Glenys said, wincing from the pain. "Goes everywhere, and it doesn't take any weight at all."

Francopan appeared and took everything in. "Oh dear."

"Here," Rocky said, stepping away, "make sure she doesn't do anything stupid, and I'll clear all the glass."

He picked up the broken lightbulb, opened the porthole, and threw it out into the sea. Then he carefully picked up all the small shards, gathered them in his hand, and threw them out. It was so thin and brittle that he couldn't avoid cutting himself.

"Glenys, dear Glenys," Francopan said, his face only a few inches from hers. "This is not your way out. Are you hearing voices?"

Somehow, they just felt like words, flat and conversational, without any emotion behind them.

"No, I don't know," she said, then choked up, sniffing loudly.

"Are you seeing things which weren't there before?" Francopan asked.

Glenys looked at him with confusion. "No, I'm– I'm just so lost." She broke down and drew out the words, then she collapsed on the bed.

"Hey, I didn't check the bed yet," Rocky warned, but too late. He turned to the camera in the corner of the cabin. "Do you hear me?"

The system clicked on. "Yes," said a female voice. It sounded slightly different from the one they'd heard before.

"You have to replace all the lightbulbs on this boat. Ever heard of LED lightbulbs? Or shatter-resistant ones? They're made of plastic or shatterproof material."

"Noted. Do we need to send in the nurse?"

Francopan inspected the cuts, then shook his head. "No, I can take care of this. We have enough supplies now in here for cuts." The sound system turned off and Francopan headed to the bathroom.

Rocky inspected the room one last time, then he closed the porthole. He turned to Glenys, lying down on her bed, in a right mess. "When he's done, you and I need to talk."

39

ANONYMOUS UPC RANKINGS

Day 39 of the Ultimate Psycho Championships (UPC)

Virgil Francopan

"Your presence is much appreciated," Virgil said, rubbing his gloved hands together.

He quickly stopped. The air had recently become more humid and hot than usual; the boat must have been travelling south. Leather was a natural material that absorbed moisture from the air, and heat caused oils in the leather to rise to the surface, all combining to make his gloves tacky. If he continued using them, he might damage the leather, so he reluctantly took them off. At home, he would have the tools and products to repair the damage, but in here, it would result in irreversible damage. He'd worked too hard to craft the perfect gloves only to let them spoil in this way.

"I thought we were making good progress," Virgil continued, "and this break will have created more bad than good."

"Yeah, sorry," Teddy said, rubbing his inked scalp, his other hand holding his red and black bandana. "Just didn't feel up to it after...you know."

"Yes, I know. About that. Where does it come from? I know you've been convicted of sexual assault before, it landed you in prison, so it's a recurring issue. Can you trace its source?"

Teddy scoffed. "Isn't it up to you to tell me this?"

"I don't know the intimate details of your past. Have you had any exposure to sex in your childhood?"

"My mates had porn magazines, and we'd sneak a porn film here and there. I probably started being sexually active around thirteen? Nothing big, but you know, fooling around."

"I meant, have you been exposed to anything you shouldn't have been exposed to? Or have you suffered sexual assault yourself at any point in your life?"

He thought for a second, then shook his head, "Don't think so. Oh, well, hang on a second. Exposed, as in seen things? Yeah, I suppose I did. When I was younger, around six or seven. Maybe before too but I wouldn't remember. I vaguely remember my dad having sex with a woman I didn't know in the house, in the living room. I was supposed to be in my room, but I was curious about the noise. I wasn't too sure what they were doing at the time, but later with hindsight, I understood. And once, he put me in the boot of the car, and I heard the noises and the rocking of the car. And it wasn't my mum."

Virgil nodded. "That certainly wouldn't help. In addition to a distorted perception of sex, sexual offences are usually driven by the need for control, power, or other deep-rooted psychological and emotional issues. Your mother emotionally abused you, and routinely shamed and humiliated you, it would explain your need for control and perhaps to punish women?"

Teddy remained silent.

"When did you first feel yourself becoming violent towards women? At school, or later? Perhaps you felt resentful towards your female teachers?"

"I've never consciously disliked women in general. Never really thought of it. School is just a big blur to me, until I got expelled because I smacked that wanker for calling me Humpty Dumpty one too many times. I've got severe dyslexia, could barely read and write, so teachers and I never got on. I tended to throw objects often. Never liked them and most were women, but I don't think it's related."

"Do you think your general violence may be partly due to your frustration at your educational needs never being considered? And as a result, it left you with no career options other than crime?"

"I suppose, yeah. I like talking to you, heh, makes me feel better about myself."

Virgil had to resist the urge to bring him back to Earth and point out how much of a rotter he was regardless. Instead he gave him a perfunctory smile. "Feeling good about yourself is the first step in reducing your violence, and being less angry towards the world."

"Yeah, I've not always been like this. I remember once when my mates shoved a younger kid on the floor just outside a McDonald's and they stamped on his glasses. They all laughed at him and then just left. I'd laughed along, not to lose face with my mates, but looking back over my shoulder, I felt awful watching the boy pick up his broken frames with a bloody nose. I was fifteen, my brother Bobby had passed away a couple of months before that, and I kept wondering what Bobby would have done. The image stayed with me for weeks. But over the years, I became numb to the daily violence around me. I stopped feeling guilty."

"I'm glad you're able to be aware of it. My job, especially if we had longer, is to help you become sensitive to it again."

The session went on like this for a good hour, at the end of which Virgil felt Teddy had become slightly more at peace with himself, though it was impossible to tell how long it would last. Before Teddy stood up, however, Virgil couldn't resist asking one last question.

"Before you go, do you mind telling me how your escape from prison took place? How did they get both you and Quentin out?"

Teddy raised his eyebrows and gave a loud sigh. "It all happened fast. I was told someone from Interpol was coming to question me in relation to an ongoing investigation, straight to my cell. So when the steel door opened I thought it was them, but it was the plague barrister's people. Four men. They must've assaulted the guards or obtained the keys somehow, and they rushed me out.

"Quentin was coming back from his hour of exercise, escorted by two guards, and when the guards saw us they grabbed their nightstick. Quentin shook them off and ran to us. The plague barrister's men were busy shooting the guards with some kind of darts, like they use with wild animals, and when Quentin tagged along they were too busy and flustered to force him to stay. He was handcuffed so he wasn't dangerous, at first one of the men told him to stay and pushed him away, but Quentin wouldn't have it. He was like a mad dog, determined to get out. One of them was going to shoot him, but the others reminded him they weren't meant to shoot anyone who wasn't a direct threat. So they just brought him with us. After that I didn't see a single guard before we got to the ground floor, and even then the plague barrister's men had all the credentials of Interpol agents, or they looked the same anyway, and when they realised something was wrong, we were already getting into the van. Then the van stormed off and–"

"That's enough," Virgil said, nodding. "Thank you, I was just curious."

Learning that Quentin was an accident, had never been part of the consortium's plan, answered some questions, but it only piqued Virgil's curiosity further. Teddy closed the door behind him and left Virgil alone with his thoughts, free to wonder yet again about Quentin McQueen and his story.

40

ANONYMOUS UPC RANKINGS

Day 41 of the Ultimate Psycho Championships (UPC)

Virgil Francopan

"You've been spending a lot of time up on the sun deck lately," Virgil said. He brought his cup of Earl Grey to his mouth. He'd made sure to bring a beverage this time, for during his last session with Jan, it had been a very long, very dry hour, sitting in silence, and something had tickled Virgil's throat the entire time but without anything to drink, it had been almost torture. "Just enjoying the sun? Trying to get a tan?"

Jan looked up, his eyes searching Virgil's, and when the hint of a smile played in Virgil's gaze, Jan returned his attention to the carpeted floor at his feet.

Perhaps he'd spent a lot of time outside, but he must

have remained in the shade the entire time, or else covered his face with his long, greasy hair, for his complexion was just as pale as it had always been.

"Here, I have a gift for you today." Virgil bent down and retrieved one of the kitchenette's bamboo cups from under his bed. He handed it to Jan. "If you don't want it, no worries. I just thought you might like it."

Jan grabbed the cup and inspected its contents. His eyes went wide. He sniffed at the cup's rim, then looked up sharply.

Virgil gave him a nod of encouragement.

Jan took one sip, then stared at Virgil again. "Are you for real?"

"Absolutely. My gift to you, Jan." He took a pill out of his jumpsuit's pocket. "Here, might as well take your medication while you're drinking something."

Jan took the pill instantly, and given the look in his eyes, if Virgil had asked him to clean his underwear by hand, he would've obeyed without a word.

Jan downed the cup in one quick gulp, then licked his lips. There was still a hint of red at the left corner of his mouth, so Virgil gestured to his own mouth to let him know. Jan wiped his lips with one swipe of his jumpsuit's sleeve.

He'd worked hard to prepare this beverage, so he was glad it was received so well.

"I hope this will prove to you that I am here to help, and I am on your side."

Jan nodded.

"So was my guess correct; you've been…thirsty, lately?"

"That's what I've been doing up there," Jan said. "Looking for birds. Fucking gulls are hard to get, though. Or I'm losing my touch. I used to catch birds back home."

"To…drink their blood?"

Jan nodded.

"Right," Virgil said. "Why do you need to do this?"

"I've always had the symptoms of anaemia; weakness, pale skin, dizziness, cold hands and feet, and that's because my body doesn't produce enough blood. My blood thickens in my veins if I stay too long without fresh blood, but as soon as I get some, I have this rush of light, of elation, and all my symptoms disappear. I even get hard."

"As in, you get an erection?"

For the first time since meeting him, Jan blushed. Even when everyone saw his request for his personal item on the first day here, the map of the human body, he hadn't shown any sign of embarrassment.

"Well," Jan said, "the blood starts flowing fast throughout my body, doesn't it? And without this fresh influx, I can't get it up."

That would make for a strong motivation to find blood. A valid explanation for the spree killings which led him to prison in the first place.

"How did you find out all this about you? Did you uncover it by yourself?"

"For the most part," he said, then avoided Virgil's gaze.

Virgil knew the telltale signs of someone hiding something. "What about the other part?"

"You can't see them, so you won't believe me."

"Try me. I am not your average psychiatrist, in case you hadn't noticed."

Jan hesitated, then glanced at the empty cup in his hand. "I have these angels, or whatever, I don't know what else to call them, but these supernatural beings who know everything, and they've been advising me. If I were to stay too long without a fresh influx, then ultimately, my blood would turn to dust and I would die. They said so, and they showed me, on the map, how it all works."

Virgil nodded. "It's more common than you think. You're lucky you're aware of them, that you can hear them. Most people can't."

"Yeah, exactly."

"So you've been keeping the voices secret this entire time, because you believe people would think you crazy?"

"They'll say I'm psychotic."

"You can't be psychotic. Psychotic patients just blurt out whatever they experience, believing it's legitimate and everyone should heed them. They are not aware of what other people may think of them, and they don't care."

Jan's face lit up. "I knew it." The semblance of a smile came on his lips; Virgil didn't think he'd ever see that.

"I'll help you get better," Virgil said, "and get what you want. You have to trust me, I'm on your side."

"I think," Jan said, looking down at the cup once more, "yeah, I think I know that now."

"Wonderful."

41

ANNA KIMPER

Life on the yacht is tense, for various reasons.

Harry is suspicious of me, I see it in his eyes, though I have no idea what he's suspicious about. I think he's curious about my medical history, and taking it personally that I refuse to put my existing doctor aside in order to ask him for prescriptions instead. Regardless of why, he's watching me, and drops hints here and there that make me uncomfortable.

But Harry's no longer an issue, because he left the boat four days ago and it's unsure whether he'll be back or not. He's had to go back to work to avoid raising any suspicion, and his mother is dying, so he needs to be by her side. Considering how things had gotten, I was glad when he announced he had to leave us. I was, however, less glad when Lawrence announced his replacement.

We were already stretched thin to cover all the shifts in the surveillance room with us three and the occasional extra member of the consortium, so without Harry it would become dangerous; we'd be too tired, we'd miss things, and we wouldn't react to emergencies with a clear head. Unfortunately, the only person who could join us at such short notice was Porker Stephen. So now things are tense because I can't stand the sight of him, and he knows it.

Lawrence picks me up outside my cabin and we walk together to the dining lounge, where Porker Stephen has asked to talk to us. We don't know what he wants now, but just being in his presence will be taxing. His aide isn't any better, at Porker's beck and call with a robotic look on his face. I know, without a doubt, that if he asked his aide to commit some atrocity in plain sight, the man would do it.

"What is Virgil playing at?" I ask as we walk down the hallway. "Have you seen his session with Jan?"

"Yes."

"Are you not alarmed?"

"I talked to Harry, sent him the audio recording. We both believe he may be trying a different tack to break through Jan's shell, since nothing else has worked so far. So he's gaining his trust, maybe to ensure he takes his medication. It doesn't look like he's been taking them after all, from what he said, so Virgil's approach may be best."

"A bit drastic, don't you think?"

Lawrence marks a pause at the top of the stairs, probably because once we go down, we'll be within earshot of Stephen. "If Virgil fails, and Jan continues avoiding his medication, then he may have to be removed from the boat. Or worse, if we're too late. So if a drastic measure is needed to make sure he complies, so be it."

I force my lips shut. Sometimes I wonder if Virgil is part of the consortium, given how much both Lawrence and Harry rely on him. I also feel like I'm being pushed out of the way; I've noticed the pattern. Decisions are made without consulting me, and then presented to me as done deals. I know if I say anything else it will look like I am focusing too much on Virgil, given how much I've spoken out against him already, so I keep quiet. But inside I'm bubbling.

We arrive at the table, take our seats, and the staff brings us a Greek salad. Stanislas is among the staff, and he brings me my plate. I like his devotion to me, the role of protector he assumed without me asking. In a dangerous environment, with a pervert sat across from me, his slave, and a powerful man whom, I've realised, could potentially turn on me and keep me from reaching my objective, having a staunch ally in Stanislas is most welcome.

When the staff is out of earshot, Porker Stephen leans back on his chair, makes it creak under his weight, and turns his attention to Lawrence. He hasn't touched his salad. "I'm disappointed in the lack of violence throughout this entire operation. I invested heavily in this, in the hope I'd secure fascinating footage you wouldn't be able to get anywhere else. A group of highly violent criminals trapped on a boat, how can you not expect violence? Blood? More tears?"

Lawrence is staring at Stephen, and when the billionaire is done talking, Lawrence doesn't reply right away. "Stephen, did you not understand the point of this experiment? We want to avoid violence, to show the world these normally violent people can be rehabilitated and trusted if placed in the right environment. In fact, I wish there had been less violence than we saw."

Stephen turns a shade of red. "I thought it was all a front! A facade, to tame the police, to gain public approval and sympathy, to fool people into thinking you're a good person, really. And regardless, I thought it would definitely fail. Lawrence, I paid big money to see blood, tears, anguish, agony, and pain. I did not get involved in this to watch them fuss over a bloody cat and waste their days away playing video games. I want my money's worth."

"There has been violence," I point out. "We've had to send the nurse in a few times, and a couple more times we didn't send the nurse in even though there had been an incident. Glenys almost killed herself, for goodness sake. It's not like they've just eaten, slept, and played cards the entire time."

"And you've received confidential footage you'd asked for in our agreement," Lawrence adds.

Stephen waves both our comments away. "None of that is worth the yacht I donated, let alone the millions I put in."

"I'm afraid it's too late now," Lawrence says. "You knew what you were signing up for, I was candid and ultimately, I have no control over what the participants do in the boat. I was – I am – genuine in my intentions, in this experiment's purpose, so I've been nothing but honest. Whatever you imagined would happen, that wasn't our agreement. I can't be held responsible for what's going on in your head."

Stephen's aide taps the side of his boss' head with a chequered handkerchief to remove the beads of sweat. "I will see more entertaining content," Stephen promises. "Mark my words. I will get my money's worth."

42

ANONYMOUS UPC RANKINGS

Day 44 of the Ultimate Psycho Championships (UPC)

Rocky Bardeaux

If they proved successful, it would be partly, if not mostly, due to this gaming console.

All of them were gathered in the lounge, even Francopan and Jan who normally steered clear of the excitement, and the atmosphere was warm, light-hearted, and playful. Banter was exchanged back and forth, with Rocky and Quentin leading the charge, and failures were laughed off while successes were cheered loudly. It was the occupation which kept them, as a group, busy the longest, and Rocky would argue it was the glue which held them together. He got up every morning looking forward to a good hour of shooting soldiers' heads off.

At some point in the game, Teddy was the group's last remaining survivor, but just before he managed to eliminate the last of the enemy's platoon, he fell down a cliff and died. He took his bandana off and shook his head in between his knees, leaning his elbows on his thighs. Edmond, leaning on the sofa just behind him, stretched to have a better look at the tattoos on his scalp, then silently pointed frantically at one of them. Rocky followed his gaze, and it fell on Francopan.

Confused, Rocky looked back at Edmond, and now he was mouthing the words 'humpty dumpty'. Had he not noticed it before? Teddy did wear his bandana often, but still. Francopan grinned, as if they shared an inside joke, but it was all lost on Rocky when a non-human shriek rang out from the other side of the boat.

"Was that from the bathroom?" Rocky asked.

"Sounded like it," Quentin replied.

"Where's Thesea?" Teddy asked.

Rocky's heart leapt; the cat wasn't here. "Who's missing?" he asked, counting.

"My brother," Edmond said.

They ran to the bathroom, but the door was locked. "Jan, open," Rocky shouted.

He looked around for an object, anything he could use to pry the door open. "Glenys, can you hand me one of the dining chairs?" But she disappeared inside a cabin before he finished his question.

Then he had a second to think, and he concluded a chair wouldn't help anyway.

"We'll just have to kick it open," Teddy said, relishing the opportunity to use violence for good. "Jan, you coming out mate?"

No response.

Teddy turned around. "Everyone okay with me doing this?"

"Uncharacteristically civil of you," Francopan said. "Fine with me, yes."

"Here, I'll help you." Rocky got in position next to Teddy.

At three, they both kicked the door at bolt-level, and it flew open in one loud crash.

A bloodbath met them.

Poor Thesea's tortoiseshell fur was spread all over the bathroom, with bloody patches and hand and finger prints scattered on the walls and sink and toilet. Jan's face was covered in blood, with a few deep scratches on his arms and neck. The cat's corpse was opened at the intersection of both rib cages, and Jan had a bamboo spoon in his hand.

"My fucking God mate," Teddy shouted, "what is wrong with you?"

Everyone expected Teddy to explode, and both Rocky and Francopan held him to make sure he didn't pounce on Jan, but Rocky realised Teddy wasn't in an angry, killing mood. He was repulsed, disgusted, and shocked. He kept looking from Jan to Thesea's remains, unable to comprehend fully what had just happened. Just like everyone else. Rocky and Francopan soon released him.

"Goddammit Jan," Edmond said. "It's happening all over again. First Skipper and now Thesea, what is it with you and pets?"

"It was the only blood available to him, short of killing one of us," Francopan offered. "The same way your dog was easy access to him all those years ago. It doesn't matter to him where the blood comes from."

"So he's not doing well at all, is he?" Quentin said, slowly backing away.

"I'm not going to jump you," Jan said at last, wiping his mouth with his jumpsuit, but managing only to create a stripe of a different shade of red on his chin and cheek. "This was...good. I feel calmer."

"What are we going to do with him?" Rocky asked Francopan, but the psychiatrist's gaze was frozen. He was watching Quentin.

"Guys," Quentin said. "My cabin's porthole is open. And Glenys isn't here."

Rocky barged past Quentin and jumped through the window, with Francopan close on his heels. He glanced at the water, but saw no sign of her. They climbed up the ladder as if their life depended on it, and they leapt onto the sun deck.

It was the end of a cloudy day, so the sun was setting behind a thick layer of grey and the light was weak. Still, the swaying silhouette against the lighter backdrop was clear.

Rocky rushed to set her down, but he knew as soon as he touched her that they were too late. Francopan helped him lay her down, and he checked her pulse and for signs of shallow breathing. Then he repositioned her neck and performed CPR, but Rocky knew in his gut that it was desperation rather than genuine hope of reviving her.

As expected, Francopan stopped and shook his head.

"It's my fault," Rocky muttered.

"Don't you start," Francopan replied in a curt tone.

His vision became blurry. "I vowed I'd keep an eye on her." And he had, he'd made sure he knew where she was at all times, he'd even sacrificed his nights, keeping one eye open and never able to fall into a deep sleep. But she'd seized her opportunity as soon as his attention had been dragged elsewhere, and in the end, he reflected, if she'd been that desperate, then she would've found a way sooner or later.

But it hurt.

"You go down and inform our masters," Francopan said, "I'll stay with her until they come to retrieve the body. And I'll undo all this."

He motioned to the rope tied around the bimini top's metal frame, the noose, and the fallen deck chair. Rocky stared at the set up. The rope, a proper sailing line, made of white and blue nylon or polyester, wrapped in a neat noose, with the right kind of knot and everything. Not only he doubted she would have had the time to set it all up, but Rocky didn't remember seeing the rope before.

In fact, a while back, he'd noticed how there were no ropes, or strings, at all on the entire boat. Until now.

43

ANONYMOUS UPC RANKINGS

Day 46 of the Ultimate Psycho Championships (UPC)

Virgil Francopan

The evening of Glenys' passing, the plague barrister spoke to them. Until the consortium collected further evidence, he said, her suicide did not affect the UPC; the championship was not yet triggered into the point system. It was clear, the plague barrister said, that everyone had tried to prevent her death, and that Glenys was unwell. She had already tried previously, and it was, ultimately, her own doing.

It came as a small relief to everyone that their future was still safe, but what worried Virgil was the initial part of the plague barrister's address: 'until we collect further evidence'. Was the decision not final, would they come back on it later?

The plague barrister also announced that Jan would have points deducted retroactively, should the championship be triggered, which placed Rocky, Edmond, Quentin, and Virgil in prime position to end in the top two, if the worst were to happen.

The mood on the boat was dark; no longer did the collective laughter from video games echo throughout the yacht, and no longer did they noisily rejoice at the marvellous meals they were served. Everybody felt Glenys' absence deeply, or acted like they did, at any rate. Jan's transgression, though not forgotten, had been placed on the backburner for the time being, for it would be seen as an insult to Glenys' memory to mourn the cat.

Two days after her death, Virgil insisted on starting the sessions again, to get back into a sort of routine and help them get through the last quarter of their journey to freedom. And he started with Quentin, for he was still an enigma waiting to be solved.

Virgil promptly got Quentin to go deeper into the circumstances around his wife's death.

"For you to understand why I'm so sure she was murdered," Quentin said, "I need to give you some background. Wendy told me, quite early in our relationship, that she'd dated an older man while she was in her late teens who was on the bad side of the law. He wasn't old, late twenties or early thirties, but a significant gap. He lived in England but he was French and she was attracted to his image and style, and she admitted it was a form of rebellion against her parents who had been quite strict. The Frenchie had a hold on her which made her do things she would not normally have done, and she told me she never actually committed a crime, but that the bloke did go to prison for theft, and that's pretty much why they broke up. Keeping this in mind, following her alleged suicide, I looked at her diaries. Her business diary said she was meeting with potential clients that Monday, as expected, but in her personal diary, she wrote down she was meant to meet 'Tank' on the Sunday evening, the same evening she arrived and checked into her Airbnb."

He marked a pause to put some order in his thoughts. Virgil sensed he was on the right trail to uncovering the puzzle's missing piece, and nothing could have shaken his focus now.

"The CCTV of the petrol station located immediately behind the block of flats where Wendy was staying caught a man walking from the station to the block of flats, at a time which fits with Wendy's estimated time of death. Looking at more CCTV footage, we traced this bloke back to his lorry which he'd parked in the petrol station, so we identified him, and guess what? He'd already done time in prison, and a nickname he went by was Tank. And Tank had been in the same prison as Wendy's Frenchie. It couldn't be coincidence, to me it was evidence, the judge disagreed, there was no hard evidence, just circumstantial evidence, and a lorrie driver parking in a petrol station overnight was a plausible alibi, so nothing happened, but–"

"Did the CCTV not record what time Tank came back to his lorry?" Virgil interrupted. "The timings could be important."

Quentin shook his head. "We scoured the footage, trust me, and he never appeared again until the next morning, where we see him walking from the lorry to the station. He must've come back on the other side of the station, where the CCTV didn't reach, so it could've been anytime. When I went to prison, I got moved around a bit and then I landed in the same prison where Tank and Frenchie had been held together, so I managed to gather all the missing information. Turns out Frenchie had stolen a valuable painting from a museum, that was why he'd done time, and Wendy had been actively involved. I don't blame her for not telling me, but Frenchie told Tank, and when Tank got out, he found Wendy and blackmailed her. I don't know what he wanted from her, but that has to be why they met on that Sunday evening, and maybe she refused to cooperate so he killed her. I'm convinced he raped her too, but we don't know because her body was too far gone when they found her."

"Tank was his nickname," Virgil said, "do you know what his full name was?"

"Yeah, Theo Bates."

Virgil grinned.

44

ANNA KIMPER

I don't know how he did it, but he did it. Virgil got Glenys to kill herself, just like he did with the nurse he became infamous for.

I add some drops to my eyes; they hurt, the light from the screens is like hot coals pressed against my eyeballs, but that is secondary. Finding proof, or at least confirmation, that Virgil is responsible is the only thing that matters right now. There must be something, in her talks with the other inmates, or in her multiple sessions with Virgil.

"Poor thing," Lawrence says as he comes into the surveillance room, eying my bottle of eye drops, "you've been watching more footage than me lately. You should take a rest."

"I'd rather not. The sooner we catch Virgil, the sooner we can save someone else."

"We won't remove him from the boat," Lawrence says, "even if we find evidence. You know that, right? It will trigger the ranking system, and he'll be at the bottom of the ranking, but that will only give him licence to unleash the monster in him because he'll have nothing to lose. So, really, it might be in our interest to turn a blind eye. Technically speaking, and perhaps in reality too, it was a suicide, and the experiment can go on."

I turn around and look at him differently. This is not the Lawrence I know. The Lawrence I know would respect transparency at all cost, and punish a criminal if he deserves it. Humanely, but still punish him.

"I want to know if it was him," I say through clenched teeth, and I turn back to face the screens.

"In that case, let me help you." He places a chair next to mine and lets his hand hover over the mouse. "Please, allow me."

I reluctantly remove my hand and let him take control.

He turns the screen away from me, enters his login details, then clicks away for a minute. He turns the screen back to where it was so I can see too, and he plays a video. It's Virgil, on the toilet.

"What are you doing?" I ask. The last thing I want to do and watch Virgil take a shit.

"The footage you haven't seen yet, because only I have access to it. Bathrooms with a lock are intimate spaces, the only room in the boat they can lock and be truly alone. It might show some things. I'll give you the rights to have access to those with Virgil and Glenys."

"I'm surprised there are cameras at that angle. And..." I glimpse the thumbnail of another video. "There is another one to watch them shower from within the cubicle? So you're violating their privacy in every way?"

"I know, I know, I'm not proud of this." He actually does look a bit sheepish. "But it's not easy to find wealthy people who are into our project, so I had to cater to all tastes in order to secure enough funds. These cameras won us surprisingly large investments, including Stephen's. And we need all sorts of unpublished footage to sell for added revenue streams."

This is where I realise he only ever considered me his business partner in name. It has been a farce, this entire time. I've been his secretary, at best. The sheer amount of things he's kept from me is astonishing. I understand this is his baby, and he's been planning it his entire life and I've only jumped in two years ago, but then why bother agreeing to call me his partner?

"Speaking of sick perverts," I say, "did you know Stephen brought a drone with him, and he's been flying it over the water, making it go quite far out at sea? A deckhand saw him." Having a second pair of eyes in Stanislas is proving more and more useful.

"Yes," Lawrence says, nodding. "But with things not going his way and his grumbling, I thought it best not to tell him off. He can play with his toy."

"But what does he do with it? Does it have a camera?"

"Yes, but just on his remote control's monitor, to guide it. I don't believe it's recording anything. And if it is...well, maybe we can use it to see what they're up to on the sun deck. I don't see any danger."

"Rocky said Glenys used a piece of white sailing line with blue stripes, didn't he?"

"He did."

"Didn't we get rid of all of the ropes on their yacht?"

"I thought we had. I wondered about that too. But then I thought, if she hadn't had a piece of rope she would've found something else, a bed sheet, something."

"It's just...a couple of days ago I noticed a length of white rope with blue stripes on the main deck that had been untidily hacked off, as if someone had struggled to cut it. And then this happened, around the time the deckhand reported seeing Stephen and his aide flying the drone towards their yacht."

"You don't think..."

I raise my eyebrows. "Having to use a bed sheet or something else requires a lot more work, thought, preparation, and a higher possibility of being seen and therefore stopped. Whereas if she goes up to the sun deck, sees a length of rope with a noose already fashioned, next to a tall metal frame...that makes it quite a bit easier, all of a sudden."

Lawrence gulps. "Oh, the swine. I'll have a word with him, see what he says."

He leaves the surveillance room. I resume my work on the screens, opening the panoply of videos I now have access to.

A notification pops up in the bottom corner of the screen. At first I ignore it, but then, just before it disappears, I notice it's an email from someone I don't know, and only the email's first line shows in the preview. It says 'Hi Lawrence'.

He's forgotten to log off.

I go to his emails and quickly scan through them, before he comes back or remembers. One catches my attention, from one of the hackers from Anonymous. The hacker just says, 'Understood'. I scroll down to see Lawrence's original email:

No, it is to remain confidential until the very end, until after it is done. No one else is to know, I will undertake everything myself. I have to prioritise the participants' safety without fear of leaks.

. . .

L

I SCROLL further down to see the hacker's previous email:

How do you want to share the successful prisoners' drop-off locations with your associates? Only in person? I would advise that, but if anything must be communicated electronically, we need to know now so we can prepare accordingly.

I TAKE a moment to process this. It changes everything.
    I must get to Virgil *before* he leaves the boat.

45

ANONYMOUS UPC RANKINGS

Day 48 of the Ultimate Psycho Championships (UPC)

Virgil Francopan

The weather improved, and where before a thick layer of light grey clouds all merging into each other had hung over them, now the blue skies and bright sun of their early days returned. Except now it was hotter, and more humid, than it had ever been. They took the fans out of the cupboards whenever they were inside, and the rest of the time they spent on the sun deck, sheltered in the bimini top's cool shade.

"There's an island, over there," Edmond said, staring at a point in the horizon.

"Is there?" Virgil asked, squinting. "Or is it a mirage?"

"Doesn't matter what it is," cut in Rocky, "I don't like where your mind is going, Ed."

"Yeah," Quentin said, "you've been doing really well, don't ruin it now."

"Did I say anything about trying to escape?" Edmond said, indignant. "I've learned my lesson, though the water does look warmer here..." Rocky opened his mouth but Edmond was quicker: "Joking! My God, guys, relax. We're almost at the end, I'm not risking it all now. And what would swimming to that island achieve anyways? Being stuck on a deserted island isn't my idea of a dream getaway, and it's not like the plague barrister wouldn't be able to just bring me back."

"Not to mention you'd be smashed against the rocks before you got there," Virgil said. "You've done stupid things, but this would beat them all."

"I wouldn't say no to a little swim, though," Quentin said. "It's so hot, and the water looks good. As you said, I don't think it's too cold here."

Teddy leaned over the guardrail and looked down. "The boat is stationary, methinks. Nothing wrong with a little dip, is there?"

"How about we all go in?" Virgil suggested.

"I'm up for it," agreed Rocky.

"Jan won't join us," Edmond said, glancing at his brother at the other end of the deck. "He hates water."

"I suppose it's good that someone stays onboard," Quentin said, "just in case."

"How should we do this?" Rocky asked. "Should we all make our way down to the stern and jump from there?"

In a single file, they used any foothold and gripping point they could find to crawl along the side of the boat and drop onto the bridge deck terrace; cleats, handrails, the edges of the shuttered windows' wooden boards, and porthole edges. Virgil kept an eye on Quentin, and noticed where in the line he'd positioned himself. He stared like a hawk, watching for an opportunity, and then it looked like he'd spotted one. He made a move.

"Oh, Quentin," Virgil shouted, "watch your step, there. That board has come loose. If you put some weight on it, it might not hold."

Quentin looked up at Virgil; there was no such board anywhere near him.

Virgil silently shook his head.

Not yet, Virgil thought.

Not just yet, Pretty Boy McQueen.

There is a time and a place for everything.

46

ANNA KIMPER

"How can he possibly take care of all the logistics by himself?" My son asks. "How is transport from the yacht to their drop-off location going to be carried out, where are they going to sleep, how are they going to obtain identity documents, how is their bank account going to be created, without your help? He's only one man, he can't do everything by himself."

"I don't know, but it doesn't matter. All that matters is that we can't wait until Virgil has been dropped off elsewhere, or we'll never see him again."

"Maybe he won't mind telling you later, after everything's been done and dusted. It won't be his problem anymore."

"Ah really? You want to wait until Lawrence *maybe* feels like revealing the location to us, well after Virgil has had the opportunity to vanish in the open? Last time I checked, you appeared more impatient than I was to get to Virgil."

A silence takes over. I'm in my cabin, Lawrence is in the surveillance room, and I have no idea and no care for what Porker Stephen is doing.

"But...how are we going to get to him while he's still on the boat?"

"It won't be easy. I've always wanted to face him in person, look him in the eye, have him look me in the eye, before I drove a knife in his guts. But maybe the only way is to get to him from a distance. If I slip some poison in his food, or something."

"That can't work, can it? The staff plate up the dishes after they get to their boat's bridge deck."

"Or swap his pills with something that would give him an overdose?"

"He's a psychiatrist, Mum. He'll know the difference, and how will you access the medication without being seen?"

"Do *you* have any ideas?"

"Convince someone, Rocky probably, that Virgil is responsible for Glenys' death, and he might have it with Virgil?"

I wince. "He wouldn't, and that's not how I want him to go."

I fiddle with a loose thread on my glove's finger. I will need to go on the boat, armed. "But if the other inmates are there, they might come to Virgil's rescue. It just doesn't work if there are other people on the boat."

"Or if Lawrence is here," Ollie adds. "He'll never let you go. And all the staff obeys him. He's their boss."

"Except Stanislas. His loyalty is to me."

"That's just one man."

"But you're right," I say. "I don't see how I can leave the yacht if Lawrence is here. I think our only option right now, is to see if the inmates make it to the end. If they don't, and they start killing each other, and Virgil is among the last survivors, then that will make it easier for us. I'll have to make something up to lure Lawrence away from the boat, and I'll strike."

"What if they all make it to the end?"

"In that case, well, we'll cross that bridge when we come to it."

47

ANONYMOUS UPC RANKINGS

Day 52 of the Ultimate Psycho Championships (UPC)

Rocky Bardeaux

When Rocky took his harmonica out on Day 52, a quiet Sunday morning, he expected the day to go as smoothly as each day had gone following the tragedy surrounding Glenys. It was as if the sadness had subdued them all, and bonded them together. They were all too aware of how close they were to triggering the championship, and just as aware of how close they were from ultimate freedom.

Not a second passed where Rocky didn't think of freedom, and more specifically, how he would go about reaching Stevie. Watching his nephew play a football game would be a miracle, a dream come true, and the more he thought about it, the more he understood how impossible it was. They would release him in a foreign country, likely very far away from England. He would need money to travel, time away from building his new life in a new and strange environment, and then enter England, with all the risks that involved. Yet his hope increased with every day. However hard it was, his determination was stronger. He would see Stevie again, he knew he would.

Their days revolved around going for a short swim in the sea, having snacks on the sun deck, listening to music, and extending their meals into long discussions, sometimes of a philosophical nature, like they did in Mediterranean cultures. They no longer played the video game as often because Glenys had loved it, and the thought of shooting virtual soldiers without her became too painful.

Some subtle signs, however, might have given Rocky pause, had he paid attention to them. Teddy had not slept much the previous night, and he'd mentioned it extensively over breakfast. He'd complained about the breakfast, which he'd never done before, with him normally being the most vocal about his gratitude for the quality of their food. Quentin had eyed Teddy with irritation multiple times throughout the morning, perhaps with more vehemence than his usual dislike of him. And Jan had skipped breakfast altogether and elected, instead, to be perched on the sun deck, watching for any oncoming birds.

Oblivious to all this, as they finished their breakfast and remained at the table to digest the food, Rocky took his harmonica out and started playing 'When the Saints Go Marching In'.

"Mate," Teddy said loudly, trying to make himself heard above the notes, "do you know any other tunes? I'm sick of hearing this same one every time."

Rocky stopped. "It's the one I know best. I can try other ones, but I'll make mistakes."

Teddy raised his hands. "Then put your harmonica away."

"Hey, settle down," Quentin said. "You're not alone here, I enjoy Rocky's music. If you don't like it, you can piss off."

"His music?" Teddy repeated, leaning forwards. "His *music*? Is he a pro now?"

"What's your talent, knobhead?" Quentin shot back. "Raping vulnerable women?"

"Okay," intervened Virgil, "you also settle down now, Quentin."

Teddy talked over Virgil. "You take that back, you cun–"

"Both of you calm down," Rocky said, placing himself in between them.

Teddy stood up from the dining table to pace in the space between the lounge and the dining area. "You guys still don't understand, do you?" he said, a fire burning in his eyes. "I wouldn't have come on to her if I didn't think it'd be reciprocra– reciprocra– if I didn't think she wanted it too."

"Teddy," Edmond called from the lounge's sofa.

But Teddy ignored him. "You didn't see everything, however much you think you did," he told Quentin.

"Teddy," Edmond tried again, "listen to me."

But Teddy didn't. "She gave me looks here and there, she flirted back with me. When we argued, it was because of the chemistry we had, because we reacted to one another."

"Teddy, for Christ's sake," Edmond continued.

"She led me on! And then she forgot to mention that bloody spike."

"Hey, Humpty Dumpty!" Edmond shouted.

Teddy heard at last. Oh, he heard alright.

His eyes turned black. He grabbed the first bamboo

knife he found on the dining table, and he pounced on Edmond. Before Rocky could get up from his chair, Teddy had already stabbed Edmond's left eye once. When Rocky reached him, he'd stabbed a second time – in the same eye.

He and Quentin pulled Teddy off and threw him against the wall, where they held him fast while Virgil tended to Edmond.

Within ten minutes, Edmond was dead.

48

ANNA KIMPER

"Ollie, are you there?"

"Yes."

"I'm exhausted..." Leaning on the surveillance room's desk, my forearm is a crutch holding not only my head but my soul. "I've watched so much footage."

"And?"

"And, well, Virgil killed Glenys. I have not a single doubt in my mind. I've gathered all the incriminating videos in one folder. It's a wonder Harry didn't bring it to our attention before, but some of them, I think the most incriminating ones, took place when Harry was away."

"So the videos Lawrence gave you access to, in the bathroom, proved useful?"

"Oh no, that was a waste of time. And I saw things I never wanted to see, and will struggle to forget. But for instance, just after the storm, Glenys told Virgil she was struggling, that she had no hope left, even if she got out and started a new life she would still be haunted by her demons, her trauma, there would still be evil men out there, and at this point in her life she doesn't want to start over with no friends and family. Virgil offered to stick with her, to ask Lawrence to be released together so he could be her friend and with enough therapy sessions, they would try and find some form of peace. But the next session, the last one before she kills herself, he says he didn't mean what he said. He said he has his own life to think about and he can't afford to have someone who knows him around, and he hopes he'll never have to do anything psychiatry-related ever again." I sigh, thinking of the footage, of the expression on Glenys' face.

"I can only imagine the blow to Glenys," Ollie says, "thinking she wasn't alone, and then dismissed like a smelly old sock."

"That's not all," I say. I don't want to see it again, or think about it, but I have to, just to put some order in my head, and talking it out with Ollie helps me process it. "Here, it's easier if I just play the video for you."

I click on it, and Virgil's voice comes through. "You can't ever fully heal from the kind of trauma you sustained. I've seen it before, countless times. You can get better, improve slightly, learn to live with it and make the right choices, but it will always be there, and in your most vulnerable moments, it will come back out biting, yearning to unleash its wrath. If you were to have a child, you couldn't help but abuse her, emotionally if not physically, and it is beyond your control. Your childhood shaped your parenthood, and it shaped who you are; you can't change it. Anyone who tells you the opposite either wants to sell you a book, or build a following to sell you a book later down the line. Or they want to keep you coming to therapy, week after week. I have no incentive to lie to you. You're not paying me, and I have no book to sell. The simple truth is that you've been damaged beyond repair, and the fault lies with your abusers."

I stop the video.

"Imagine saying this to someone who is known to have had suicidal thoughts in the past," Ollie says. "I've been watching that first session over and over again, looking for the thing which bothered both you and me, and I've put my finger on it. Virgil went on the attack from the very start; he established that her father was the pillar in her life, the only thing that made sense and which brought comfort in her childhood, the one positive thing throughout her life, and then he smashed it. Absolutely reduced him to pieces, pointing out how he'd been as useless as everyone else, destroying his character. Must have challenged her entire life perception and belief system. Can't have helped."

"Yes, makes sense. In that same session, do you remember when he described the pain in a very...odd way, saying she needed to feed it and love it and let it grow before being able to shed it? Well, listen to this. That was in their very last session." I click on 'Play'.

"You are now as intimate with your pain as you can be. It is now so big it is weighing you down. It's a part of you, and it will never let go. The time has come to kill it."

"How do I do that?" Glenys asks, her voice small and fragile.

"The problem is, you've absorbed it. It is as much a part of you as you are a part of it. You must eliminate its host. Cut its life source. Starve it."

I close it.

"Quite clear, isn't it?" Ollie says.

"If that wasn't enough, I've checked the medication Virgil recommended for Glenys, it's in Harry's notes. He left a copy behind when he left, in case we could make use of them. I've done a bit of research; they're antipsychotics which make anxiety symptoms worse. Virgil knew she was not becoming psychotic, he knew full well it was just her anxiety ramping up, and he knew this medication would make things worse."

"Shouldn't Harry know that too?" Ollie asks, frustrated. "He should know better than to listen blindly to a serial killer. Is he secretly working for Virgil?"

"Harry didn't listen to Virgil, he never prescribed the medication. He wrote in his notes that her anxiety had become severe, and he prescribed the right medication for it. But as I was scouring the footage, I recognised Porker Stephen's aide among the staff delivering the medication one morning, and he gave boxes directly to Virgil and Glenys. So perhaps Stephen saw Harry's notes and got the medication somehow, I'm sure it's not hard for someone like him, and decided to meddle?"

"That bastard is as guilty as Virgil for her death."

"He really is, and what else will he do? He has no intention of leaving until the end, he said so to Lawrence."

"Have you told Lawrence all this?"

"I'm meeting with him when he takes over from me, in half an hour. We'll see what he says."

49

ANONYMOUS UPC RANKINGS

Day 53 of the Ultimate Psycho Championships (UPC)

Virgil Francopan

The evening following Edmond's murder and after they'd taken the body away and done the necessary cleaning, the plague barrister came on the PA system.

"Participants, the championship is triggered. As things stand, this is the ranking: Tied in first position, Rocky Bardeaux, Quentin McQueen, and Virgil Francopan with sixty points. In fourth position, Jan Van Helmont with fifty-three points, and in last position, Teddy Brandt with twenty-five points. Teddy: put one foot wrong, and you will face execution. One last thing: the sessions with Virgil are cancelled. No one is to meet with Virgil in private again, until the end."

The rest of the evening had been a quiet one; Teddy skipped dinner and shut himself in his cabin, Jan ate but then also shut himself away, and Virgil read a book at the dining table while Rocky and Quentin watched a film. Though they usually chatted away like a pair of old spinsters, this time, they watched in silence and then went to bed.

Day 53 was another hot day, so they climbed up to the sun deck immediately after breakfast. Teddy elected to have his breakfast after everyone else had gone, and it was a good thing too, for the rest of the inmates may not have left him anything to eat if they'd had to suffer his presence.

"That's a pleasant surprise," Quentin said, looking to the east.

"A stony outcrop," Rocky commented. "Is it pleasant? Or a surprise?"

"I think I'd like to have a look.'

"There will be a lot of nice sea shells there," Virgil said. "We could even make a dinner of it."

"Really?" asked Rocky, making a grimace.

"Well, maybe not a dinner," Virgil conceded, "but maybe a nice homemade starter. There is a beauty in scavenging and harvesting your own food and eating it. I'd be happy to prepare it with some salt, pepper, and perhaps some lemon and butter."

"Why would we do that, though? We've got a professional chef preparing us a five star meal three times a day."

"Virgil's right, actually," Quentin said. "It's nice to fish your own meal. Those rocks must have some molluscs."

"How are you going to cook them?" asked Rocky.

"We can eat them raw," Virgil replied, "or boil them in

the kettle. The water here isn't polluted, and we'll eat them fresh, so no real risk of food poisoning."

Rocky took a step back and raised his hands. "Up to you, mate. Can't promise I'll have any, though."

"Do fish have blood?" Jan asked, perched on the booth's backrest.

All three heads turned to look at him.

"Mate," Rocky said, "are you...getting thirsty?"

Jan shrugged.

"Yes," Virgil said, "they do have blood. Though it's unlikely you'll catch large enough fish without any equipment."

Virgil turned back to the other two and they exchanged a look. "Stony outcrops like that will also have sea anemones and sea sponges," Virgil said, staring Quentin down. "They're ever so pretty."

Quentin stared back for a moment, then nodded. "Do we have a bag? Or something to bring back the produce?"

"Here," Virgil said, and he started taking off his jumpsuit. "I'm too hot in this anyway, and I've got two spares in my cabin."

Quentin took the indigo jumpsuit and used the sleeves to tie it around his waist. "Right, I'm off then."

"I'll come with you," Jan said.

Quentin looked unsure, but then Jan started climbing down to the stern at the back of the yacht, so he followed.

"Do you think they'll free all three of us as first place winners," Rocky said when they were gone, "if we end up with sixty points?"

"Good question," Virgil replied. "I think they should. If we were all good enough to play by the rules and get no point deductions, why shouldn't we be rewarded for it? The first place prize is already worse than if we'd been successful, so their point is made."

"Can't believe that wanker," Rocky said, shaking his head. "We were so close to making it out, with precious help. Now we're doomed to a life on the run, at best."

"Yes, it's a real shame."

Rocky cast a sideways glance at Virgil. "Why did they cancel your sessions?"

"Do you want to file a complaint? Do you miss them?" Virgil let his playfulness come through.

"No, but it was odd, wasn't it? Why go through the effort of cancelling them?"

Virgil shrugged. "We're close to the end, a week away, give or take one day. Nothing major can be done in therapy now. Maybe they want to keep all the juicy footage outside the privacy of my cabin."

"Hmm, I suppose. You know, Quentin talks as if he won't make it out. He was upset about Edmond, but he didn't seem all that bothered by Teddy ruining it for us."

"Maybe he plans on beating Teddy up, which would put him in third place." Virgil chuckled.

Rocky did not laugh.

"Jan is not doing well," he said. "Do you know what could trigger him to attack us? What happened in his last killing spree?"

"There's no way to know what will do it. He's in his own world, the illness working its magic, plunging him in a different reality. I don't know the details of what happened last time."

"Is Quentin safe, there?"

"In the water, yes," Virgil said, "that's probably where he's the safest, I'd say. Quentin's a good swimmer, and Jan is not. As we can see." Quentin was about a hundred paces ahead of Jan.

"What about us?" Rocky said, a hint of worry in his eyes. "Are we safe, when he comes back? Should we find a way to lock our cabin at night?"

"Hard to tell. Which means there is a risk; he has a precedent of attacking people, after all. It's probably best to stick together, the three of us, whenever we're around him. If he tries anything, we'll overpower him."

"What about the other one?" Rocky muttered as the metallic sound of someone climbing up the ladder reached them.

"If we don't trigger him, we should be fine," Virgil whispered. "And by not communicating with him, as we've done so far, we won't risk any trigger."

Teddy emerged from the side of the yacht, and climbed over the guardrail.

"Where are the other two?" he asked.

Virgil pointed in the distance. Quentin was already hoisting himself onto a rock.

An awkward silence took place.

And it lasted until Quentin returned with Virgil's jumpsuit bunched up in his fist. When he reached the bridge deck terrace, he threw the jumpsuit to Virgil, who managed to catch it without dropping the harvest.

"What did you find us?" Virgil asked.

"Have a look," Quentin said, out of breath, crashing onto the booth to rest.

Virgil carefully unfolded his wet jumpsuit. "Limpets, two sea urchins, and a good deal of periwinkles." As well as a razor clam, but Virgil noticed there was no flesh inside. "It will make for a nice amuse-bouche. This was good to hone your survival skills," Virgil told Quentin. "You might need them when they throw us out into the wild with no money."

"You missed the best bit," Quentin said, and he got up from the booth and walked over. "I put it in the jumpsuit's pocket, to make sure I wouldn't lose it."

Even Teddy stepped closer, intrigued by the hidden treasure.

"Ah, there we are." Quentin held it in the palm of his hand. It was a pale yellow lump with a porous, irregular surface covered in many small holes, giving it a bumpy, textured appearance. "A sea sponge. It feels all soft and squishy. Want a feel, Teddy?"

He stepped in his direction, but as soon as Teddy caught a glimpse of it, he screamed and leapt back, almost falling over the guardrail. "Get that away from me!" He turned around to climb over the barrier. "I've got trypophobia, mate. Can't be around this shit."

He climbed down and out of sight.

Quentin plopped the sea sponge in his soaked underwear, grabbed the razor clam, and followed Teddy down the side of the boat.

Rocky turned to Virgil, his face pale as a sheet. "I think..." He was so stricken, so shocked, that he could barely speak. "I think Teddy's killed Quentin's wife."

Virgil smiled. "Teddy, or the name he was born with, Theo Bates?"

"They're downstairs, alone!" Rocky shouted, panicked. "We need to stop Quentin."

He rushed to the guardrail, then looked back. "Aren't you coming? I don't want Quentin to go back to prison."

Virgil moved his gaze to Jan, in the distance.

Rocky waited another second, then he climbed down.

50

ANNA KIMPER

The staff serve the bowls of gazpacho. Only Lawrence and I are here, Porker Stephen and his aide now eat at different times. A rift separates us; he is on his own bloodthirsty mission, and we can't kick him out. We physically can't kick him out. Our only advantage is having the boat's staff on our side, so we can try to keep an eye on him and block his meddling. His aide is now strictly forbidden from joining our staff when they leave the boat. He had never been allowed, but we'd never explicitly mentioned it because we simply didn't think it would happen. Lawrence has had to take the distasteful step of informing the staff he will turn them in to the authorities if they accept a bribe from Stephen and help him against our cause. He's confident of most of his staff's loyalty – that's why he chose them in the first place – but a couple of deckhands could potentially be persuaded, for the right price.

"That will teach us," Lawrence says, sprinkling some more salt over his cold soup. "Quentin was not in the plan, but we allowed him to join anyway. We allowed him to bring his own agenda, and infect our experiment. This is what happens when we don't stick to the plan." He breaks off a piece of sourdough bread and dips it in the gazpacho. "And I've only got myself to blame."

"No, I'm taking some of that blame too. I should've done my research, it wouldn't have been too hard to find their connection. I thought he was just an opportunist, jumping on the one chance to break out of prison. I would never have imagined in a million years that he actually didn't want to let Teddy get away from him. Did you know that Teddy was involved in the case of Quentin's wife's death?"

Lawrence taps his white napkin on his lips. "Yes, I found out once he was already on the boat, so it was too late to back out. But watching him, he didn't give anything away, so I was naively hoping he hadn't realised it was the same person, since Teddy changed his name *and* he got his tattoos after that happened. But clearly, he knew all along."

"What's the plan now?" I ask.

"Everything remains the same. We watch how it unfolds. The experiment ends in a failure, sadly. The monsters have proven they can't not kill if given some freedom. I'm still proud of our achievements, I think there is something to learn from what we've seen, but perhaps I was slightly over-optimistic. Selecting the world's most dangerous prisoners may have been a step too far."

He still doesn't blame, or even mention, Virgil. So I make a concerted effort not to mention him. "Are we leaving Jan in?"

Lawrence nods. "He hasn't shown signs of violence towards the inmates. I'm reluctant to reduce their numbers further, after so many have left already."

"But he has killed before, and he seems more and more in need of blood. Clearly the medication isn't working, if he's even taking it."

"Indeed, but he was ill for years before he killed his first person."

The first one is always the hardest. After that, the floodgates open. Not such a stretch, anymore.

But I can see Lawrence is set on this, and whatever I say won't change his mind. Another case of not truly being his equal partner.

I can't wait to finish this lunch so I can go back to the surveillance room and talk to Ollie.

51

ANONYMOUS UPC RANKINGS

Day 53 of the Ultimate Psycho Championships (UPC)

Virgil Francopan

The four remaining participants took a seat at the dining table for dinner. The food delivery man entered through the lounge's door, balancing three bell dish trays on one arm, and placed them in front of Virgil, Rocky, and Jan. Then he came back for Quentin.

They removed the silver bell lids; Rocky scoffed, Virgil smiled to himself.

"The special treatment is over," Virgil said. A plain sandwich lay before them, made with pre-sliced packaged bread, full of preservatives and devoid of flavour.

"What's in this?" Quentin said, grimacing as he lifted the top layer.

Rocky sniffed it. "Tuna. Thanks, mate. Not only did you fuck your future, but you've turned our luxury feasts into lunchbox-fucking-tuna sandwiches. Was it worth it?"

"Absolutely," Quentin said, and he took a large bite.

"Was it really?"

"Twelve years I've been waiting for this," Quentin replied with his mouth full. "I'll go back to prison now, I know, but I'll be at peace in here." He pointed to his head. "I'll stop being violent towards the guards, so I'll get out of solitary, and live out my sentence in as much peace as I can find."

"Is that what you did, then?" Rocky asked. "You acted out to end up in the same wing as Teddy?"

"Everything I did was for him. For justice. I drove over a random drug dealer so that I'd end up in prison and then I didn't rest until I landed in the same prison as him. Took a while, but I was eventually transferred to Wandsworth. And then I made sure I would be placed in solitary."

"Even then, it would've been hard to find an opportunity to attack him," Virgil said.

"I know, but it was even harder when we were in entirely different parts of the facility. And that's why when I saw him being broken out, I simply couldn't take no for an answer. It was now or never. I had been working towards this for so long, I couldn't let him get away now."

"I both admire and curse your determination," Rocky said.

"Hey, I'm not the one who ruined your chances in the first place. Teddy is. Even better reason to make him pay. And now you're both firmly in the top two. You should thank me, really."

"Jan," Virgil said, "you haven't touched your sandwich."

"Not hungry."

"You should make an effort."

"Yeah," Quentin said, "we don't want you to be hungry later."

In response, Jan silently stood up, walked away from the table, and headed towards his cabin.

Rocky shook his head. "He is creepy."

"He is ill," Virgil corrected him.

"One doesn't exclude the other."

"Fair point."

"Remember," Rocky said, "place your chair against the door at night. That's when vampires come to life, isn't it?"

DAY 55

Early in the morning, Jan started showing signs of restlessness. Virgil was enjoying his morning cup of tea – first up in the boat, as he had always been even when all seven participants had been present – when Jan emerged from his cabin. He looked like he hadn't slept at all; dark bags under his eyes, bloodshot eyes, his face was more gaunt than usual, and his shoulder-length hair resembled a bird's nest. He stumbled through the hallway and across the dining area, and came straight to Virgil.

"Do you have another cup for me?" he asked.

Virgil had to virtually pinch himself to make sure he wasn't in an alternate reality where a drug addict was asking for his fix. But in a way, that was exactly what this was.

"I'm afraid I don't," Virgil replied. "It wasn't easy to prepare that cup for you the other day."

Jan stared in silence. His stare was blank, but Virgil prepared himself for an assault. There was something in his eye which felt off. Who knew what he was imagining?

"You sure?" Jan asked at last. He cast a brief glance

behind him before leaning closer to Virgil. "My blood's getting real thick. I can feel it. My heart's on overdrive, it can't pump through the sludge."

"I can't help you, Jan." He was sure that in Jan's mind, he could help him – or his blood could, anyway – which was why he remained on high alert. "You want to try coffee? It might give you a boost."

Jan did not react. He stared blankly for a moment longer, then he turned around and hobbled into the hallway's darkness.

"Stay hydrated," Virgil called out after him.

He had to get up from his chair to double check Jan wasn't entering one of the other cabins, but he went back to his own, like a good boy.

The next time he re-emerged from his cabin, it was shortly after lunchtime. He stood by the dining table, staring at the lounge, his eyes no longer bloodshot but looking as gaunt as ever. Rocky and Quentin had started playing on the gaming console again, reasoning they needed to make the most of their last five days. Virgil was reading a book at the dining table, a biography of the surrealist painter René Magritte he'd requested from the consortium, but he kept an eye on Jan the entire time he stood at the other end of the table. With his dishevelled hair concealing half of his face, he might've been recreating a scene from 'The Exorcist'.

He'd rarely acted this strangely before, and never for this long, so Virgil suspected he was on the verge of some form of crisis. The other two, fools with their controllers, did not notice any of it.

Virgil grabbed a piece of paper and a pencil, jotted something down, then slid the note over to Jan's side of the table. Jan glanced at Virgil, then at the note. Then his head shot up, like a robot's, and his eyes fixed on Quentin.

Quentin offered Rocky a drink, then got up and headed to the kitchenette.

Jan grabbed the pencil which lay next to the note, and walked over to the kitchenette.

Virgil slowly stood from his chair.

Jan lunged and stabbed the pencil in the side of Quentin's neck from behind. Virgil rushed forward, his training in Krav Maga taking over instinctively. With precision, he grabbed Jan's wrist and twisted it sharply, forcing him to drop the bloodied pencil. In the same fluid motion, he delivered a swift elbow strike to Jan's face, disorienting him. It was almost unfair, as Jan was so slow, but Virgil swept his leg and sent him crashing to the ground. With his knee pressed firmly into Jan's chest, Virgil kept him pinned down.

"Check on Quentin," he told Rocky, who looked in shock.

"Plague barrister," Virgil shouted. "Plague barrister, do you hear me?"

A second passed, then the PA system turned on. "Yes, we are sending help right away."

"Take Jan away from here," Virgil said, "he needs help. Serious help. He's too ill to be around people."

"We agree. Is Quentin alive?"

Virgil glanced at Rocky.

Rocky was a big man, and most of the time he was in control of his emotions, so it was a sight to see him sobbing like a child, holding Quentin's head in his arms and covering himself in blood. He wailed and wailed, as if Quentin had been his brother.

Virgil stretched over to feel Quentin's neck while holding Jan down, for he preferred not to press Rocky further.

There was no pulse.

52

ANNA KIMPER

Patience is not my forte.

I've tried to zoom in on Virgil's note to Jan. It looked, on camera, as if this note was the trigger for Jan. He'd acted strangely, walking as if he were injured, and no expression on his face. Eerie is the word. But he didn't look like he was actually going to do anything until he read that note, and if we can read what it said, I think it will be very telling indeed.

So I've sent the footage to an expert in our Anonymous team, and I'm waiting for him to get back to me. I should be doing other things in the meantime, coordinating with our supply team on the ground, in Brazil, checking my emails, calling Ollie, but I'm too anxious to know what it says. I check my WhatsApp; still no reply. 'Any news?' I send. He's received the message, but not read it.

I check the live streams on the screens. Our team has just finished cleaning and tidying everything. There was a lot of blood this time; Jan must've hit an artery. He must be on his way back now, if he's not already arrived. He'll be locked in a cabin, with a locked porthole and shatter-proof glass. We've only got one cabin like this, to use as a prison, just in case. That's something I should be doing; organising his handover to a secure psychiatric unit. The problem is we're far from the United States. We'll have to put him on the helicopter, then arrange a flight to American soil using our network to go undetected, probably land in Florida, his homeland, and drop him off near a psychiatric hospital. Our people will leave, and then we'll call the hospital and inform them of Jan's location.

Ping. New message.

I'm so impatient I fumble with the phone.

With 96% confidence, the note says: Quentin is vegetarian. His blood is lean and pure.

Of course it says that, of course it does. Not the shade of a doubt in my mind they've deciphered this correctly.

I tap a few more times on my phone.

"Ollie," I say, "are you ready? Are you sat comfortably?"

"Sure, go on."

"I've gathered evidence pointing to Virgil being responsible for every single death and elimination we've had. While I was reviewing footage, I noticed that about two weeks ago, Virgil started collecting the boxes of medication directly from the staff and distributing it to the inmates. It made sense to everyone, I suppose, because he's a psychiatrist, but one time I noticed he only took two boxes from the staff. I checked Harry's log, and that day only Jan and Virgil got medication delivered. I noticed that during previous deliveries, Jan's box of antipsychotics had some red on it, and this time the box with red on it was there, but Virgil gave him the other one, and kept Jan's. And in Harry's log, Virgil's medication was just a mild anti-anxiety pill which would do nothing for Jan's psychosis. And Jan did get worse recently, didn't he? Not to mention the strange session Virgil had with him, where he went along and gave him the cup of blood, which could only make things worse."

"Oh, I remember well," Ollie says. "I remember Lawrence saying Virgil was doing that to trick Jan into taking his medication. I swear I could throttle him for insisting on seeing only the good in Virgil."

"I know, me too. So Virgil manipulated Jan's psychosis to his will, made it a lot worse, and got him kicked out."

"What about the other ones?"

"Glenys we already know. Teddy, well, it's mostly down to Quentin, but Virgil understood some time ago that this was Quentin's plan, and he provided the perfect moment for Quentin to make his move, coming up with the sea sponge and letting Quentin join Teddy below on the main deck without hindering him. He stepped out of his way, where he could easily have stopped him."

"What about Edmond?"

"That took me a while to find, but in one of his sessions, when Edmond caved in and started talking about himself for the first time, Virgil called Teddy a Humpty Dumpty. He planted the seed in his head, knowing full well it was Teddy's most sensitive trigger. Without Virgil, Edmond would never have thought to call him that. And Quentin... the clearest of all." I tell him about the note.

"Wow," Ollie says. "And I bet that note no longer exists, he'll have destroyed it, or swallowed it."

"We've got footage, but what use is it? I'll go in soon and end it with him anyway. So that's everyone, except Rocky. I need to get there before he turns on Rocky."

"Are you going to tell Lawrence you've figured all this out?"

"No, it won't change a thing. It might even be a risk; what if he decides to end the experiment early, and to send Virgil back to the British authorities? No, all I need to do now is get on that boat. I reckon I can convince Rocky fairly easily, if I mention the evidence I've got, and then maybe he'll help me. He'll want to avenge Quentin."

"And if not, you've got the gun."

53

ANNA KIMPER

"Yes? What is it?" Lawrence asks.

He seems flustered, irritated to have to talk to me. He's hovering by the door, not coming into the surveillance room. That is not the mood I wanted him to be in for this.

"Sorry to bother you, is Jan making trouble?"

"Not him specifically, but I can't get hold of anyone who will facilitate our flight into the US. I'll get back to it as soon as we are done here." He gives me an expectant look.

My heart is pounding. I'm not a born deceiver.

"I'll try to make it quick. We are in Brazilian waters, and a Brazilian senator's team has just gotten in touch. They urgently want to know who we are, what we are doing here, how long we'll stay here, etc."

"Haven't we already given our usual speech to anyone who enquires?"

"Yes, to the Brazilian Coast Guard, and they've clearly chosen to escalate this to a senator within the committee responsible for territorial waters." Now, I have to be careful how I phrase this. This is where my plan lives or dies.

"Should we leave immediately and reach international waters, where they can no longer do anything? The new Brazilian president is not friends with the US and the UK, very anti-West, so they'll probably be hostile to a British crew."

Up to now, Lawrence has hung around the door frame, itching to turn around and leave, but now he leans against it and a thoughtful look comes into his eyes.

"That's irrelevant," he says, which I already knew, but I'm glad he underestimates me. "Our boat is Russian, and I myself have acquired Russian citizenship."

"Have you?"

"Courtesy of Alexei," he says with a wink. "We could use direct contact with a senator to see if his government would be happy to help us, if needed. A safe harbour in this part of the world could prove very useful. And I'll bring up both my connections to the Russian government and Joao. Can you make sure the senator himself meets with me? Or at least in a video conference?"

"Sure, but...do you not want a deckhand, or someone else of your choosing, to go on your behalf?"

As I had expected, he categorically refuses.

"I'll even go, if it helps," I say, clenching my left fist, driving the nails into the palm of my hand, hoping with all my being he won't like the suggestion.

To my horror, he squints and studies me for a moment. A brief moment, but to me it feels like an eternity.

He shakes his head at last. "No, I must do it myself. I've only relied on myself so far, and I won't stop now. Besides, we need you here; you're the one I trust the most to take care of things in my absence."

"But at this stage of the experiment, you need to be here." It's hard not to overdo it, easy to betray myself with the wrong facial expressions. "And it could prove dangerous, we don't know what they're like. Besides, I would rather not be left alone with Stephen." That, at least, is true.

"I'll talk to the staff before I go, make sure they look out for you. You'll be fine."

"Okay. I'll get back to them now and ask for the senator to be present. They did ask to meet later this afternoon."

Lawrence thinks for a moment, then nods. "Fine, I'll take the chopper out. How long to the meeting point?"

"They've suggested a government office in the city of Salvador, which is not very far from our supply spot, so it should take about an hour and a half."

He checks his watch. "It doesn't leave me much time, but that's fine. I can keep working on the chopper. I only need my phone, really. I'll leave as soon as you hear back."

He leaves, and I can finally breathe.

For now.

Soon, the moment of truth.

54

ANONYMOUS UPC RANKINGS

Day 57 of the Ultimate Psycho Championships (UPC)

Rocky Bardeaux

A boat glided past in the distance, which was the first time Rocky had noticed one – other than the man-bird's. Were these waters busier, or was it just a coincidence?

The two days since Quentin's passing had been morose and miserable. Francopan and he barely talked, as if they knew the only thing left to do was to wait until the experiment ended, and there was no point faking a friendship that wasn't there. Quentin and he had made plans to find each other if they gained their freedom, and that would have been some life. Free and settled with a friend by his side, a dream he'd never dared to dream. But that had been before, and Quentin had probably never meant it. It hurt, but not as much as seeing the life seep out of his eyes had.

He'd lost a friend, maybe his only true friend ever, to a man who was ill, so he couldn't even be angry with his killer. Who was he meant to direct his anger against? The man-bird for leaving Jan in here when he clearly should have been removed earlier? Probably, yes.

But perhaps he was missing the point altogether, and he shouldn't be angry at all. What would anger achieve for him? Bugger all. What he needed to do was cherish the memory of Quentin and their friendship. And be grateful Quentin had achieved peace just before he'd passed.

Rocky chuckled to himself, sat alone on the sun deck's booth, cool in the bimini top's shade and the sea breeze. Look at me, he thought. Becoming all philosophical and emotionally mature. Maybe now he could get out and become a Buddhist or something, in his new life. There were still so many things to discover, to experience, to feel. He could do it all in Quentin's name. Or in his own. It didn't matter, as long as he did.

He was now assured to end in the top two, so freedom was his to take. What would he do, though, once released? With no money, no bearings, no contacts in a foreign place. The authorities would assume he left immediately to try and lose them, so should he stay put? He needed to eat, though. He wasn't much of a forager or survivalist, so he'd have to steal until he found some way of making money. Which meant finding a hub of people, some town or city, where he could melt in the crowd. So many unanswered questions, so much uncertainty.

Francopan emerged from behind the guardrail.

"Am I ruining your peace and quiet?" he asked, walking

over to the booth. He grabbed one of the chaises longues and placed it next to the booth Rocky sat on.

"A bit, yeah," Rocky replied.

"I won't be long." Francopan leaned forward and scratched the metal pole of the bimini top's frame with an unusually long thumb nail. "I think now is a good time to deliver on my promise," he said, staring at an imaginary point next to Rocky's eyes.

His nail produced a high-pitched screech; Rocky couldn't keep his attention away from it. Did Francopan know the mic was right there, next to the pole? What was he playing at?

"Is this really necessary?" Rocky asked, glaring at the offending thumb.

"Do you remember," Francopan went on, ignoring his question and lowering his voice, "when I told you I'd tell you one of my deepest, darkest secrets, in exchange for everything you told me in our sessions?"

Rocky nodded.

"I've told you about my crimes, what motivated me, where and how I selected some of my victims, but I didn't tell you everything. You wouldn't expect me to." His voice was barely above a whisper, and with the metallic screech ringing in one of Rocky's ears, it was a struggle to understand what he was saying. "Some of the victims...were not adults. Some of them were minors, and with the minors, my purpose was not the same as with everyone else. With them, I unleashed my darkest self." His eyes moved away from the imaginary point, and bore through Rocky's own. Chills ran down his entire body. "I brought them to my basement, my leatherworking workshop, which I had thoroughly sound-proofed. And I raped them. Boys and girls, it didn't matter."

Rocky shook his head. He didn't believe him. He didn't

know what he was doing, or why, but it didn't resonate with him, with what type of psychopath Francopan was.

Francopan moved his head up and down in rhythm with Rocky's shaking of his head.

"We have one point in common, you and me," he continued. His eyes shone, as if they had a magical property to ensnare the prey's attention. Rocky no longer heard the metal screeching. "Whenever I did what I did, I liked to play a lullaby."

Rocky tensed. The left corner of Francopan's mouth stretched upwards, ever so slightly.

He started humming a melody.

By the time he moved to the second note, Rocky had recognised Rock-a-Bye.

It was like a beast had awakened inside Rocky's chest and unfurled its tentacles throughout his body, taking over against his will. He saw the reflection of a six-year-old Rocky in his old bedroom, terrified and helpless, and he swung at Francopan.

But Francopan was prepared.

He moved swiftly out of the way, and he struck Rocky across the throat.

Just once, but it was enough.

55

ANNA KIMPER

About twenty minutes after Lawrence's helicopter took off, Virgil and Rocky started a strange conversation. Without audio enhancing tools, it is impossible to understand what Virgil is saying, but the mere fact he tries to conceal what he is saying is enough for me. By the time we've made sense of what he said, it'll be too late, and he might have a plan to escape. We have to leave now.

I go down to the main deck and seek out Stanislas. He's in the store room, moving boxes around. "Virgil is up to something, we need to go there and check on him."

He puts a box down. "There? As in, the prisoners' boat?"

I nod. "You said you'd help me if I needed anything, didn't you?"

His turn to nod.

"Well then, I need you now. I need you very much. I have been waiting for this moment for a long time, ten years in fact. And it all hinges on you helping me."

He stares at me in silence for a moment. I wonder if images of my Wimbledon title appear in his mind, me hitting the forehand winner on his television screen, falling to the ground, covering my white clothes in grass and dirt, lifting the trophy with a huge smile on my face, my cheeks wet with tears. I wonder if he feels like a child again, admiring a champion and dreaming of becoming one himself one day, remembering the emotions my unexpected victory stirred in him.

Whether it was this or not, he nods and steps out of the store room. "What's the plan?"

"We need to take the Zodiac and go there now. With Lawrence gone, we can't waste a single second."

We run towards the stern, and perhaps that was our mistake, for another deckhand, a young Canadian man, sees us, and soon, just as we reach the stern and swim platform where the inflatable boat rests, the captain, the engineer, and the nurse, along with the Canadian deckhand, appear.

"Is everything okay?" the captain asks, though his tone is not caring or concerned. "Mr. Lawrence asked us to keep an eye on you, for your safety." He is clean-shaven, with an impeccably ironed uniform, sharp features, and a similar aura to Lawrence's.

"Yes, all good here, thank you, Captain." Now go away.

Nobody says a word, and the four pairs of eyes shift their gaze between Stanislas and me.

"Are you going somewhere, Mrs. Kimper?" The captain has a Scottish accent, and for some reason it makes him more authoritative, more menacing.

"Yes, to the participants' yacht."

I give Stanislas a look, and nudge my head towards the yellow button which will lower the platform and make the Zodiac float.

He steps forward, then stops as he glances at the captain.

"I don't believe you are meant to go to their yacht," the

captain says, staring at Stanislas. "The tender is only to leave this yacht under express command from Mr. Lawrence."

"In his absence, am I not in charge?" I say.

His gaze moves to me, and I hold it. I will not be intimidated, not now. "The tender is part of this yacht, which falls under my direct command. Mr. Lawrence employs me, not you, so unless he wishes to send someone out, in which case he always informs me, then I cannot, in good conscience, allow it."

His three mates aren't moving, however.

"Are you going to stop us?"

"No," the captain says, and his gaze returns to Stanislas, "but I will have to let Mr. Lawrence know."

"Fine," I say, though it could potentially ruin everything. "Brandon," I call out to the nurse, "we could use someone your size. Would you like to come with us?"

He shakes his head instantly. "I will not go unless Mr. Lawrence asks me."

"And Stanislas," the captain says, "if you go with her, you are fired. You will never work on a boat again."

I hold my breath. I wouldn't blame him if he ditched me.

Stanislas stares back at the captain, then he looks at me. I think I see regret in his eyes.

But then he raises his hand and presses on the yellow button. As the hydraulic platform slowly lowers into the water, the captain and his crew go back inside the main deck.

When the platform reaches the water level, Stanislas presses on the button again to pause it and we get busy untying lines and undoing straps.

"What are you doing?" asks a familiar voice from behind.

I turn around to see Porker Stephen, leaning on a cane, and his aide, lean and about a head taller than his master.

I ignore him, and continue working on a strap.

"You may or may not have heard, but an altercation has just taken place on the boat," Stephen goes on. "Virgil's calling for the nurse."

So that's how he plans on escaping. "There was no way to know what happened from what we heard. He made sure of that."

"No, indeed." The way he says this makes me look up. He knows something I don't, and he's enjoying it. "My drone had a view of their sun deck. Not a perfect view, but good enough to see that Rocky clearly swung at Virgil, and Virgil avoided and retaliated. He's the sole survivor, he's gravely injured, and if we want the project to make as much noise as it should, we need at least one survivor."

I abandon my strap and straighten. "I am not letting the nurse take this tender. I am taking it, end of discussion."

"Oho," Stephen says, then he nudges his aide with his elbow. "The woman has spoken. Her word is final. Or so she thinks. If you want to go there, be my guest. I won't say no to more drama. But take my aide with you."

Out of the question. I am not letting that snake anywhere near my revenge. I don't even take the trouble of replying.

"Anna," Stephen says, louder than before, "if you do not take my aide with you, we will have to stop you leaving at all."

I bet the crew is watching this, and the bastards are choosing not to intervene. So much for Lawrence asking them to keep me safe from this perv.

"Enough," Stanislas says, and even I am surprised by his tone. "Mrs. Kimper wants to leave by way of this boat, and she will." Then he turns to me. "There's one strap on your side, and when I finish untying this line, we can lower the platform further and leave."

I go back to working on my strap, but keep watch on the other two from the tail of my eye. Stephen's aide moves to a loose line, and he loops it around a cleat. Stanislas lunges over and gives him a violent shove.

I didn't think he had it in him, but I'm glad he does.

The aide, however, is no pushover, and jumps right back with a blow to Stanislas' ribs. They quickly lock into wrestling positions, neither letting go of the other, slamming each other against walls and guardrails.

Then Porker Stephen lifts his cane, points it at me, and starts lumbering over to me with a vicious look on his fat face. A sense of panic seizes me; there is water behind me, the Zodiac to my left, more water to my right, and a four-hundred-pound man is slowly hemming me in.

I feel like I'm in a video game, except here I have only one life.

56

ANONYMOUS UPC RANKINGS

Day 57 of the Ultimate Psycho Championships (UPC)

Virgil Francopan

As soon as he confirmed his blow landed as expected, Virgil let go of the razor clam – the second half of the one Quentin had brought back – and he smeared Rocky's blood all over himself. He rushed back down to the main deck, limping and faking an injury or three, and knelt before the first camera he found, in Quentin's cabin.

"Rocky lost it," he cried. "He attacked me, he thought I'd killed children as well as adults, but he misunderstood. I– I had to defend myself, but not before he got me." He barely touched his abdomen, which he'd soaked with Rocky's blood, and winced in pain. "You need to send the nurse in."

He scrambled to get back onto his feet, then placed his hands around the camera as if holding someone's head to make sure they listened carefully. He got up close to the lens, and repeated, "Send in the nurse, I'm losing a lot of blood, and weakening. Hurry."

Then he deliberately pulled the camera off the wall, hoping they'd think he'd accidentally put too much weight on it.

He climbed back up to the sun deck, then made his way back down to the stern, at the back of the boat. There, he opened a storage locker and fit snugly inside, pressed against the life vests and fenders.

And he waited.

The distant buzz of a motorboat echoed, and grew louder and louder. He opened the locker's lid slightly, but couldn't see the boat approaching, so he opened it a bit more.

Then he saw it, the same yellow boat the nurse had used every time he'd come over. Everything was going to plan perfectly so far, and in a way, he couldn't believe his luck. The hardest was still to come, but that was the exciting part.

As the Zodiac grew closer, however, he spotted two people aboard. And none of them was a tall black man.

One was a lean white man who could've been one of the cleaners; at this distance, it was hard to tell.

The other, he waited until they got closer.

It was a woman. But strangely, incredibly, impossibly, unbelievably...she looked like a former patient of his.

57

ANNA KIMPER

(a few minutes earlier)

I'm soaking wet; as we speed forward, Stanislas with one hand gripping the tiller, the wind penetrates through to my bones.

I escaped Stephen by diving in the water, just as Stanislas knocked the aide out and put him out of service long enough to undo the Zodiac's last line and strap and push it away from the yacht, where I swam to him.

Astonishingly, my phone survived the swim. This is where I'm grateful I chose the latest model. But as soon as we zoom away from the yacht, leaving Porker and his slave behind, my phone rings. It's Lawrence.

I ignore it.

He calls again.

I ignore it once more. My pulse quickens, a sense of impending doom taking over my senses.

He calls again, and this time my finger hovers over the

screen. I trace the swiping motion, but an inch above the screen, and in the end it stops ringing.

We can see the participants' boat in the distance, now. Not long before I face Virgil.

My phone pings. A voice message.

I bring the phone to my ear and listen to it.

There was never a meeting with a Brazilian senator, was there? He's seething, I hear it in his voice. I've never heard him this furious. *If you go on that boat, I will divulge publicly that you were in a psychiatric institution, and everything that entails. I know you had a public injunction so that it would never be made public, so you must want to keep it quiet. And I know you have history with Virgil. You didn't think I would accept your participation as my partner in this project without doing my due diligence, and having some form of leverage over you, did you?*

I hang up and put the phone away, then I take the gun out of my inside pocket. I'm surprised he knows, but at the same time...not. He chose the wrong type of leverage. I don't care. Not anymore, and not right now. Do what you will, Lawrence.

"Are you sure about this?" Stanislas asks. When I turn around, I notice he's staring at the gun in my hand. A small semi-automatic pistol, the slide already racked.

"We can't face Virgil without one," I reply, "so yes, quite sure."

"Do you have experience using one?"

"I've shot in a range before." I'm not telling him I shot for the first time in my life a month before coming here; I sense it would not go down well. "Have you?"

He shakes his head. "Despite what I did so far, I am not a fan of violence. I never got in a fight before today."

I nod and glance at the boat, getting bigger and bigger.

Not the most reassuring thought, but I've got the gun. How could it go wrong?

~

THE STERN IS CLEAR.

Stanislas places the Zodiac along the stern and I jump out, holding a line. I tie it around a cleat, then Stanislas jumps off and ties his line around another cleat. Just as I take my gun out of my inside pocket, one of the storage lockers behind Stanislas opens wide.

I try to warn him but I'm too late; Virgil is holding him from behind, pressing some kind of blade against his throat. I point the gun at Virgil. His eyes find me from behind Stanislas' petrified stare, and my muscles tense up, as if I've just ingested some poison. Virgil looks terrifying, his face covered in a thin layer of dried blood and dark patches all over his jumpsuit.

"Anna," he says, a grin etched on his lips. "How wonderful to see you here. I knew that voice rang a bell. I just couldn't quite put my finger on which bell."

"Let him go, or I'll shoot," I say.

He laughs. "No you won't. You're not that good a shot. Not to mention the stress will affect your accuracy, and you don't want to risk his life."

He's right. "I know you're behind all the deaths and Jan's elimination, so you won't get out of here with your freedom."

"Well aren't you a clever one. You even know about Rocky?" He sees through me straight away. "No? Not that one? Oh well, I'll save you the work. I killed him too, although I did enjoy my little performance. You'll understand when you look back at the CCTV footage and audio feed. Well, if you get out of here safe and sound, that is. Speaking of which, I won't hurt a hair of either of you if you let me board this Zodiac in peace. Do we have a deal?"

"Not a chance." I take aim at his forehead, but he keeps moving in and out from behind Stanislas' head.

"That's a shame. It's a beautiful glove you have there. Are those patches made of leather?"

I can't believe he's bringing that up.

"I see you're wet. I hope you didn't jump in the sea, because the saltwater will dry and crack the leather."

How dare he bring this up. We're standing about four metres from each other, close enough to get the shot right, surely? Perhaps I should shoot his shoulder first, much easier to get, and then his face.

"It could stain it too, potentially permanently. You don't want that, do you? In fact, you should remove it now and dry it. Whatever it's hiding, it can't be comfortable to keep a wet glove like that on."

"Whatever it's hiding?" I say at last. "Are you having a laugh?"

"Oooh," he says, then whispers into Stanislas' ear: "I hit a nerve." Back to me: "What did you do to yourself, Anna?"

I can barely believe my ears. "What *you* did to me, you monster."

He raises his eyebrows in surprise, and it doesn't appear fake. "Pray tell me, what *did* I do to you?"

What is he playing at?

Still aiming at his face with the gun in my left hand, I pincer the glove in between the fingers of my right hand and the side of my body, and manage to pull it off. I let the glove fall to the ground, and I hold my arm in front of me. Let him deny it now.

Stanislas' eyes go wide. Then he peers at me, and something has changed.

"What are we meant to see?" Virgil says.

"This," I say, shaking my arm.

"Your arm," he says flatly.

"The scars from your flaying." My voice is high-pitched, because this is ludicrous, unreal. How can they not see the...

I glance at my hand, my wrist, my forearm, the skin once red and raw and covered in unnatural folds and white scar tissue, now a milky white, smooth and free of marks or other evidence of his bestiality.

"Oh dear," Virgil says. "Here we go again."

"Mrs. Kimper," Stanislas says, leaning back in Virgil's grip and uncomfortable, yet still finding a way to talk. "What is happening?" The fear in his eyes has made him drop ten years.

"I...I'm not sure." I grip the gun again with both hands, aiming at Virgil's right eye.

"Go ahead, shoot."

Not right now. If I miss, it could all go wrong.

"If you don't, it will definitely go wrong." Ollie's voice.

But his head is too close to Stanislas'. I'm not killing this young man.

"He's irrelevant. Shoot, Mum!"

"No," I shout. "Leave me alone."

Virgil's eye glints. "They're back, are they?"

"Who's back?"

"The voices, those forces which are more powerful than anything else. I believe that's how you described them, back in my office."

"No, no, not that, I was ill then. This is Ollie. My son."

"Which son?" He tuts. "You have no children, Anna. You had a baby, which you killed, and unless you immediately recovered from your trauma and got very busy since I've been incarcerated, and your son is what, seven? Eight years old? Then you have no son, and your psychosis has returned with a raging vengeance."

My world crashes down around me. I seek confirmation from Stanislas, with my eyes. When he just looks at me as if I'm a freak of nature, I ask: "Is it true?"

"I– I didn't think you had children, no," he says.

"But," I shake the gun at Virgil and Stanislas flinches. "You killed my son! And you flayed him."

Virgil laughs out loud.

Stanislas makes a go for the sea, but Virgil quickly seizes his arm, twists it behind his back, and presses his makeshift blade harder against Stanislas' throat. "Don't do this again," Virgil whispers, "I'll just slash. I don't care about you, you're more of a hindrance than anything else here." Then he directs his evil eyes at me. "I never physically harmed your body or your offspring."

It's like there are two parallel universes. I remember the past ten years as they happened; tortured by Virgil's murder of my baby boy and the mutilation of my arm. Ollie supporting me throughout, my rock, my friend, my blood. It's my reality.

And yet, I can also remember another reality, one I'd almost forgotten, one I still want to forget. The one I share with everyone else.

How can they both exist?

"I don't get off killing babies, or children," Virgil says. "There's no power in that, no sense of accomplishment. However," his grin grows larger, "causing a mother to kill her own child…now that is rewarding. You were my first, and my last. You are special to me. But I did not kill your son, Anna. You did."

"I was ill."

"Yes, yes you were. You had postpartum psychosis. It was too easy for me, but I couldn't resist. I should have given you different medications, stronger doses, but instead I played along. After your murder I should have reported you to the police, but where was the fun in that? And there was always a risk it could be traced back to me. So I backed the story of the tragic accident, said you were improving and taking your medications before the tragic night so you wouldn't have been so severely affected. It must have been a tragic case of the baby accidentally wrapping the monitor's cord around his neck, and pulling, pulling. Your grave relapse afterwards was only natural, and I recommended your hospitalisation."

My arms start shaking, my vision blurs, my teeth chatter. The past ten years of my life have been a nightmare, a slightly better nightmare than reality, but a mare of falsehood after falsehood. I block Ollie from my mind, I hear him try to bring me back to his fold, and I want to, I want so badly to talk back, to tell him how much I love him, and how sorry I am. How I am not worthy of being his mother, and how much better off he would've been had I never been born. Regardless of the illness, I was his mother, and a mother did not...

Virgil pushes Stanislas to the side and drives a punch to his face, then he leaps at me. I pull the trigger, blindly, hoping I will get lucky.

The gun doesn't fire, and before I've even fully realised, Virgil has knocked it out of my hand, grabbed it, racked the slide, and he points the barrel at us both. Stanislas is crouched at the other end, rubbing his jaw.

"I was right, in the end, not to tell anyone the truth about us, wasn't I?" Virgil says, slowly stepping backwards towards the Zodiac. "None of this would have happened otherwise. It would have been a great shame. I'm sure I have you to thank for my presence on this boat. Unfortunately, I will not be able to actually thank you. My plan all along was to gain my freedom, and I can't do that while having to continuously look over my shoulder, worrying that Psycho Anna might be after me. Again."

"Virgil Francopan," comes Lawrence's voice on every single one of the boat's speakers. "Stop immediately."

"Or what? I think I have the upper hand now. I'll be the one making demands from now on."

"I have something, on our yacht, that I believe may change your mind," Lawrence says.

"I highly doubt it, Mr. Masked Bird. No single thing can stop me now."

"Not even your red leather armchair?"

Virgil freezes. No more sardonic smile, or grin, or glint in his eye. His cheeks drop, despite his skin being stretched taut over his bones. "How do you know about that?"

"That is irrelevant," Lawrence says. "It is in my possession, and I know how much it means to you. Drop the gun, and wait patiently for us to come and collect you, and you will see it again. Very soon."

"What if I don't?"

"It's just an armchair to me. An unfinished armchair, at that. I have no qualms destroying it, and never again mentioning it. Letting it be forgotten, and no one ever knowing about your project."

Virgil directs the gun at Stanislas.

"No," Lawrence says. "Drop. The. Gun."

Virgil looks around. "There are no cameras here."

"Look up."

We all do.

"Now to your left."

Stephen's drone.

I hear a click. Virgil has pulled the trigger on Stanislas, but just like it did with me, it fails to fire.

He hurls it into the sea. "I always feel more comfortable relying on my bare hands, anyway," he says, then turns to me. "You jumped in the water with the miserable pistol on you, didn't you? Silly girl."

Then he contorts in rage, doubling over himself, and lets out a shrill cry. "I did everything right." His voice is muffled by the jumpsuit and his knees. "Everything ended how I wanted. I could just leave," he adds in a lower tone, "but my red leather armchair..."

The wait is excruciating. Virgil continuously mumbles to himself, sometimes raising his voice, and every time I fear he'll lash out and kill us both. I slowly make my way to Stanislas; I have this thought that if we stand together, it may make it harder for Virgil, were he to lose it. Stanislas inches away from me when I approach him, but then he glances at Virgil and stays put, perhaps judging I am less of a danger than a madman serial killer.

My muscles relax only when Lawrence arrives in a lifeboat, flanked by the nurse, the Canadian deckhand, and the engineer. The deckhand and engineer grab Virgil immediately, and the nurse drives a syringe in his buttocks. Then they haul him inside the Zodiac and hold onto him until he is fully sedated.

I climb into the lifeboat, wishing to keep as far away from him as possible, even though Lawrence is there. I hesitate to look into his eyes, fearing his reaction, the judgement on his face, but when our eyes finally meet, I only see affection. He wraps a space blanket over my shoulders and gives me a gentle rub.

A strange feeling creeps in. Perhaps it's a sense of safety.

58

ANNA KIMPER

Lawrence hasn't said a word yet, but I feel like it is to give me space, not because he's cross.

I am grateful, because I need time to process everything. I am still hearing Ollie's voice, and being aware it is probably a hallucination does not make it any less real-sounding. Same as when I first heard voices, following Oliver's birth. It all makes so much sense, and yet...my head is a muddle.

One thing is clear, though: Virgil is to blame for all of this. He was the professional assigned to my case, he could have prevented all of it. He should have protected Oliver from me, not used us as a sick game. He might as well have driven a knife into my son's heart, he would've caused less pain overall. The journey back to the boat serves one purpose, and that is to strengthen my resolve. He must pay.

When we step out of the lifeboat and back onto the yacht, Stanislas cannot get away from me fast enough. Just before he turns the corner and I know I won't see him ever again, I call out to him: "I'm sorry, Stanislas. So very sorry.

And thank you, from the bottom of my heart." He gives me a cold stare, then goes on his way.

The boy has lost his job because of me, and worse, he will be traumatised for life. As soon as I feel better, I will send him a generous check. It won't erase what happened today, but I hope it will give him some form of relief.

Lawrence leads me to an empty cabin – or at least, a cabin I thought was empty until now. When I step inside, Virgil is sat on a chair, his head leaning to one side, his mouth open, heavily sedated. The nurse and the Canadian deckhand are standing on either side, but Lawrence dismisses them. "Keep an eye on the CCTV feed," he tells them as they leave. "Just in case."

Just then I realise Virgil is sitting on the famous red leather armchair, and I am thrown into the past. It is the very chair I used to sit on, when I visited his office for our therapy sessions. It brings me back to a time where my son was alive, and though I can't avoid but feel pangs in my heart, I'm also grateful for the vividness of the memories this chair triggers. For a fleeting moment, it's like I'm with my baby boy again.

When I come back to the present, Lawrence is placing straps around Virgil's wrists.

"May I?" I ask.

Lawrence nods and steps away.

Two thick cable ties on each wrist, and two more for each elbow, wrapped around his limbs and the chair's armrests. There's something therapeutic about attaching this monster to his deathbed. I stare at his sleeping face while I do it, hoping he feels my presence in his sedated dreams.

"How can such an ordinary object hold so much power over a man like this?" I ask as I attach the last cable tie and step away. "The lengths he went to in order to have a stab at escaping, and yet he gave it all up for...this."

"I'm sure you've figured out this is no ordinary leather," Lawrence says. "I've spent a great deal of time researching Virgil Francopan and the workings of his mind. You're not the only one who's been obsessed with him, though in my case, I have no personal vendetta against him. I broke into his house, the one he keeps clean and maintained even though he was going to end his days in prison, and he knew it. There had to be a reason why he did that, it had to be both to protect something, and in case he ever escaped, so he could come back to his treasured possessions. Serial killers like to keep trophies, don't they? So I looked for his. I read his files, combed through the books he owned, read his emails, the articles he wrote and submitted under a pseudonym. I drew a fairly complete picture of him, not only because I was, and am, fascinated by him, but also out of necessity. If I was going to bring him into my life's project, I needed to know him inside and out. I failed, clearly, but it wasn't for lack of preparation."

"And that chair was just resting in his basement?" I ask.

"Yes, in his workshop, next to a painting – a replica in oil – of the Red Leather Armchair by René Magritte, which is how I put everything together. This armchair, right here, is his trophy, containing a piece of all his murder victims.

"In the painting, the armchair is placed in a vast desert landscape. The image of a luxurious chair in the middle of a barren wasteland contrasts comfort and opulence with isolation and emptiness. And Virgil's armchair is identical to the one on the canvas, with a few patches missing. He is a great fan of René Magritte, a Belgian surrealist painter. His life's work was to create his own surrealist work of art, a real life production of Magritte's painting, with a few twists."

"That's sick." What's surrealist is watching Virgil sleep on a chair from my past, made of human skin, in a cabin on a boat in the middle of the Atlantic ocean.

"Leather is full of symbolism which Virgil likes; it's associated with wealth, power, and authority. Magritte frequently played with the idea of identity, facades, and the human condition. An interpretation from Virgil was that the leather armchair could represent a protective barrier or an artificial covering, echoing themes of disguise or masking true identity, which he identified with: a serial killer disguised as a psychiatrist."

Virgil stirs, but he remains asleep, a string of drool slowly forming in the corner of his mouth.

"Magritte was known for his ability to transform familiar objects into something uncanny or unsettling by placing them in unusual contexts. By using an object like a leather armchair, which is typically a symbol of comfort and domestic life, Magritte might be encouraging viewers to question its ordinariness and see it in a new, surreal light. He believed that ordinary objects could be presented in ways that disturb their usual meanings, encouraging viewers to question their assumptions about the world. Making the chair's leather out of human skin was Virgil taking this to a whole other level; visually an ordinary object, a symbol of comfort, but once we know the source, the surreality of it all is gobsmacking. Patients sitting down on previous patients' remains. In the open.

"By distorting reality and bending physical laws, the surrealists questioned the boundaries between what is real and what is imagined, and who controls that boundary. Which brings us to *control*, Virgil's favourite subject. Because control and power are synonymous, to him."

Virgil looks peaceful, asleep in front of us, his cheek

twitching every now and then. It would be so easy to walk up to him and stab him. What keeps me from doing it? I don't have a knife on me, for one. Or anything else which could serve as a weapon.

"But Virgil did not agree on everything with Magritte; he liked that there was no sexual dimension to Magritte's work, but Magritte didn't aim to shock viewers with strange or grotesque imagery, and Virgil quite enjoys the grotesque. However that tended to be the domain of the sexually obsessed surrealists. He wanted to shock people in the way Man Ray wanted to shock people. He wanted to show his ability to manipulate both the body and the mind, the very things Man Ray focused on in his photography. Man Ray played with the idea of objectification and sexuality, simultaneously celebrating the body's beauty and turning it into something utilitarian. Just like Virgil took great care to produce the highest quality of leather, something beautiful to him, and he literally turned the body into something utilitarian. Where surrealists stuck to art to express their ideas, Virgil took things literally and acted out surrealist notions and concepts."

Could another reason why I'm not killing him right now be that I want him awake for it...? I think so.

"Virgil's obsession with surrealism bordered on madness. He wanted to create a masterpiece, to surpass his master, shock not only Magritte, but other surrealists too. Shocking the general public wasn't something to be proud of, but shocking the masters of shock themselves, those who studied the art of shocking for decades and had mastered it, to him that would be the pinnacle of his existence. He had no natural painting skills, but he believed his form of art was just as worthy, if not more so."

"As far as shocking goes, yes," I say, "what he did is slightly more shocking."

"Exactly. I was elated when I found this chair, and understood its importance. I needed something Virgil could lose, to have some form of leverage. When you and I met in Wimbledon, I had already done all that. I already had this armchair in my garage. I knew taking Virgil on was madness, it posed too much risk, not only to break him out of prison but also and especially to keep him in check during the experiment, but I knew the rewards would be just as great. The publicity he would generate, and if he somehow lasted until the end without killing, managing to turn a man like him tame would be proof that I was onto something. That would have given the public a good shake. I thought I might use the red leather armchair as the carrot, or the stick, to make him behave. But he fooled me."

I realise, just now, that the entire time he *was* just a naive bastard. Where I never trusted Virgil, Lawrence did. He knew the beast he was dealing with, and yet he still fell for it. I thought he was in league with Virgil, somehow, because I just didn't imagine Lawrence capable of being such a fool, but he was blinded by his hope that Virgil had indeed been tamed, and how positively that would have reflected on his experiment.

"I truly thought we would reach the sixty days without having to take out my joker," Lawrence goes on. "And then it unravelled all too quickly. And until today, I wasn't even sure he'd had a role in the deaths." He rubs his eyes with one hand, and I see from up close just how old he looks. I swear he didn't look this old this morning.

"So...do you think the way this experiment turned out for him, his plan, the way he wanted to escape, was a statement on surrealism?" I suggest. "The ultimate demonstration of his ability to manipulate both mind and body, in front of an audience?"

Lawrence stops rubbing his eyes but the hand stays pressed against his face. Then he mutters, "I should have seen it coming, shouldn't I?"

A moment passes, then he calls for Brandon.

"Time to wake him up," Lawrence says.

The nurse returns with his medical kit, prepares the syringe, then injects Virgil intravenously.

Within a minute, Virgil opens his eyes.

59

ANNA KIMPER

His eyes are bloodshot. At first he doesn't know where he is.

Then he sees his armchair, and just as quickly as it all comes back to him, he turns a bright shade of red.

"How dare you damage it?" he mutters through clenched teeth. He's staring at the cable ties cutting into the armrests' leather.

"You'd better not struggle, then," Lawrence says.

"This is more valuable than both of your miserable lives put together," Virgil says, his face contorted by rage, but his body still as a leaf.

"Isn't it poetic?" Lawrence says. "Trapped in your own creation. I'm sure there are lots of metaphors which are lost on me."

"Was your goal throughout this experiment to create a surrealist masterpiece to rival this armchair?" I ask.

The rage fizzles out. "In a way, I did it. You can't ever take that away from me. I am the sole survivor, and I orchestrated it all."

"You forget about Jan," I say.

"I got him out. I am the last to survive the experiment. And everything went to plan. I could have escaped."

"No," Lawrence says. "The Zodiac didn't have enough petrol to go much farther past our yacht."

"Who said I was planning to go past the yacht? You underestimate me, Mr. Plague Barrister." He peers at Lawrence and studies him for a moment, as if properly looking at him for the first time – which, in fact, it probably is. "Regardless, I couldn't resist being reunited with my one and only, even if it meant being tied to a chair. Again."

"That was your only mistake," Lawrence says. "This armchair is both your life's purpose, and your greatest weakness. And your undoing."

Virgil squints at Lawrence. "I recognise you. Where from?"

The slightest grin forms on Lawrence's thin lips. "Do you?"

Then Virgil's eyes go wide. "My trial. You were the judge."

"Bingo. Who would've thought we would see each other again? Here, of all places."

A deafening silence settles as they eye each other. I would kill to know what is going on in Virgil's head.

"Right," Lawrence says at last, "the time has come to decide your fate. I think it only fair that the decision rests with Anna. Both about Virgil, and what to do with the armchair."

Virgil's gaze falls on me. Not an imaginary point next to my head; on *me*. His eyes bore into mine, and for a moment I waver. He intimidates me, I can't deny it. But then Ollie's voice rings in the depths of my mind, and I take strength from it.

What makes me pause is not what to do about Virgil; he will not live to see the moon rise again. I don't know whether I should destroy the chair too, or not.

Destroying it would symbolise my freedom from his manipulation, a final act of reclaiming power over my past. The chair is also a symbol of his victims' violation and dehumanisation, and keeping it would feel like perpetuating the memory of their suffering. Destroying it would metaphorically lay those victims to rest, offering them a sense of justice and closure. It would honour their memory.

Preserving it, however, also has some upsides. It would represent my decision to confront my past rather than run from it. By keeping it, I would transform the armchair from something Virgil used to symbolise his dominance into a symbol of my strength and survival. A physical reminder of how far I've come.

Virgil intended it to be a surrealist statement, but by preserving it, I could make my own counter-statement: it no longer belongs to Virgil, or represents his 'art', but rather becomes a testament to my agency over my reality. It can be my piece of catharsis rather than an object of fear or power.

"I've decided."

Lawrence looks at me expectantly.

"Can we move him to the stern?" I ask.

Lawrence nods, and calls for Brandon and the Canadian deckhand.

Once on the stern, Lawrence and the crew stare at me. Virgil has closed his eyes, as if resigned to his fate. He is facing the agitated sea, the armchair positioned right on the edge of the stern's swim platform.

I stare right into Virgil's closed eyes. "You were worried about saltwater damaging my glove's leather. Let's see how it treats your chair."

He wakes up, our eyes meet.

I gesture to the sea.

"Drown in your legacy."

The final image of Virgil floating away in his red leather armchair, head and feet above water and the rest of his body submerged, carried by the tide, eyes closed, will forever stay with me.

I've read once that what goes into the sea always comes back up.

I wonder where he will turn up.

60

ANNA KIMPER

"What now?" I ask.

We are in the main deck's saloon, and besides feeling lighter because of Virgil's sealed fate, I also feel a lot more at ease on this boat without Stephen here. He and his aide fled as soon as we apprehended Virgil.

"We're navigating back towards England," Lawrence says, crossing his legs in front of him, "and once the chopper is back from dropping Stephen off, and we're close enough to the continent, we'll fly back home."

I nod. I sense there's something else Lawrence wants to say. I give him the time he needs.

"Anna, you're not well," he says at last, giving me a fatherly look. I see genuine concern on his face. "You are aware?"

I nod. I want to say something, but my mouth isn't allowing me. A ball has formed in my throat, and my lips tremble.

"Please, *please*," he goes on, uncrossing his legs to lean

towards me, "as soon as we get back, get all the help you need. Take your medication."

"I have been," I manage to say, though my voice quavers. "That's why I had no idea, I thought I was fine."

"Go to your psychiatrist, and do everything he says. Do you have a good one? Would you like me to recommend one?"

I nod. "I– I'm sorry. For tricking you, going behind your back."

Lawrence dismisses it with a wave of the hand. "You weren't yourself, I know that. We'll go back to England, I'll be by your side, and we will put all this behind us."

I hope we can. I hear what he isn't saying; if the authorities don't crack the case, if we manage to get away with it.

As if he can read my mind, he says: "Don't worry about anything else related to this project from now on. I'll take care of everything; it's my mess to clean up. You must focus on your recovery. That is your only priority, I'll make sure of it. So long as you promise you'll take care of yourself."

"Of course. I've let you down, I've let everyone down. It's high time I shut myself away and healed."

"No, you didn't let me down. I'm–" He marks a pause, looks away, and swallows hard. "I'm the one who created a mass torture from scratch, and now I'm responsible for six deaths. I wanted – I want – to improve thousands of prisoners' lives, get rid of all inhumane treatment, and yet I've created my own form of inhumane treatment. I placed individuals with a great deal of hope for rehabilitation in the same room as a dangerous, hopeless madman. What was I thinking?"

Is it tears I see gathering in his eyes? He swallows hard again, blinks a few more times, and they vanish.

"I've failed," he continues. "I've made mistakes, I trusted

them, and I shouldn't have. Not to that extent. Of course not. I've been blinded by my idealism, and in the end cost them their lives, and wasted a lot of money, other people's money. Am I no better than them? A criminal of the same ilk?

"Am I?"

THANK YOU

Thank you for reading this book. I take great pleasure in writing, but having people read what I write takes it to another level.

If *Sixty Days of Virgil* kept you turning the pages, I'd be incredibly grateful if you took a moment to leave a quick review on Amazon.

It helps more than you know — and I read every one!

Thanks again for reading,
 Orion

ABOUT THE AUTHOR

Orion Grace holds triple Canadian, French, and British citizenship and lives in Wales with his wife and three children. A former professional tennis player, he has a bachelor's degree in finance and a master's degree in international studies. He previously published a science fantasy novel in French. He has published another psychological thriller, *Thirteen Graves*, available on Amazon.

Visit his website at oriongracebooks.com and follow him on Twitter @OrionGraceBooks.

ALSO BY ORION GRACE

Enjoy a free preview of my psychological thriller *Thirteen Graves*.

Tristan

Rebecca assured me long driveways are very common in the countryside, though she admitted not *this* long. The private driveway leading to her ancestral home is thirty-eight miles long. To put this in perspective, that is roughly the diameter of the M25 ring road around London, or three times the length of Manhattan Island. Or a farm track in the Scottish Highlands, I guess.

It took just under an hour in a car from the moment we entered their estate until we could see the house. I mean, think of the cost of just filling in the potholes. By the time you've fixed all of them, new ones have popped up. And does the postman drive all the way down to deliver the

Advertiser Monthly brochure, or do the residents have to drive an hour to pick it up from a post box at the top of the track? It took us two days to get here from London to make the six hundred-mile drive more bearable, but this last hour was by far the longest – and the most fascinating.

The Morrison estate spans ten thousand acres of pure wilderness. All the lochs (yes, plural) we drove past, the glen, the herds of cattle, the wide open spaces, all part of the same estate. The entire way down the private track, I couldn't help but wonder if I was going to spend a week with the laird and lady of a grand Scottish castle. As we park at last on the bank of a shallow river, opposite the lone house in the distance, Rebecca assures me her great-aunt is not titled, and she says the family isn't wealthy.

I give her a look.

"Well, *technically* I suppose they are," she says, getting out of the car and buttoning up her winter coat.

There are other cars parked here, which comes as a relief. I always find comfort in the presence of other people, especially when tucked away in the butthole of Britain.

"There's a lot of money in the land," Rebecca goes on, "if they were to sell. But the family's owned it for generations, bought it to farm it back when the land was cheap." She hands me her suit case and I shoulder my bag. The wind is frigid but I leave my gloves and scarf in my coat pocket, we'll be inside a warm house soon enough now. "But Great-Aunt Norah and Dickie were not farmers, and I don't think Dickie's parents were either. Norah rents the land to a tenant farmer for a pittance, and the house costs her each year. She has to keep it in a decent state of repair so we can spend Christmas here all together every year, but nobody has lived there since Dickie was a little boy, so it deteriorates quickly."

She stops abruptly and points to an oddly shaped metal bucket in front of us. "Luggage in there," she says.

I stare at her. "Why?"

"The house is still some way away, no need to break your back carrying our bags. It's much easier with the wheelbarrow."

Only now do I notice the wheel under the rusty bucket. "That's alright, I can carry the bags to the house." I'm not sure I'd be able to remove the rust stains if I shoved my suitcase in there.

Rebecca sighs impatiently, then grabs the bags from me and throws them inside the wheelbarrow.

I seize the freezing handles and push after her. "Every time you come here," I say, "you have to make sure you've got over seventy miles' worth of petrol in the car. Talk about planning your trip! It's a logistical nightmare."

"And the closest petrol station is in Stradorroch, another twenty minutes up the main road. My dad used to always keep a can of petrol in the boot, just in case. Probably still does. His car's here, by the way."

An entirely different sense of dread fills me at the thought of meeting her father. There's nowhere to run if things go bad. We've only been together for six months. Is it too early to meet parents?

It takes me a few moments to realise we're walking away from the house. "Where are we going?"

"There." She points vaguely ahead. "How did you think we were going to cross the river?"

I can't see what she's pointing to. Only trees bordering the river, and intimidating mountains rising on both sides of the valley. "Isn't there a bridge somewhere?"

"*There*, you numpty. Don't you see it?"

Now I do. It is a bridge, I suppose, though not the kind I

had in mind. It's a string of wooden planks held together by thin ropes, suspended over the river and tied around tree trunks on opposite banks. The whole concoction swings in the wind, and though the ropes turn out to be thicker than I thought as we get closer, my hands moisten around the wheelbarrow's handles despite the freezing gusts.

I step on the first plank and I'm surprised to see it holds my weight. I can't hear the wood creak with the screaming wind and the rush of the water below, but I can feel it under my foot well enough. There is a rope on either side at waist height to hold onto, but that's useless to me and my wheelbarrow. The wood beneath the wheel and my feet sways dangerously from side to side, and I've never been so scared of falling to my death. Twice I think of turning around and giving up, but how humiliating would that be? And where would I go, anyway?

"Don't worry, Tris, it's a perfectly solid bridge," Rebecca says after a quick glance behind her. "We've used it my whole life and no one has ever fallen over. Just think of the warm eggnog waiting for us when we get inside. Great-aunt Norah always has some ready to greet us."

I make it across the bridge dry and in one piece, and my heart settles down. We walk in silence as I take in the scenery. A clump of tall and straight pine trees to our left, with a large wood store, the logs piled all the way to the roof. A rather large axe is planted in a tree stump by the store, and a few stray logs are scattered over a bed of pine needles. A circular well stands to our right, the stones stained by time and neglect, and behind it a barn and an old tractor.

Something on the floor by the barn catches my attention. I put the wheelbarrow down and take a few steps away from the well-trodden path to have a better look. A row of mounds of freshly dug earth lines the cow shed. Rebecca stops too when she doesn't hear the squeaky wheelbarrow behind her.

"Is that...are those graves?" I ask. I get closer and...yes, the holes are perfect rectangles. I count thirteen of them.

Rebecca keeps quiet for a moment, then she gives a disbelieving laugh. "Norah has acquired a grim sense of humour. Either that, or Billy, the tenant farmer, is preparing to bury some animals."

But she doesn't sound convinced, and though I know nothing of the inner workings of a farm, I doubt farmers ever bury dead animals so close to a house. "How many will we be, in total?"

"Strip that look off your face," she scoffs. "You've watched too many films."

"How many?"

She takes a moment to count in her head. "Sixteen. Dangerously close, I'll admit. A creepy welcome for you, my dear." She gives a nervous laugh. She's being uncharacteristically awkward, which does nothing to reassure me. "Let's go have that eggnog, my nose is about to fall off."

The thought of a warm mug in my hands in front of a fire helps to shake off the feeling of creepiness, but as Rebecca opens the front door and announces her arrival, I sense that things aren't right.

No wave of heat to greet us, no smell of eggnog or mulled wine, and no jolly hubbub of Christmas music and family laughter.

A well-dressed man appears, hugs Rebecca, and says, "No sign of Mother, I'm afraid."

So I'll have to appease the sense of eeriness with a cold house, a smell of stale damp, and the terrifying prospect of meeting my girlfriend's father for the first time.

Printed in Dunstable, United Kingdom